D1008648

Fire's Edge

To Ken
Best
Alan Sip

a novel by

Alan Siporin

Wounded
Bear Press

ISBN 0-9722806-0-X

Printed in the United States of America
Published by Wounded Bear Press
P.O. Box 50822
Eugene, Oregon 97405
suspense@fires-edge.com
www.fires-edge.com
October 2002 First Edition

Book design by Jerril Nilson

For my sister, Roz, and my brother, Steve.
Without their input this book wouldn't be nearly as good.
Without their love, neither would I.

Acknowledgments

Blue Heron, my original publisher, folded one week prior to the scheduled release of *Fire's Edge.* Nevertheless, their role remains primary. Dennis Stovall, Martha Ruttle, and Daniel Urban, thanks for your faith in writers, and your hard work and effort on my behalf.

Daniel deserves the lion's share of credit as the primary editor who helped shape this book, and in the process, made me a better writer. But others contributed, as well. Lesley Kellas Payne, in particular, thanks for an incredible edit and a hard shove in the right direction.

Wounded Bear Press picked up where Blue Heron faltered and brought *Fire's Edge,* home. Thanks to Diana Wells, Opie Snow Heyerman, Jeffrey Flowers, and Jerril Nilson.

Special thanks to fellow Eugene writers, Elizabeth Lyon and Bill Sullivan, for your guidance and support.

And thanks to the following who played some role, ranging from love, friendship, and encouragement, to feedback, advice, and just plain pointing. Julia Siporin, Megan Craig, Roz Stein,

Steve Siporin, Ona Siporin, Eric Ward, Marion Malcolm, Bayla Ostrach, Karen Lackritz, Bill Nelson, Jeff Stier, Martin Acker, Tracy Bernstein, Barbara Branscom, Barb Newcombe-Stevens, Barbara Heyerman, Grace Morgan, Sallie Tisdale, Garrett Epps, Stacy Creamer, Elie Wiesel, Ken Kesey, Jane Ellis, Jenny Root, Thom Chambliss, Maggie Herrington and Haystack, Rich Wandschneider and Fishtrap, the Mid-Valley Willamatte Writers, B.J. Novitski, Carol Busby Cricow and the National Writers Union—Oregon Local, Chuck Palahniuk, Valerie Miner, Kate Joost, and Bill Johnson.

I would also like to acknowledge Michael Thoele's *Fire Line, Summer Battles of the West*, and Norman Maclean's *Young Men and Fire*. Although the hundreds of hours I spent covering wildfires as a reporter provided my background for reality-based fire scenes, I am, nevertheless, grateful that I had these works to refer to for confirmation; and, as it turned out, for further inspiration.

And, to all who stand against hate.

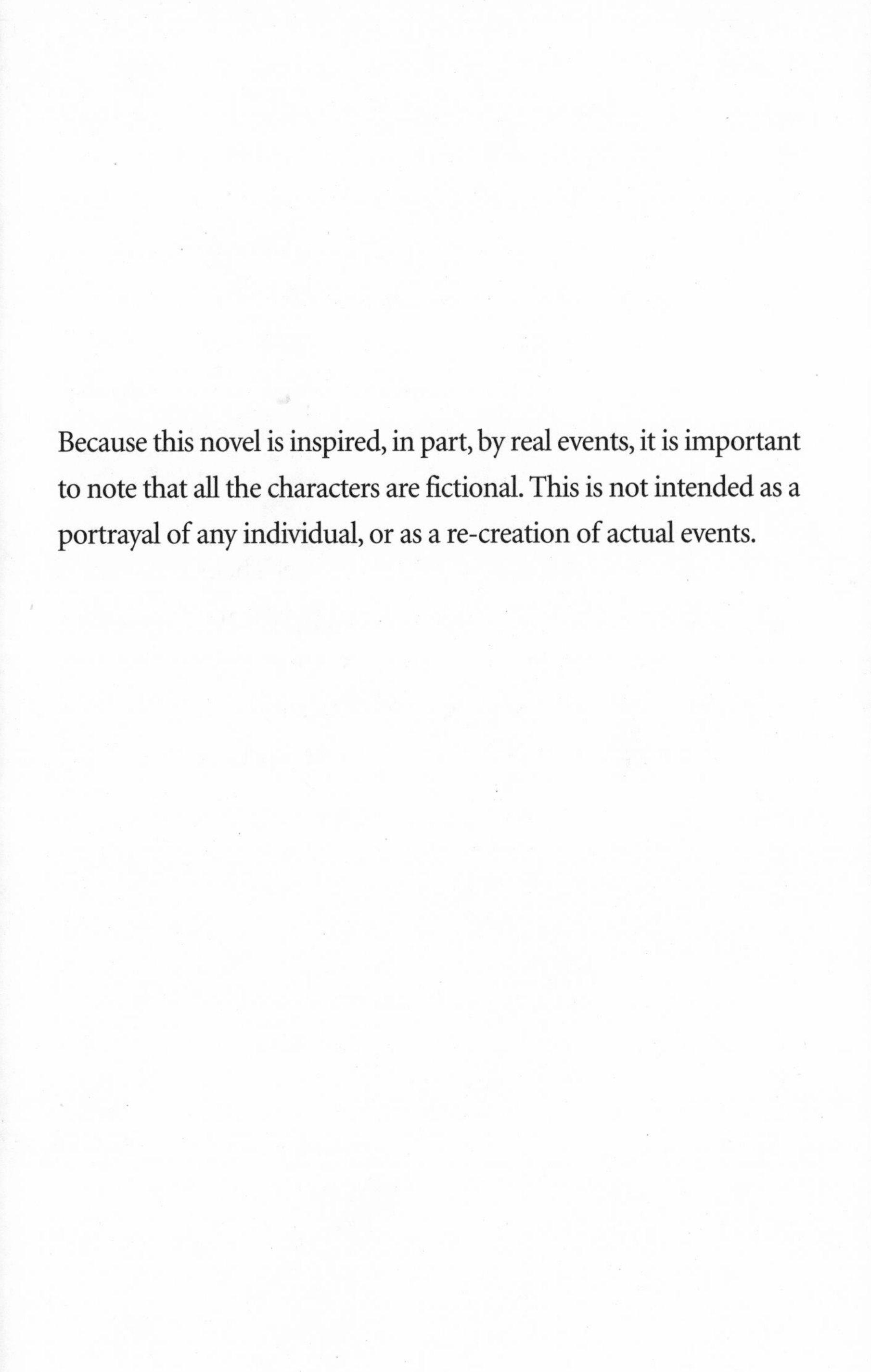

Because this novel is inspired, in part, by real events, it is important to note that all the characters are fictional. This is not intended as a portrayal of any individual, or as a re-creation of actual events.

Prologue

A large black woman sprawls across her couch, napping. At the other end of the sparse room, a thin pale man dozes lightly in his wheelchair, his head nodding, waking him. In the late afternoon, their basement apartment offers a cool escape from the summer heat.

A Coke bottle shatters a window above the man, strikes the floor and explodes. He jerks his head back hard. Gasoline glides across the room, a light blue flame riding atop the liquid. The fire incinerates a stack of newspapers. Swollen yellow flames quickly diverge, sucking up the oxygen, leaping to chairs and a table. The blaze locates things hidden from the eye, beneath the couch, in the cracks and crevices, nurturing its hunger on everything that can burn. Thick black clouds of smoke swarm the corners.

The pale man screams, bellowing out air. When he breathes back in, thick dark matter surges into his lungs. He heaves the black smoke back out, emptying his lungs again, leaving them unnourished. He shakes and writhes. He grabs his wheels with his hands, discovers he has no strength. He's out of breath, gulping for life. Epinephrine courses through his veins. And fear. Desperately, he sucks the smoke back in, vomits it out again. Reflexively, he gasps again, strangling himself on the finest particles of ash.

In the black woman's dream, she is held by men in white sheets. A man is lashed to a cross. They are about to torch him. Jovial and arrogant, the men in sheets have no faces, but the woman feels their demonic grins. She smells the smoke and kerosene wafting from torches. She can't make out the man who is tied to the cross. Could it be her grandfather? Or is it her brother? He appears strong and calm. Her fear is fused with pride. She observes her brother clearly now; a light brown man in his twenties, his jaw set and determined, his eyes glinting and defiant. But she hears him scream — a weak and mournful cry for help. The dream changes. Her brother is only five years old — a little boy — helpless and pleading. She reaches out to help him, but she can't budge.

She's strapped to the cross. No, she's bound to a tree. The fire sears her, soot clings to her nostrils, terror overwhelms her. In her dream, she is screaming.

Outside, passersby glimpse three young men running from the side of the house. Later, these witnesses will tell police the arsonists were skinheads: shaved heads, leather jackets and Doc Martin boots. One big kid, two smaller ones, laughing.

Part One

1

Hannah Turnfeld tastes the stale courthouse air, and a wet-dog aroma from wool moistened by the Oregon drizzle, mingling with whiffs of floor-polish, perfume, and sweat. She feels as if she could sink into the deep ruts of the worn, wooden stairs. She hesitates, then mounts the last few steps and turns into the expansive corridor. A hubbub of voices echo off the high ceiling and marble walls. The line is more of a mass than single file, with some people standing by themselves, most gathering in groups of two, three, or four, facing each other, talking. As many as fifty people wait for a seat to watch the Robert Hanson trial.

She hurries around the corner to the back of the line in the isolated side hall, where another thirty people cram into the more limited space. Some wear jeans and sweaters, others suits and ties. A few bright-colored, waist-length rain slicks provide splashes of green and purple. They remind her of Anthony's black, nylon jacket with lime green trim around the pockets and collar. Her throat tightens.

She knew the Hanson trial would evoke him. She's suffered

worse losses — her mother and father, taken in the same instant. But Anthony's murder stole her passion for teaching.

Hannah starts to rummage through her last encounters with him, except something nags at her — a strange yelping that isn't quite dog-like. The insistent barking intrudes, yanking her from her thoughts, like an alarm rattling a dream. She focuses, glancing quickly from one person to the next, until she spots the source of the disruption — a teen in full Nazi uniform stands five or six places down the line from her. The boy's head is shaved. His brown coat bears a red Nazi arm-band with a white circle and the twisted, black cross. Hannah feels the sudden thump of her pulse.

She glances around to see how other people are reacting, but no one else seems to notice him. Perhaps because the boy's growl sounds more prankish than threatening. Or maybe they avoid him out of fear. He's with two friends, smiling and laughing. If not for his shaved head and Nazi garb, Hannah might see him as playful. Her heart backs off her throat, but queasiness lingers.

She expected to see skinheads at Hanson's trial — not Nazi dress. To her, Nazi uniforms belong in the past — in films or in the Holocaust stories of her grandmother and great aunt. She tries to turn away. She can't. She's drawn to the boy. In a way, *he* is what she came for.

His friends have shaved heads, too, and wear similar Nazi attire. One is short like him, the other tall and massive. But something strikes her as out of place. The uniforms on the two smaller boys are too big for them — their shoulders hang loose and the sleeves droop nearly to their fingers — and the big skinhead is bursting out of his tunic. The odd fit makes her chuckle, inwardly, soothing her for a moment.

She follows the fix of the young Nazi's stare to an old man who slumps forward as if he were leaning on an invisible cane. His thin shoulders curve inward, and a thick tuft of white hair stands atop his head like a rooster's comb. She glances back toward the young Nazi, who whispers something to his buddies and gestures with his head. They nod in agreement. The three skinheads brush past a couple in front of them, strutting toward the man. A woman with a baby in her arms moves closer to the man she's with, and, together, they move away from the boys, closer to the wall. The boy emits his yelp again. The old man glances at him, then quickly looks away, rocking back and forth, from heel to toe.

Hannah searches for allies who might assist the man, but the crowd remains turned away, in private enclaves. She wonders if people are oblivious, or if she is making something out of nothing. The din from the crowd around the corner cascades off the walls. Her great aunt and her grandmother told her the Holocaust began with isolated acts of intimidation. Hitler's thugs, they called them, grew bolder because no one stepped forward to hold them accountable.

The boy and his buddies slip closer to the old man, until no one stands between him and them, and they're only a few feet away. Hannah's heart races. Her legs feel heavy. But she urges her body forward, slides out of her place in line, past a handful of people, and places herself between the boys and the man. The kid glares at her.

His eyes are red. Not a dull, bloodshot maroon — but an icy crimson.

She winces.

The boy smirks.

She measures his distance. Could he take a swing at her and connect? It's close. She takes a breath, straightens her spine and shoulders, and stares back — hard, with her scolding teacher's scowl.

Undeterred, the teenager puffs out his chest and shoves past her. His buddies follow. She looks down at her own, shaking hands. The three skinheads surround their mark. The big one hulks behind the old man; the red-eyed kid takes up a post directly in front of him, face-to-face. The third one hesitates, a shoulder's length behind. Hannah, to the kid's side, feels a sudden urge to rip his swastika arm-band.

She wonders if the last image Anthony saw was a swastika. She swallows hard. And, again, she questions her reaction. The kids are playing with the old man, like older brothers teasing a younger sibling. After all, the courthouse hallway is filled with people. But when she looks at the man, she sees his arms and shoulders tremble. His head wobbles. Hannah feels a bead of sweat run down her side as she psyches herself to act. Fear cements her feet as if she were in a nightmare with a monster on her heels, her legs unable to move.

She focuses on her self-defense training, centers her energy, tightens her stomach, and slightly flexes her knees.

Steadied, she encroaches on the threatening trio, wedging herself between the man and the boy. This time the boy's strange eyes are inches away; hard and dark, emanating a reddish tint as if fire burned behind the blackness. A tiny swastika tattoo is blazoned below his left eye. His breath descends on hers.

Her trembling, barely at bay, easily returns. She fights an exacting knot twisting at her gut, twisting around and around, forming a larger and more entangled gnarl.

But she finds the strength to make her voice firm. "Leave him alone."

The kid grins. She stiffens, braces for whatever will follow.

She feels something brush her shoulder, and she jerks. A man slides past her. He sticks a microphone in the young Nazi's face.

The man's voice is strong and compelling. "If you're with White Nation, I would like to ask you a couple questions."

The red-eyed boy tenses his arms, forms his fists. But he hesitates and looks down. Then he belches out a barely audible grunt before he backs off a couple paces. The kid appears as a vampire to Hannah now, cowering before a priest with a cross.

The man, at first glance, is not physically imposing — a dark brown man of medium height wearing thick, black-rimmed glasses. His hair is part dreadlock, but mostly just unkempt. He presses his advantage. Pivoting, he thrusts the microphone in the face of the huge kid behind him. "How about you?"

The big Nazi kid shakes his head. Again, no words. Hannah feels the tension between them, but the standoff ends as quickly as it began, and the three invaders slink slowly back to their places in line.

"I can't believe these guys." The commanding intensity is gone as the man addresses Hannah and the old man. His voice turns light, though it holds a hint of disgust. "They act so tough, but you can't get a word out of them. At least a black guy can't." He laughs, then shakes his head from side to side, flip-flopping his dreadlocks.

She wants to say something, but the man doesn't give her a chance. "Actually, I'm not sure these fools are capable of talking. They fight you at the drop of a hat, but they're scared to death to debate you. Underneath that bravado they're just scared, little kids."

The old man smiles. "I'm afraid I'm the scared one here."

"Are you all right?" She lightly touches the old man's arm.

He sighs, and his body droops. "I'm okay now. Thank you."

Hannah turns to the black man. "I'm not sure they would have done anything here, but I'm glad you stuck your nose in there. Thanks. I was a little freaked-out."

He laughs, short and halting. "I hear that. These kids can be scary. But they wouldn't hurt you here. This place is crawling with cops."

She glances around in a quick attempt to spot the police. More people have squeezed into the side hall, compacting the line. But she doesn't see any comforting blue uniforms. Only the boys in their brown, Nazi garb. They huddle together, now, talking in hushed tones; still too close for Hannah to relax. She twirls a lock of hair and tucks it under her bangs.

"My name is Hannah." She shakes hands with both men.

"Earl," the old man says.

"Fil." He shakes hands with the old man. She looks Fil over. His dress is disheveled. And he's so talkative he's practically bubbly. Probably because he's young, she thinks.

"So what brings you folks to the trial?" He looks back and forth, from Hannah to Earl and back to her.

"That's kind of a long story," Earl shrugs.

Fil grins. "This line doesn't seem to be going anywhere."

"I got a kind of personal interest in seein' this trial." Earl pauses, looking back and forth from Fil to Hannah. "My neighbor is the grandmother of Tommy Larson."

Fil and Hannah look at Earl, then at each other, but no one says anything. She feels a lump well up and fill her throat. After a moment, Fil asks, "One of the kids who killed Anthony Jones?"

"Yeah."

Hannah looks away, but she can still see Fil glancing at her, then back toward Earl, as the old man continues.

"I haven't seen the boy in years. Seemed like a real nice kid when I seen him last. He was maybe ten, then. His grandma is the salt of the earth. She's awful shook up."

"I can't imagine," Fil says. "I've often thought about Anthony Jones' parents. But that's gotta' be rough, too."

Earl cocks one eyebrow. "Nothin' I'm gonna' see here is gonna' make her feel any better. Nothin's gonna' take Tommy off the hook. I know that." He sighs and shakes his head. "But I want to see this Hanson get what's comin' to him. You know what I mean?"

"Sure," Fil says. The two men look directly at each other. Then Earl looks away and shakes his head.

"Tell me more about his grandmother," Hannah says. She thinks her voice will crack, but it comes out fine. "What does she say about her grandson?"

"At first she wouldn't believe it. But, you know, all three of those boys admitted they done it." Earl shakes his head. "That set her back. She was a lively, happy gal before that. She keeps to herself now. Won't go out." Earl raises his voice and his shoulders and arms shake. "I know I can't help her, but I thought maybe I could see this Hanson for myself and come back and tell her the guy is a snake in the grass, and he coulda' got the next kid as well as her Tommy."

Fil glances at Hannah. She creases her lips, attempting a half-smile.

Earl's head wobbles, his eyes blink, then close. His body slumps toward the floor. Fil and Hannah grab him and hold him up.

"Are you okay?" Fil asks, still holding him up.

Hannah wonders if Fil is taking all the weight — the old man feels so light and frail. After a moment, Earl opens his eyes. He looks back and forth from Fil to Hannah, but he doesn't say anything.

"Earl. I think you blacked out for a second," Fil says.

"Yeah, things are a little fuzzy."

"Maybe you should sit down," Hannah says.

"I think I'm okay now. Thanks."

"Are you sure you're okay?" She pats his arm." There's a place to sit over there." She gestures toward a well-worn bench along the wall, about ten feet away.

"That's a good idea. This hallway is still movin' on me."

Fil and Hannah each hold onto an arm and slowly guide Earl toward the bench. She notices a hand-painted no smoking sign on the wall and a metal ash tray nearby. She wonders what the three skinheads are doing, but she can't see them without being obvious. Earl turns around and eases himself down to the seat. He looks up at Hannah.

"I'll be fine. Don't give up your spot in line on account of me. I ain't too sure everybody's gonna' get in. There's a lot of folks here, and that's a small courtroom. I seen it before."

"Are you sure you're okay?" Fil asks.

"Positive."

"We'll be right over there," Hannah says, gesturing toward their previous place in line. "If you need a hand, let us know."

"You're very kind. But I'm fine."

As they return to the line, she glances at the skinheads. They don't seem to be paying any attention to her or Earl.

"What a sweet, gentle man," she says to Fil.

"I didn't realize you didn't know each other."

"I can't believe I'm the only one who saw those kids." She raises her voice.

"I think the cops would have intervened before it got serious."

"I thought it was serious. That old man — Earl — could have had a heart attack. Those kids were intimidating him, at the least. And I didn't get the feeling anybody, police or otherwise, were paying any attention."

"You were." Fil smiles.

"Apparently you were, too."

Fil shakes his head. He seems a little embarrassed. Hannah smiles, then looks away. After a second she glances back toward him. Fil is still looking at her. He flicks his hair out of his eyes with his flip-flopping motion, smiles and asks again what brought her to the trial.

"Checking it out, like everyone else. How about you?" She points to his microphone and tape recorder. "I thought you must be a reporter. But you haven't been recording any of this, have you?"

"I work with an anti-racism organization in Eugene. I document connections between groups like Hanson's and the skinheads." He looks down, then back up, making eye contact again. "I bet you a cup of coffee it's more than curiosity that brought you here."

"I'm not really sure what brought me." Hannah glances at the skinheads again, still in their spot. "I mean there's a number of reasons."

She tries to imagine Anthony running into Tommy Larson and his friends in the alley. But, other than a fuzzy news photo, she doesn't know what Tommy Larson or his friends look like, and she doesn't want to let herself drift while Fil is waiting for her answer.

"I don't know. I guess being Jewish has something to do with it. I'm not exactly sure."

"I guess that makes you more curious about Hanson's trial than your average white guy, anyway." He laughs.

His laugh lights up his eyes, and makes her laugh, too. Hannah thinks the sound of his laugh is a bit dorky, but the smile and the way he shakes his head when he laughs engages her.

"I guess that's part of it," she says. "But there's a lot of reasons for being here."

Hannah isn't sure why she's reluctant to mention Anthony. Probably because she'll start sobbing. She recalls her first day back in the classroom, two days after his murder. She had canceled her planned lessons and held a circle meeting. The kids were quieter than usual, obviously aware the feeling-sharing session would be about Anthony.

She could feel a flood forming inside and thought her voice would waver when she invited them to talk about him. But she sounded composed, and the expected catch in her throat failed to manifest. The kids remained quiet. Finally, Mickey Serano, usually one of her more gabby kids, whispered that Anthony showed him how to get in front of ground balls. Mickey sounded more like four than twelve, and her repressed tears almost burst out as laughter. But she was grateful for any response because it allowed others to follow.

Four or five boys prattled on with more sports-related connections, until Joyce Chapman suddenly shouted, "What's the matter with you? This isn't about baseball. Anthony was murdered for being black." She sobbed, and the girls on each side of her embraced her. Other kids wept.

Fil stares at Hannah with an earnest gaze. "Are you okay?" he asks.

She shakes her head. "Yes. I'm fine." Her voice cracks, slightly. If Fil notices, he doesn't let on.

"You were saying there are a number of reasons that brought you here."

"Hope." She pauses. "Fear. But not fear of these guys. I mean — I am afraid of them, but that's not why I came. I guess fear of them is just a bonus." She laughs.

Fil laughs, too, his eyes lighting up again. Then he sets his jaw and his voice takes on an urgency. "These guys scare the crap outa' me."

"I thought you said they were just scared little boys?"

"Oh, they are, but they're like cornered beasts, too. Their fear won't keep them from lashing out. Like I said, though, I don't think they would do it here with cops everywhere."

"Don't bet your life on it, nigger." The red-eyed kid is at Fil's shoulder, with a mocking grin. It all seems like a big joke to him, Hannah thinks. But she's afraid he won't stop at verbal threats. She feels the big skinhead crowding her from behind. She turns. He looms over her, staring down. She had been glancing at them and can't believe they managed to get so close, undetected. And she wonders how much they heard.

The big kid says something to Hannah, low and muffled.

She can't make it out. He whispers it again.

"Race-mixer."

Before she can move or speak, she's pushed aside by two men, one in a dark-gray sport coat, the other in dark blue. They place themselves between Hannah and the kids, moving Fil to the side as well. The hall feels packed, Hannah realizes. Suffocating.

"Is there a problem here?" One of the men asks Hannah, but he rivets his gaze on the young Nazi. His voice holds a booming, commanding authority.

"No —" Fil starts to respond.

"Yes," Hannah interrupts. "I think there is."

The man has a receding hairline and a hard, square chin. He's a big man, but still considerably smaller than the massive teen. He presses close to the big kid.

"Back off. Your business here is finished. Understand?"

"It's a free country." The big kid fidgets, but stands his ground.

"Oink, oink." The red-eyed Nazi wedges near his buddy.

"Back off, unless you wanna' spend the night locked up."

The other man, dark-haired with a stern, angry face, shouts his command.

The big skinhead leans his chin and chest forward. "Fuck you, you motherfucking pigs!" he shouts in their faces.

Everyone in the hallway turns, looking at the plainclothes cops and the skinhead kids. More spectators from around the corner crowd into the side hall, gawking. Three more men, two in plain brown suits, the third in a plaid sport coat, quickly emerge from different parts of the crowd and are immediately in the faces of the three young Nazis. A crackling, walkie-talkie sound cuts through the corridor.

"Get some uniforms up here right away. Second floor, side hall."

Hannah isn't sure which detective is talking.

"We're on our way." The answer is broken up, but easy to make out. The big Nazi stares at the cops, daring them. The red-eyed kid glares at Hannah instead of his immediate adversaries.

"You've been warned." The cop looks right at the big skinhead.

"You're either on you're way out the door, or you're on your way to lockup."

"Fuck me, pig."

The words are barely out before the two officers pounce on the big Nazi. One goes low and takes the kid's legs out from under him. The other grabs the teen's left arm. When the boy crashes to the floor, the officer goes with him, yanking the kid's arm behind him and cuffing it in a swift, practiced motion.

The other officers hold the two remaining skinheads at bay with their presence. The red-eyed boy tenses. His companion backs up. Police in blue uniforms arrive and together with the detectives, hoist the big kid to his feet.

He wrenches back and forth, spits and curses, but he can't break loose. "Fuck you!"

Hannah has never been this close to anything so violent and frightening. She feels a shiver, and her body trembles. She thinks of her self-defense course, how lame her kicks and blocks would be in the face of this boy. Then she remembers the red-eyed Nazi, but when she looks for him, he's gone. She looks around to make sure he's not behind her, but she can't locate him.

The hallway buzzes with chatter. Fil jerks out a little laugh. "I never thought I would feel good about having cops around."

Hannah is quiet.

"Are you all right?" he asks softly.

"Yeah. I've never seen anything like this. You know? I'm okay, though." Hannah sighs and takes a breath. She feels her body sag. The hallway feels hot, the air stagnant. The clatter of the crowd simmers back to a low, constant murmur.

"What is wrong with these kids?" Hannah suddenly blurts out, catching herself by surprise.

"I don't know." Fil clenches his jaw and his voice hardens. "That's part of what I'm trying to find out. But I'm not optimistic."

He hesitates, as if he doesn't know what to say next. Hannah realizes her most disruptive students are a breeze compared to these hard-cores, and finally understands why Anthony was no match for kids like them.

At the circle meeting after his murder, none of the kids ever mentioned things Anthony might have done to them— hitting them or bullying them. Hannah wondered if the kids were observing a don't-speak-ill-of-the-dead rule, or if Anthony had really changed that much. She had no doubts that, at his worst, he was one of her most disruptive students — stealing, picking fights. He never seemed vicious, though, and she believed he was turning it around. He hadn't been in a fight, that she knew of, in three months. He was reading, and completing his assignments. But she would never know if he had turned it around.

2

Billy the Kid hurls his jacket into the wall, charging into his apartment as if he were storming a barricade. His two friends are on his heels. "Goddamn niggers," Billy wails and heads for the kitchen. The odor of rancid milk tweaks his nostrils. Brown paper sacks, two high, filled with garbage, lean against the wall. Sunlight streams through a curtainless window, highlighting food-caked dishes that overwhelm the sink and mass on the stove.

"Fucking pigs," Hulk shakes his head back and forth.

"They porked your butt pretty good, Hulk." Billy's red eyes twinkle.

"I hope you don't think that's funny."

"Kikes and pigs and piggy little dykes," Billy playfully sing-songs.

"Pigs were everywhere, Billy. I didn't have room to spit."

"Yeah, yeah." Billy snatches a beer out of the refrigerator, an old Hotpoint, painted black. He glares at Hulk. "They're gonna' fuck Hanson for sure. They're gonna' fuck Hanson 'cause he's white."

Hulk grabs a beer for himself. "I know that. Don't you think I know that?"

Billy mouths the words. I know that. Don't you think I know that. But Hulk still faces the refrigerator and can't see his mockery.

"Man, this place is beginning to stink," Joe says as he finally slips around Hulk to heist a beer.

"It always has, dude. Portland's a dump," Billy says with his Valley voice imitation.

Joe starts to say something, but Billy winks at him and Joe chuckles.

Billy moves past him toward the living room, his back to both his friends. "Dumb-fuck Hulk and piss-ant Joe," he mumbles.

He hits his stereo button on his way into the living room. The top shelf of a mahogany bookcase holds the amplifier and the CD unit. CDs fill the bottom shelves. Billy slides a Skrew-driver CD in the slot and gives the volume control a full-twist, steps over a pile of bottles, boots, and comic books, spins around on one foot and slides into a spot on his couch. Two wooden crates with a door on top serve as a coffee table. He shoves a bunch of empty beer cans over, clearing a spot between soup bowls filled with ashes and cigarette butts and a pile of comic books and matches, and hoists his steel-toed boots up onto the table and crosses them. Hulk moves into a dilapidated, but cushy old chair perpendicular to the couch.

Billy reaches under the couch cushions and pulls out a Sucrets tin. He opens it, wets the tip of his little finger and dips it in. He holds the white-tipped finger up, displaying it for Hulk and Joe.

"Crank it up, dudes," Billy shouts over the bass-heavy cadence. The stereo speakers can't handle the volume and distort the sound.

Hulk smiles. "Skank it down, bones." They both laugh.

Billy snorts the speed up his right nostril, dips his finger back in, and holds it up. He dangles a limp wrist and puts on an English accent. "Skunk it up, chums."

Hulk and Joe laugh. Billy hands the tin to Hulk.

"Here's to my mom," Hulk makes a toast with his white-coated finger tip. "For coming through with the fifty bucks that put us over the top."

"To us, Hulk." Billy rivets a long, hard stare at him. "Me and Joe wasted the whole goddamn day hustling your fuckin' bail."

"Okay. To you, too, then. What's your problem?"

"Our problem is, we missed the day, Hulk. Portland was wacky. Skins were kickin' ass." Billy fumbles around with the clutter in front of him.

"I missed the day, too, you know. "

"Marble mouth." Billy mumbles so Hulk can't hear him. He thinks Hulk sounds as if his mouth is full of marbles when he gets excited. He smirks and shakes his head, finds a pack of cigarettes with a couple left.

Billy raises his voice. "Joe and me sat in that shit-hole police basement waitin' forever for some geeky clerk to do your goddamn paperwork. And the whole fucking time cops are creepin' all over the place like slimy cockroaches." He lights a cigarette and takes a drag.

"I'm the one who was in the slammer, Billy. You just gonna'

sit here bein' pissed?" Hulk shouts his challenge. "You wanna' kick some shit? Let's go."

Billy can hardly keep from cracking up at his marble image. The more excited Hulk gets the more the marbles bounce around. Hulk takes a snort up one nostril. He rubs his fingertip on his gums. He offers the Sucrets tin to Joe who declines with a shake of his head.

"We missed the window," Billy says. "We'll get on it later."

"Easy for you to say. You didn't spend the day in a fucking cage."

"That's cause you're a fucking idiot. You knew there were pigs everywhere. Like Hanson says, you gotta' choose your battles, man. And like I said, me and Joe spent the fuckin' day in the pig basement. Cause of you, we were as good as locked up."

Hulk glares at Billy. Billy stares back at Hulk, then at his blank television screen. Joe gives the music control a quarter-twist down and looks away from Billy's glare.

"How about a little more light?" Joe asks as he puts his hand on a heavy cotton curtain draped across two large, wood-framed windows. A single window on an adjacent wall lacks a curtain or blinds, allowing the evening's fading light to graze the pale plaster walls.

"There's enough light already," Billy responds.

Joe releases the curtain. "What time is it, anyway?" he asks as he squeezes into a spot at the end of the couch.

"Hanson said now isn't the time." Billy says. "Portland is crawlin' with pigs doin' overtime."

"Shit, man, they can't be everywhere," Hulk says.

"They were on top of you, weren't they? Fuckin' slow down, will ya?" Billy shoves some junk on the door-table to the side, reaches under a mass of comic books.

"No. I won't fuckin' slow down. Will you pick it up? Man, I wanted to stick that bitch, and I was ready to. I'm not just talkin' it. Like some people."

Billy feels the blood in his neck. He tenses his muscles, and his eyes turn cold. He looks away. He fumbles among another pile of junk, then glides his hand under a pile of papers. He finally finds his remote control. He points it at the tube, flicks it, and jerks his hand back like he had just fired a gun. Twice, in quick succession, turning it on and hitting the mute control. He waits for the picture, then fires again. "Blazers, dude."

"Fuck this, man. You gonna' waste all this juice watchin' a bunch of niggers suck each other off?"

"Fuck off, H. I told you, it's early. We'll go out in a few hours. Chill, already." Billy rubs his right eye with his index finger. His eyelid twitches as he pulls it away. Then he holds a beer can to his eye for a few seconds — a habit that gives him a short respite from his itching.

"Hey, check the news, Kid. There might be something about Hanson." Joe slouches forward.

Billy puts the beer can down and gives Joe a hard look. Joe fidgets and looks away. Billy breaks into a grin. Hesitantly, Joe grins back. Billy flicks his channel gun in rapid succession, flying by a couple movies, a quiz show, a newscaster, and stops on a panel discussion. He quickly fires again, backing up to the newscaster, and fires again, bringing the sound to its maximum volume.

"Not much happened at the Robert Hanson trial today..." the newscaster intones. With the volume cranked to compete with Skrewdriver, his polished voice crackles at the edges, and distorts.

"Perfect timing, du —" Joe starts to shout over the competing noises.

"Shhh." Hulk and Billy jump on him. Joe slumps back and remains quiet.

"...Hanson's lack of courtroom experience was evident, however, and his decision to defend himself could wind up costing him ten million dollars, the amount of the civil suit brought against him by the family of Anthony Jones, who was killed by four skinheads two years ago..."

Billy fires again, and the screen goes blank. "Fuck this."

Hulk goes to the kitchen, grabs a full six-pack out of the Hotpoint, walks back in to where Billy and Joe are sprawled, pops one beer off the plastic mold and drops the remaining five onto the table with a crash. He opens the can and swallows about half in one gulp.

Billy looks up at his big friend. Even as a high school freshman, Hulk dwarfed his older football buddies. And Billy remembers many of them as bulky guys. Now, with his head shaved, multiple tattoos of swastikas, spiders and eagles, and wearing his usual dress — steel-toed boots and a leather jacket — Hulk is a frightening monster. The skins generally use names of outlaws or super heroes, and Hulk seemed like an obvious identifier. When he and Billy started reading some neo-Nazi comics and magazines, they picked up on "H.H." for Heil Hitler and after a while

Billy started calling him H.

"So, are you ready to split, man, or what?" Hulk rocks from one leg to the other.

"How many times do I have to say it? It's too early."

Hulk takes a few steps toward the door, then turns back toward Billy. "Let's go over to Patty's."

"Patty's? No, fuck that."

"What the hell is wrong with that, Billy?"

"You guys go without me," Billy says flatly.

"C'mon Billy, what's your trip? Patty says Debbie's got the hots for you. I'm sure she'll be there, too."

"Yeah, I don't have the hots for her, okay?"

"Hey okay, but she's got humongous tits. You don't have to like her to fuck her, dude."

"Man, what is your trip, tonight? Just split, okay? I'll catch up to you guys later."

"You're acting like some goddamn fag."

Billy glares at Hulk. Hulk moves toward him, scowling. Billy looks away, flicks the TV back on, fires past the news, a quiz show, an old movie, the Blazer game, and stops on another old movie. He tries to back it up to the game, but the remote sticks. He can't get off the channel with the movie. He points the remote and presses harder. Nothing. He aims it directly at the TV and presses again. The Blazer game appears on the screen. Billy relaxes his grip on the remote. Skrewdriver has finished, and Billy turns the game volume up.

Hulk stands with his hands on his hips, staring at Billy. Joe looks from Hulk to Billy to the game.

Billy ignores his friends, concentrating on the game. Inside his head he mimics the play-by-play. The Kid breaks loose, he's going in for the lay-up. No, he stuffs it over the seven-footer. Look out, folks, Billy the Kid steals the in-bounds pass. He stuffs it again. And the crowd goes wild.

"Fuck you," Hulk shouts.

Billy stares at the screen. He tries to focus on the game. The color commentator, a black man, praises a drive by Damon Stoudamire. "Fuck you," Billy mumbles out loud, raising his voice with each word. "Get a goddamn white announcer, and get that fucking monkey out of there."

"I'm outa' here." Hulk guzzles his beer, tosses the can at Billy, and picks up another full one as he moves toward the door. Billy just stares at the tube, like Hulk isn't there.

"Fuck you." Hulk spits it at him. Billy stares straight ahead. Joe is quiet, slouched back in the corner of the couch.

"Well, Joe, how about you?" Hulk looks right at him. Joe looks at Billy, who stares at the television. Hulk taps his foot and turns his gaze back to Billy.

"Split, Joe. Go with Hulk. I wanna' be alone for a while."

"If you're sure, Kid?" Joe asks, softly.

"Positive," Billy deadpans, looking straight ahead at the tube. "Check me later."

"Where?" Joe asks, "When? Do we come back here for you?"

"I'll meet you at the Paradise sometime after 11:00.

"Okay, man, catch you then." Joe looks at Hulk, who heads out the door without saying a word.

The door slams shut, leaving Billy alone. "Asshole," Billy says to Hulk's vacated space. "If you think I'm afraid of you, you got another thing comin'."

#

Billy started getting into fights on the playground in first grade. He would rather choose a kid to a fight than play a game, like dodge ball or softball. Fighting was more fun.

His first assault charge came at twelve, and another at thirteen. Both times the charges were dropped, but the police were on to him. He was still thirteen when he was charged with arson for a warehouse fire. They might have known he lit the blaze, but he didn't think they could prove it. The charges were pending, when a kid called him out. Billy beat him badly, landing the kid in the hospital. The district attorney offered to drop the arson case if Billy pled guilty to the assault.

Billy was enraged. It was a fair fight, he said. He was being punished for winning. But his court-appointed attorney told him he would only serve thirty days, and if he got nailed on the arson charge he could go away for a year. He agreed to the deal.

As he remembers it, the judge lectured him about starting a fire that wasn't supposed to be part of the charges, and then burned him with a six month sentence at MacLaren. His attorney said the judge had that kind of discretion.

At thirteen, Billy was one of the youngest and smallest kids at the juvenile detention center. He had only been there three hours when Mike Bullard, the most feared kid at MacLaren, confronted him. The muscled, square-faced seventeen-year old stood in the doorway, grinning ear to ear. His braces reminded Billy of

Jaws, the James Bond villain. Billy's sister took him to the movie when he was seven, and he pretended to be the tough, cool, British secret agent.

A couple of Bullard's buddies were at his flanks.

"We're the official greeting committee," Bullard said and his friends laughed.

"Nice to meet you." Billy said it evenly, his defensive gaze flitting from one guy to the next.

"Welcome to the booger room." Bullard turned and swept his arm across the doorway, revealing the room behind him. His buddies chuckled. Years earlier, the adolescent inmates had dubbed the all-purpose space the booger room because of its dull yellow walls and pallid green trim. It served as the cafeteria, meeting room, and, with the pale green tables folded into the walls, the center's cramped exercise space.

Billy cautiously stepped forward, but Bullard whipped his arm back up, planting his hand on the doorjamb, blocking Billy's way.

"Almost forgot, kid. Booger room toll gate. Cost you a quarter."

He smiled. Billy looked at him and back and forth at his two cohorts before he tried to duck under the outstretched arm. Then Bullard stuck his elbow into Billy's ribs and shoved him hard against the doorway wall. Billy knew the drill. Give in to the older kids, pay homage, pay your dues.

But to Billy a fight was a fight, and Jaws Bullard one more villain in a long line of foils.

"Fuck you," Billy shouted and shot out his left hand. Bullard blocked the thrust, except Billy had pulled his punch and was running his hand through his hair. The old, junior-high-trick made Bullard look foolish. Billy laughed. The older boy scowled.

Bullard tensed, ready to retaliate, but Billy already launched his right fist. This time he didn't pull his punch. He nailed Bullard square on the mouth. Billy felt his knuckle tear on the braces. He followed with a left to the gut, taking the wind out of Bullard. Quickly, Billy smacked him again with a right cross to the chin, knocking him back. Before Bullard could regain his balance, Billy was on him, flailing with both fists. Dozens of kids scrambled to the doorway, screaming and cheering. Bullard's buddies hesitated.

The guards were on them by then, anyway. The seventeen-year old didn't get a chance to use his strength and size to overcome Billy's initial flurry. One of the guards grabbed Billy. Another guard laughed at Bullard as he shoved him to the side.

"Looks like you got what was coming to you, tough guy. And as a bonus, you get to spend a month all by yourself."

"This new punk jumped me. I never even swung, let alone landed a punch." Bullard sounded whiny. He was talking fast. "Ask anybody." He nodded at his friends and a dozen other kids crowding around.

The guards looked at each other and back and forth between Billy and Bullard. The guard who laughed at Bullard shrugged his shoulders.

"Okay, you get a freebie," he said slowly. Then his voice became stern. "Next time, I don't care who starts it, you owe me double. You got that Bullard?"

"Yes, sir."

"First one's free, kid." The guard turned to Billy. "You heard what I said. It doesn't matter who starts it. The next fight will cost you."

Billy had been at MacLaren less than half a day and he was already the talk of the center. He figured he was in for it. Bullard couldn't let it stand.

Billy stayed awake most of the first night, fretting over a possible attack. He relished a good fight, but what if a bunch of them rushed him, held him down and raped him? He had to stay alert. He didn't mind the six-foot by four-foot cell, which consisted of a toilet, a sink, a metal bed and a metal desk. The door that locked him in the barren, cramped space, also kept him safe. But he thought Bullard might have a way to spring his lock and burst in. Lying there, he questioned his own defiance. He wondered if paying Bullard would have been the smarter move. Nothing happened that night. If Bullard could get to him in his cell, he was saving it for another time.

MacLaren didn't offer much space, anywhere. The cell area funneled into two hallways. One led to the showers, the other to the all-purpose room. Beyond the universal space were a couple classrooms, offices, and the visiting rooms.

Billy spent his second day checking every corner. Once he got his bearings on his new terrain, he realized there were only a few places Bullard and his crew could ambush him. He also realized six months was too long to avoid his due. Eventually, he figured, Bullard would get him — probably in the showers. Billy decided his best bet was to strike first.

On the third day, he picked his spot at lunch — with everybody watching. The tables were down in the all-purpose room, crowding the limited space. Billy walked up to Bullard as he left the food line with a full tray.

"We got some unfinished shit, don't we tough guy?"

"Not here, you little fuck. We'll both get nailed."

Billy shoved Bullard in the chest and raised his voice. "Oh you want me alone somewhere with your bodyguards to back you up. One-on-one I had your punk ass. You know it. I know it. And now everyone knows it. You're chicken shit."

Billy tensed for the battle he knew was coming. But Bullard didn't oblige.

"Nobody's buyin' that bullshit, kid. And I ain't goin' to the hole to make you happy." Bullard flicked his eyes toward the guards. They were close, and like everyone else, watching every move between the two. If Billy threw a punch he would pay for it. He wasn't sure what to do next.

Bullard smiled. "I got a better idea, kid," he continued. "Why don't you join me?"

"Fuck you," Billy snarled, ready for battle.

Bullard remained slack. He flicked his eyes toward the guards again. "Don't be stupid. The hole is a drag."

Billy hesitated. How bad could solitary be? He looked around the room. The guards were watching them. He could land two or three punches at most before they would be on him. Was it worth it? He looked back at Bullard, studying his expression. "Why the fuck would you want me to join you? And what's in it for me?"

"I was just fuckin' with you the other day, kid. I don't give a shit what you do. But now that I see what a tough little son-of-a-bitch you are, I wouldn't mind having you backing me up."

"And what's in it for me?" Billy stared straight at Bullard, ignoring everyone else in the room.

"That's up to you. I'm king of this roost. You hang with me, good things happen for you." Bullard leaned to within a few inches of Billy's face and whispered. "Plus, I won't have to kick your ass." He smiled again.

Or go to the hole. It finally dawned on Billy. Bullard was willing to take his shit to avoid doing time in solitary. He looked around the room again. Everyone was watching. He didn't trust Bullard for an instant, but this is what Billy was after in the first place — not letting Bullard and his little gang bully him. Billy figured nobody would think he gave in to Bullard. After all, Bullard was the one who made the offer. It was Bullard who backed down.

"Okay. Why not?"

Bullard switched his tray to one hand and put out the other. "What did you say your name was kid?"

"Billy."

"No shit? Billy the Kid?" Bullard laughed again.

For a long time Billy couldn't shake the feeling that he had chickened out. It was three years later that he put it together, when Hulk gave him one of Robert Hanson's White Nation pamphlets. Sometimes making allies, Hanson wrote, is better than conquering enemies. As long as they're white.

3

Pain rouses Max Turnfeld. It's still the middle of the night and he knows he won't get back to sleep. He's not sure which throb grabs him first — the back, or the knee. Once he's awake, they both hurt. And now his bladder demands attention, too.

Reluctantly, he gets up and hobbles into the bathroom, past the toilet, through the back door onto the wooden walkway to the woodshed. His knee still stiff, he limps to the end, stands naked in the cool, early morning air and relieves his nagging bladder. The knee and back aren't as easily placated. A few stars are visible through the partially cloudy sky; and Jupiter, big and close. The giant planet looks like a tiny moon.

Max walks back into the bathroom, dimly lit by the kids' night-light. He glances in the mirror. Despite his imperfect surgeries, Max is a powerful, muscular man. Gnarled. His dark brown hair curls behind his ears. His beard is short. Flecks of gray are beginning to show here and there.

Feeling chilled from the frosty night air, Max slips back to bed, and pulls the blankets around him. He waits for his body to warm before rolling onto his side toward Gretchen, deeply asleep, facing away from him. It's still too early to wake her. And too dark to see her very well. But he imagines. He imagines his hand stealing softly to one of her breasts and cupping it gently. No movement, just lightly embracing her softness until her nipple grows hard. He loves her small breasts that fit so nicely in his palm. His imaginings of her nipple, erect with its own longing, stirs him, and he moves toward her.

There was a time when Max doubted the prudence of his middle-of-the-night maneuvers. Until he asked.

"Are you kidding?" Gretchen had responded. "What woman wouldn't want to be awakened softly to a good man's love?"

"About ninety percent of them wouldn't, from what I've heard," Max had responded, giving her room for an out.

"Ninety percent?"

"Sure. For some once a month is too frequent, for some even once with any man is too frequent, then there's your control freaks," he had smiled, "Then, of course, there's your morning haters."

Gretchen had laughed joyfully, and playfully said, "Well, you lucky dog, you've got a woman in the top ten percent."

That I have, he thinks, as he moves along the curve of her rump, guiding his hand along her thigh, across her belly, finally cupping her breast. The fronts of his thighs lightly graze the backs of hers, softly tingling her awake. Max fights his penis — less restrained than the rest of him — from seeking an unsolicited entry. He waits, patiently, instead, just holding her, taking in her softness. Her nipple responds, he hears her low sigh, not an irritated go away, but a wake-me-some-more purr. "Hmmmm."

"Good morning, my sweet."

"Good morning, Max."

"What time of the month are we?"

"We," she pauses with a half-smile, half-waking-up-yawn, "are completely safe."

Gretchen rolls around, snuggling into Max's body and arms and reaches for him with both her hands.

"Oh, God."

"What?" Gretchen demands, and squeezes him just enough to let him know who's in charge.

"I mean, oh Goddess."

"That's better."

#

Crisp, early morning air chills the house. Max shivers. But he doesn't think it's cold enough to start a fire in the wood heater. The heat from the cook stove should be sufficient.

"It's goddamn June already," he mutters to himself. He lifts up the stove round with one hand, tosses some wadded up paper in the long narrow box, and snatches a few pieces of kindling from the stack by the side of the stove. He adds a couple slightly larger pieces of fir before striking a wooden match on the stove top and lighting the fire. He quickly replaces the stove round.

His knee and back begin to loosen, and he runs the seventy yards down to the garden and unearths a few potatoes, pauses for a second to marvel at the big red jewels, and bolts back to the kitchen. The fire crackles, the stove top is heating up, the water beginning to murmur. In minutes Max has the iron skillet hot, the potatoes washed, cut, and sizzling in a stream of olive oil.

"Gretch," Max shouts toward the bedroom, "if you want eggs you better head down to the hen house. The potatoes are going in any second."

No reply. Her late-rising habit still gets to Max. He takes a deep breath. You can't have everything, he reminds himself, and sex in the morning makes up for a lot of other deficiencies.

"If you can hear me, I'm going to wake the smooches so you can stay in bed. You can make your own breakfast later."

Max heads for the girls' room. Michelle, the eleven-year-old, is still asleep. Five-year-old Heather looks right at Max as he comes in the door and talks to him as if they had been in the middle of a conversation.

"I had a dream about Cinderella, Daddy."

"Cinderella, the cat?"

"Of course." Heather says matter-of-factly.

Max grins. He sits down on the edge of the bed.

"Of course." Max concedes. "What did you dream?"

"I dreamed she came back." She says it with the same matter-of-factness.

"She's not coming back," Michelle, now awake, interjects. "She's been eaten."

"Daddy," Heather pleads. Her chin quivers.

"Michelle, you know better than to say that to your little sister. We don't know that. She could be on a long cat trip." He gives the older girl a hard look.

"Probably right. Sorry, Heather."

Michelle's apology starts out snooty and ends up whiny, but when Heather grins and hugs Max, he decides to let it go.

"Hey, smoocharoonies," he says, "school's not out yet. You've got four more days, so up and at 'em. Do you want cereal or eggs and potatoes?"

"Cereal —"

"Cereal," Heather shouts right on top of her sister's answer.

"Hot or cold?"

"Cold." This time Heather manages to say it nearly in unison with Michelle. Max laughs.

Heather grins. Max pokes her in her stomach and she giggles and squirms away. Her face is round, made rounder by short brown bangs. Max insists they stay out of her eyes. Michelle, at eleven, is already beginning to elongate like her mother, and her face is narrower than her moonfaced sibling's. Max is happy to see her acting like a kid. Lately, she's become moody.

"Teenager stuff," Gretchen had speculated.

Max groaned. "You mean this is going to last for the next several years?" But the moods aren't steady; more like episodes.

"In a few more days we'll have fresh strawberries with our cereal," Max says.

"I want strawberries now," Heather demands.

"Can't rush Mother Nature, sweety. When they're ripe we'll eat them." Heather scrunches up her face in a fake pout. "Hurry up, or you'll be rushing after the school bus next thing we know."

Max heads back to the stove and checks the potatoes, now crusty on the bottom. He flips them, and sprinkles them with salt and pepper. The heat from the stove cozies the kitchen. Max inhales deeply. The aromas of olive oil and potatoes mingle with the scent of burning wood. He places a couple bowls of cereal on the table and heads back to the bedroom again. Gretchen's long dark braid snakes across his pillow. The rest of her head is buried under the quilt. "Let sleeping dogs lie," he chuckles.

#

After breakfast, Max walks the girls toward the bus stop. The dirt road out runs one hundred yards, disappears around a curve, and goes another couple hundred yards before reaching the nearest neighbor and the highway where the school bus stops. A steep barren embankment forms a wall to their left. The land slopes downward to the right, lush with spring growth where viny maple, blackberries and conifers create a temporary railing against the deeper forest. Max marvels at the rapid spring growth. The blackberry vines couldn't have doubled since yesterday, he thinks. A white-crowned sparrow greets them with its distinct whistle, followed by several more trills. Heather spots the black-streaked gray and brown bird on a low branch and runs toward it, but the bird takes flight before she can reach it.

"Why did it fly away from me, Dad?" Heather whines.

"You know they're afraid of you, sweetheart," Max says. He strokes her head as she comes back to him.

She twists her head around and looks up. "But I would never hurt it."

"Birds don't know that."

Heather scrunches her forehead. They walk along in the quiet. At the road, he kisses and hugs his daughters good-bye, and watches as they walk across to the other side and down thirty yards to where the bus stops. Michelle is becoming more angular, but not at all gangly. Heather walks with her stomach pooched out the way a teen jock might strut his chest. Max gets his morning paper and heads back.

Because Max and Gretchen's twenty acres are in an isolated little hollow, radio and television signals don't find their way in clearly, which is fine with them. But Max still likes to keep up on current events.

He tosses the paper on the front porch and ambles to the garden. He lifts the black nylon netting off the strawberry bed, squats down, and lifts a clump of leaves, revealing berries dangling free. He picks a couple moldy ones off and pitches them, then reaches between two tiny green berries and plucks a medium-sized, ripe, red fruit. He tosses it in his mouth.

He cleans out several moldy berries and weeds grasses and other unwanted competition. After only fifteen minutes of weeding, and sorting out the moldy fruit, Max's left knee hollers at him. He gets up in two parts, lifting his whole body straight up, with his back still bent forward, then pulls his torso back, aligning it with the rest of his body. "Fuck," he grunts to get things started. "Goddamn it."

He heads back toward the house, hobbling for a couple strides until his knee loosens up. He turns the faucet on and walks around the side of the house to a dark shaded area in the back. Fifty logs, ranging from two feet to four feet in length, are loaded with shitake mushroom spores. Some of the mushrooms have already sprouted, popping out of the wood like elves looking for mischief. Max checks to make sure all his logs are wet. In the dry, hot weather he has to keep the dark, rubbery-looking oriental mushrooms wet and cool. If he could only stagger the harvest a little better, he thinks, it would make things a lot easier. His only two customers, a health food store and a Chinese restaurant, don't create much demand between them, and Max hasn't worked on marketing them beyond his local area.

His rocking chairs are a much better income-producer. They're plain, made with local, white oak. Max has a one-page flyer on the bulletin board at the feed store with his phone number and the phrase: "They rock real nice." The requests come in at just about the right pace. And when the demand slows, the chairs don't go bad like mushrooms.

Max ambles back around to the front porch and eases into a weather-beaten old chair, the first rocker he ever made. He looks out at the garden and, settles back to read the morning news.

The Hanson trial is front page. Same old shit, Max thinks. A lot of speculation about how foolish Hanson is to defend himself. Max hears a triumphant call from a blue jay and looks up to spot two birds swoop down to the berry patch. He's left the netting off. Another bird joins the first two, then another. Go ahead, he thinks, have a few. Soon, the four vandals move on, having wreaked their damage and savored the booty. Teenagers, Max thinks with feigned disgust. He laughs, puts the front section aside and dives into the sports section.

#

By the time he finishes the paper, his morning-savoring mood is beginning to give way to impatience. Max is about to head out on his own as Gretchen emerges, coffee cup in hand and a very happy look on her face. She reaches down and kisses Max on the cheek.

"What's the plan, man?"

"The sun is breaking out. May not last, though. I figured if you got up in time we could take a little walk." He barely manages to keep anxious and scolding tones out of his voice.

"Let me get my boots and finish this." She waves the mug at him, "And I'll be ready to stroll."

#

Max and Gretchen's home is about a three-and-a-half hour drive from Portland. Three hours south, straight down the Willamette Valley and the I-5 corridor past Salem, Eugene, and Roseburg; then a half-hour of curving and twisting on side roads heading east into the mountains. Their house sits on a flat piece of land at the foot of a steep bluff. Sloping hills surround the homestead, forming an isolated little hollow. The drainage forms a creek that divides the home, yard, and garden from the wooded hillsides. Their acreage is steep and forested.

A flat bridge with no railings spans their creek. The walkway consists of a series of cedar two-by-sixes laid across two ten-foot long yew poles, each nearly a foot around. Max and Gretchen cross the four-foot wide bridge and meander up the road, side by side. The road succumbs to forest growth, and narrows, still running several hundred yards into the woods as a wide walking path before dead-ending completely.

"Heather dreamed Cinderella came back," Max says.

"And you didn't spoil that notion, I suppose?"

"No, but Michelle couldn't wait to."

"Well, she's probably right. At some point we have to tell Heather that her cat is dead."

"Does that mean you've given up?"

"You haven't? It's been nearly two months, Max."

"I know, I just —"

"Oh shit." Gretchen jumps sideways into Max. She's looking down at the spot where she was about to step. "Oh, it's a slug."

"What did you think it was?"

"I thought it was a dog or coyote turd, or something like that."

"It is a turd," Max says excitedly, "It's a living turd."

"God, it's huge. It's the biggest slug I've ever seen." She crouches lower for a closer look. The fat, slimy, brown creature is at least five inches long and covered with black spots.

"Look, Max." Gretchen points out two little antennae. He bends over, resting his hands on his knees. A barely discernible undulation propels the slug across the ground.

"It's not moving much faster than a pile of shit, either," Max says putting on his Groucho Marx voice.

Gretchen laughs, and they move on, walking quietly for a while, taking in the trees and space. Low-lying shrubs fall away with the sloping land. Thicker growth forces Gretchen to slow down and pick her way. After several plodding steps, the density of thick, viny maples obstructs her vision, forcing her to stop, completely, and consider her next move. Beyond a thicket of twisting limbs, vines and thorns, the forest floor is less crowded.

Once they get around this little stretch, the going will be easier.

"Let's head up to the madrone," Gretchen says.

Madrones are everywhere, but Max knows Gretchen refers to a particular, favorite tree of hers. When she stands next to this long and elegant madrone, Gretchen and the tree look like sisters to Max — sisters who share a grace and resilience. Max sees himself as more of an oak, knotted and arthritic, but the sturdiest creature in the woods.

A wide marsh obstructs a direct route to the clearing. Even in the driest years the low-lying spot remains wet and marshy, and the past year has been wetter than usual. Max figures a rich spring fuels the gusher. On their first few forays into the quagmire, they sank into the muck and mud up to their thighs, and mosquitoes had buzzed about in the shaded marsh. Ever since, they've avoided the area, walking around it. As usual, they decide on the longer route through the woods.

Gretchen slips past an entanglement of blackberry, the thorns grabbing in futility. Max follows, crushing the thorns rather than avoiding them.

"I don't remember the blackberries being this thick in here," Gretchen says. She squeezes a fat vine between her thumb and finger, delicately avoiding the thorns, and hoists it up over her head. Still holding on, she twists and slides her body under the vine, like a dancer twirling under a long silk scarf. Once she's past it, she lets go. The thorns latch on to Max's blue jeans and green flannel shirt, but they scrape off as he pushes his way through.

"They weren't this thick before," he says. "They're taking over."

Gretchen angles around an area rendered impenetrable by

viny maple. Max stays close behind. They enter a stretch of woods forested with tall trees, keeping the sunlight out and the ground snarls to a minimum. Firs dominate with madrone, maple and oak interspersed. The mercurial leaves of the maples and oaks join with the evergreen foliage of the firs and cedars. No longer impeded by low-lying growth, the couple moves swiftly.

"Oh, no." Gretchen grabs as if to pull her hair, but her hands freeze in the air, constricted. "Oh my God, it's been cut."

Max hurries to share Gretchen's view. "Goddamn it." Max rests his hands on his hips, staring. "Son of a bitch."

"I loved that tree," Gretchen whispers.

"Those damn idiots — Jesus —"

"Max?"

Gretchen's eyes seek comfort. Max doesn't want to comfort her or to be comforted.

"Shit. You'd think we would've heard these bastards."

Gretchen doesn't say anything. She just looks at the cut tree. Max wonders if she's going to cry. He puts his arm around her and draws her to him.

After a long quiet, Max resumes muttering about the bastards and sons-of-bitches.

Gretchen finally asks, "Why would they cut it and leave it? Did they get it hung up?"

"Damn idiots." Max's grumbling gains more volume. "They didn't have the slightest idea what they were doing. Just look at that."

The madrone had grown straight up, then stretched outward toward several towering old maples. Its color was chocolate brown until the bark went through its annual peel, turning the tree tan.

The way it set off the little clearing had made it special to Gretchen. Now, Max and Gretchen stare in disbelief. The tree is cut at the base but isn't dislodged; instead, the cut end of the tree is still resting on its stump. The thick arms of a huge white oak cradle the slain madrone and hold her aloft.

"That's dangerous, Gretch," Max finally surmises aloud.

"I've got to get my chain saw and bring it down. Can't leave it like that."

"Why don't you wait till you can get some help from Frank or somebody? Doing it alone is dangerous, too."

"I'll be careful. I'm afraid the kids'll come up here and we'll have a major disaster." He doesn't look Gretchen in the eye. He knows the look she's giving him, knows what she's thinking — that he's obsessing and that it's useless to try to talk him out of it. Finally, he looks at her and smiles.

Gretchen gives him a smirk; she takes a last look at the little clearing and the suspended madrone. "I'll see you back down at the house."

She turns and slips back into the woods.

Max puts his hand on his hips and studies the tree. "These damn idiots," he murmurs aloud. Just beyond the clearing the land rises sharply to a crest. Max climbs up to get a better view. He still can't see much, but he hears more. The creek rushing down the other side bubbles its rhythms up to him, and a red crossbill trills from a nearby spruce.

#

Max sniffs in the gooey smell of yeast as he enters the kitchen. His arms strain from a load of freshly split fir.

"Say, Gretch, have you seen the ax? It's not by the shed and I already looked around the porch. I just used it this morning."

"No, I haven't seen it. You're not going back up there, are you?" Gretchen asks. "Let it go 'til tomorrow, hon."

"If you're worried, come along and keep me company. I could use your help."

Max doesn't think Gretchen is seriously considering his proposal. They're just going through the ritual invitations and excuses of a twenty-three-year relationship.

"I've started a batch of bread; you go ahead. I'll just worry a little." She smiles. "You be careful."

Max slips his arm part way around her back and gives her half a hug. "Sure thing."

He makes another pass at obvious places where the ax might be hiding and grabs his big splitting mall off the front porch.

#

Max figures the danger will begin after the cut reaches some depth. He paces around the big madrone, studying the probable stresses. He plants his left foot near the stump and crouches on his right knee to study the placement of an undercut. The stress is actually upward, he reasons. A big wedge at the top and an undercut — then it should fall away. He pauses. Right on top of him. He shakes his head. Max studies the site for another minute. Then he yanks on his starter cord, and the Huskavarna purrs into motion, the well-sharpened chain slicing rapidly through the madrone. Once the wedge is out Max whips into the undercut.

He stops, clicks off his saw and surveys the site one more time. He wraps a coarse, thick rope around the smooth bark of the madrone and secures it in place, walks several paces back and gives a hard tug. Nothing.

Max starts up his saw again and proceeds with the undercut. He pauses again, goes to the rope and tugs hard. Nothing. Not the slightest budge.

This time he cuts deeper before pausing. The tree creaks and groans. The grains of wood tear and separate from each other, screaming. As it finally falls, it pivots first, the cut-end smashing directly into Max's misplaced foot before rebounding off it. The once-elegant madrone shudders before resting with a thud.

Max lets out an anguished cry, but even in his agony Max knows it won't reach Gretchen's ears. Sounds travel up the hollow, not down.

#

Gretchen, scrubbing the cutting board, perks up. She thinks she hears a faint sound in the distance. She turns the water on, rinses the board under the faucet and turns the water off. The sound is closer now, and obvious. She hears a vehicle turn off the main road and proceed up the long, narrow drive. She wipes her hands on a cloth hanging above the dish rack and walks out to the front porch.

A wiry, unshaven man is already out of his pickup — a beat-up, early fifties Ford. He approaches the house, his gangly shoulders dipping up and down with each step. Another slightly less scraggly man leans on a half-opened door, peering studiously at

Gretchen and the house.

"What can I do for you?" She compels her voice to be firm, but cordial.

Gretchen's eyes dart back and forth between the two men. The closest man twitches his shoulders up and down and glances back at his companion.

"Well — ah — we got this here load a firewood — thought you might be interested."

Gretchen takes a quick glance for any madrone, but mostly pretends to survey the load of wood while she studies the man by the pickup. The bill of a faded green, John Deere baseball-cap shades his eyes. His face is clean-shaven, with a gaunt, haggard look. "My husband and I gather our own wood like most folks back this way. Maybe you should think about advertising instead of driving around with a load, gas costing what it does these days."

"We just cut this here wood on a piece over yonder and we thought we might run into somebody who could use it — maybe some woman what needs an extra hand. You could have it cheap."

He's speaking more confidently now. His shoulders are still, but his eyes fidget to the side and down, then dash back toward her. She stares back firmly, and his eyes glance away again in retreat and discomfort.

"We don't have money to spend on wood we can gather for the cost of running our chain saw." Gretchen's earlier firmness wanes, replaced with an edginess.

The slamming of the truck door startles her as the other stranger suddenly approaches with a confident walk.

Gretchen is outnumbered. Be calm, she tells herself. Be calm and forceful. "I have work to do, so you'll excuse me."

"Maybe we could just hang out for a spell." The second man isn't asking a question.

"I'd prefer you did not." Gretchen finally allows her irritation to show. "Since you have no business here and I have things to do, I'll have to ask you to leave."

The first stranger studies the scene; his shoulders move up and down again, as if his body wants to bolt. But he doesn't leave.

His companion edges closer to the porch and says, "Ain't very neighborly, is she?"

"Maybe she thinks she's better 'n us," the closer one responds.

Gretchen eases beneath the overhang, looking for an escape route or a weapon. She knows she can't whip open the door, rush inside, slam it, and lock it before they can catch her. She sees no weapon. She remembers Max looking for the ax, not finding it.

Gretchen inches backward. The men lunge for her. Desperate, Gretchen goes for the door, but she's too late. She swings at one attacker. He smacks back, stinging her cheek. Momentarily stunned, she regains her balance and brings the full force of her knee straight up between the nearest attacker's legs, but as he goes down, the other is upon her, knocking her to the deck with a hard blow from his fist. She tries to get up, but he's on top of her, restraining her wrist. Occasionally, Gretchen has pictured herself fighting off an assailant. She has never allowed herself to envision defeat, but then she has never thought to envision more than one attacker, either. The one who went down rejoins the attack.

Gretchen feels like she's driving a car that just lost its breaks and is careening off the road. Everything in slow motion.

Her right wrist burns from the grip upon it. She struggles to rip it free. She flails with her left arm, hitting her attacker again and again. She wrenches away from the foul breath on her neck. She's inches from the second attacker. Face to face, Gretchen sees a blackened tooth next to a gap where another tooth is missing. She jerks her head away from the sight and the stench, writhing and twisting, but her body can't move. Her head is turned away from the attacker. Her eyes focus on the door, but she still sees the image of the black tooth and the gap, and she smells the foul, whiskey-coated breath. They pin both her arms. Her left leg is still kicking, but the right leg has gone numb from a knee digging deep into her thigh, pushing the one leg away from the other.

"Bitch. Bitch."

"Not too good for us now, are you?"

Rough, dirty hands are everywhere — on her body; on her face. She feels herself slipping, her will draining under the onslaught. She grabs at her last recourse. Gretchen screams.

4

"Paranoia strikes deep. Into your life it will creep." Hannah sings the Buffalo Springfield verse as she climbs the stairs to her second floor apartment. She can see Max in their basement the summer after his first year of college, mouthing the lyrics and strumming on an imaginary guitar, but she can't remember the rest of the words. She repeats what she knows. This time her elongated emphasis on "creeeep" makes her sound more like Bob Dylan. She laughs for a second, before tension returns to her face.

Two days after the courthouse encounter she's still peeking over her shoulder, bracing for the next blind corner. She puts the key in her apartment door lock and glances at the *mezuzah* mounted on the door frame before closing and bolting the door behind her.

She walks to one of several second floor windows, runs her hand along the smooth, polished wood of the sill, and peers out. The big maple, its trunk off to the side and out of her view, spreads its branches into her gaze and, aided by a breeze, seems to wave at her. She leans forward, looks from side to side. Nobody is in sight.

The overcast skies have darkened, and a light rain dampens the leaves and branches. June is doing its usual schizophrenic thing: sunny one minute, overcast the next. Oregon weather can drive people's moods up and down; Hannah thinks of it more as outward and inward. The sun lures her outdoors. The cloud cover turns her contemplative.

She considers Fil. But the image of his smile — with his dreadlocks flip-flopping back and forth as he shakes his head — gives way to her father's icy expression. Her father would never say "nigger" but the way he used, "shfartza," a Yiddish word for black, always struck Hannah as derogatory. She was nine years old when her suspicions were confirmed. Max and Hannah and their parents were dining out at Pitigliano's, their favorite Italian restaurant. She had a deliberate way of eating her meatball pizza, nibbling to the edge of the meatball without biting into it, savoring the sweet tomato sauce and creamy, melted mozzarella. A gulp of Seven-up followed. Her parents wouldn't let her have Coke until she turned twelve. Max, at fourteen, sat across from her, sipping his Coke. She didn't understand the restriction. None of her friends were prohibited, but she didn't mind because Pitigliano's served the Seven-Up with a maraschino cherry, Shirley Temple style.

After her sip of Seven-Up, she took her second bite of pizza, this time sinking her teeth into the middle of the tiny little meatball. The sauce on the meatball was different from the tomato sauce on the pizza — richer and tangier. She was relishing her first bite of meatball and barely noticed the maitre' de seat a black man and a white woman at the table next to them.

Hannah thought she saw her father roll his eyes toward the couple. "I think I'm going to be sick," he said.

His eye gesture puzzled her, and, for a second, she wondered if the pizza made him ill. Then she saw her mother trembling.

"Michael, please. They'll hear you." Her mother looked directly at Hannah's father, and quickly at Max and Hannah, before looking down. Her face was red.

"I hope they hear me." Her father raised his voice. His face hardened.

Hannah gazes out her apartment window. The memory of her mother's embarrassment tugs at her, momentarily, before she returns to the image of her father, sitting at the restaurant table, stone-faced.

Besides an enigmatic need to placate her father's ghost Jewishness had not been an issue for Hannah. Not until two days ago. She rarely goes to the synagogue anymore. The *mezuzah* in the doorway is more of a cultural icon than a religious observance. She keeps kosher by default, Max had teased. "Vegetarians are kosher," he said. But she violates the kosher laws, too, when she visits Max and he coaxes her into eating his pork spareribs.

One single event impacted Hannah's attitude about being Jewish more than anything else — another argument that haunts her. She was only six. Her Great Aunt Sonya scowled as she told Hannah God used Hitler to punish the Jews for not practicing their religion, "for trying to be like goyim."

Her grandmother, Sonya's sister, had interrupted. "Don't put such nonsense in her head." She turned to Hannah, ran her hand tenderly along her cheek. "The good, pious people — the most religious, the cantors and the rabbis — they all were killed. Not because God punished them, but because good men didn't stop the evil ones."

Aunt Sonya had snapped back, "Then why didn't God stop them?" The scene had frozen, vividly, in Hannah's memory, perhaps because it was the only time she ever saw the two sisters angry with each other. But what she remembered most was that her grandmother didn't answer. She just shook her head back and forth as tears welled up in her eyes.

Hannah walks into her bathroom and looks in the mirror. She's always liked her hair. When it was long, when it was short, and now more than ever, the way it hangs just above her shoulders. But she avoids a glance at her nose, and a few lines nearby. Too long a stare and she'll be reminded of the imperfections of her genes, and perhaps worse, the crevices of age. She's okay, she tells herself. Sure, another internal voice answers sarcastically, and she shoots a nasty stare at herself. She flares her nostrils in defiance, pokes at a few loose hairs, and tucks a silver strand of bang back under another.

Hannah had always thought she passed for a WASP. Her hair, most of her life had been light, almost blond-brown, and straight. People never identified her as Jewish by her looks. Now she wonders. Did the young Nazis detect her origin? She thinks perhaps age is exposing her roots. She hears Aunt Sonya, "They didn't consider themselves Jews, but Hitler did."

Hannah goes to the kitchen, pours a cup of water into a small saucepan and stirs a one-third cup of oat bran grains into the pan on a small front burner. She makes a face.

The water starts to boil. She stirs the bran a couple times, watching to make sure lumps don't form. As the water boils and the hundreds of tiny little grains bounce about the pan, Hannah sees red eyes glaring out at her from beneath the liquid's surface. She blinks. The eyes are gone as quickly as they appeared.

She lifts the pan and switches the burner off, plops a couple big forkfuls of Nancy's yogurt on top of the cooked bran. She heads out of the alcove, past her big table where she would eat if company were present, and settles into her overstuffed chair. The flavors are bland, but the textures engage her, the warm grainy bran against the cool smooth yogurt. In another week, she'll add strawberries.

Hannah finishes, sets the pan down, picks up her phone, and tries Max's number. After several rings she wrinkles her brow. Her brother and Gretchen don't have an answering machine because they are almost always there. She gets up, paces back to the window.

Everything has seemed great for Max and his family, which triggers a superstition. Hannah believes if things are going really well something awful will happen. She knows it's a terrible belief. It means you have to hope that little, bad things will happen every so often in order to prevent a total calamity, like small tremblers preventing the build-up to a massive quake. She doesn't recollect anything that had happened to her as a child to have created the belief. She seemed to always feel this way. For a long time she wondered if it was a Jewish thing or her own perverse superstition, until she discovered Max felt the same way, too.

She was twenty-nine, then, and finally beginning to accept the notion that life could be good without necessitating disaster, when the unimaginable occurred. From the moment the stiff, wooden voice on the phone asked her if she were Hannah Turnfeld, she knew something terrible had happened. The man's voice was neutral. But she knew, anyway. Maybe she heard the slightest tremble in his words, after all. She instantly started hoping for specific bad things — Max getting hurt, but not too severely; her father being diagnosed with a serious, but non-fatal illness — anything but someone's death, as if she sensed the depth of the still undelivered news.

When the voice asked her if Michael and Helen Turnfeld were her parents, she said, "Yes," and felt the word catch in her throat. She heard her own voice trembling. Each second seemed like a minute. A voice inside her head started shouting, get on with it, already.

"I'm sorry, Ms. Turnfeld." The stranger's distant facade cracked ever so slightly. "I'm officer Bill Henderson with the Illinois State Police. I don't see any other way to say this." His voice quavered.

Now the voice inside Hannah pleaded, no, no, no. Let them be hurt. Let them be hurt, badly.

The officer's tone deepened. "There's been an automobile accident." The clatter inside her head was deafening, voices upon voices screaming, no, no, no. She could barely hear the voice from the phone. "Both of them were killed. We believe they died instantly."

The voices fell still. Her body convulsed, and spewed its torrent. She was alone, shivering, holding herself, bawling forth an endless flood of tears.

It took less than a day to get to Max. But the time between the phone call and when they finally embraced seemed endless to her. Sometime during the days that followed, when they held each other and cried, and she confided her secret fear — that if things are going too well, something catastrophic will happen — Max said he had always felt the same way.

Eight years later, she thought she had finally loosened the grip of her superstition. Life could be good without disaster. Not perfect, but not catastrophic either.

Then Anthony was murdered.

Hannah walks to her desk, a beat-up, wooden, Goodwill purchase painted an ugly, glossy blue. She had planned to sand it down to its natural wood finish and stain it, but she hasn't gotten around to it. She pulls a manila folder from the center drawer. A plain white label reads: Jones, Anthony.

She settles back into her chair and rests her hands on the folder without opening it. Student folders weren't supposed to leave school grounds. She would take them home, anyway, combing them for clues, hoping to find any edge that might help her reach a troubled youngster. In her most severe cases, including Anthony, she made copies and kept them.

After Anthony's murder Hannah quit bringing folders home. Then she quit looking at them at school. She was ready to quit teaching, too, but Max talked her out of it. They were sitting on his front porch, Max in his old rocking chair, Hannah trying out a new rocker. They wore sweaters and wrapped themselves in blankets, cozying up against the spring night chill. Hannah sipped on a cup of tea, allowing the steamy fumes to warm her face.

He reminded her she was ready to quit halfway through her first year. She said that was different; she didn't have the hang of it yet. Then Max recalled what Hannah termed her "fuck you" episode, and they both laughed. Her first year of teaching she lost it and screamed "fuck you" at a kid who had interrupted her one too many times. Brenden Lane, who became Brenden the Brat in subsequent recollections — her first ever class clown. Max said that should have earned him a special place in her heart. She said she still grits her teeth when she thinks of him.

"You were ready to quit then," Max said.

She admitted she was overwhelmed, but she said her errors were rookie mistakes. She learned a lot from the experience, she told him. The next year she instituted her three strikes rule. Kids knew where they stood. Thanks to Brenden, she expected at least one kid would test her at the start of each year. And once she suspended one kid, the rest tended to shape up even more. Two years later she started her contract system. The kids and Hannah spent the first few days drawing up class agreements. Her students not only knew where they stood, they had a hand in making the rules.

Max told her she was doing a great job — by her own account. It's not the teaching that was getting to her, he said. It was Anthony's death. She needed time to get over it.

"I don't think you'll ever feel right about this if you quit now," he said. "Maybe later the time will be right. For now, you have to stick it out."

Maybe later has arrived, Hannah thinks. She did stick it out. For two years now, she's arrived at school an hour before the kids, preparing for each day's lessons. And she often stayed well into the evening, too. More often than not, she came in on Sundays to plan the week in advance. Before Anthony's murder she did all that, too, but she didn't notice how much time she was putting in, because she couldn't wait to be in the classroom, and she hated to leave. After Anthony was killed, she forced herself in every day, because she felt it was her duty. That's what feels dangerous to her.

Hannah sets Anthony's folder down and walks back to the kitchen.

She fills the sink with hot, sudsy water. The warmth is comforting, the cleaning ritual meditative. She takes her dishcloth and wipes more than scrubs a glass, a cup, and a couple plates. She rinses them along with a handful of silverware she pulls from the sudsy sink. Her small iron skillet comes clean. Hannah leaves the dishes to drain.

She dries her hands and looks at them. They're younger now at thirty-nine than they were at twenty-seven. Fighting wildfires left them carved and cut; darkened by dirt and sun. At least the classroom has been good to her hands. They're smooth and soft, now. They were already soft a few years ago. She pictures them, with Anthony's thin, dark fingers cradled momentarily in her white hands. School was out for the day. The classroom was empty, except for the two of them. She was holding his hand, speaking softly. She thought he had calmed down, when he jerked away in an angry outburst.

"Fuck you, Turncoat," he screamed.

She told him she was his friend. He said that was bullshit, that friends don't turn each other in. Hannah could see Anthony fighting back the tears.

"We had an agreement," she said. "All the students signed it, including you, Anthony. First time you violate class rules, you get a warning. Second violation I call your — "

"And third violation I get suspended. But you could've given me another warning."

"Anthony." She raised her voice to compete with his. Then lowered it when she realized he was listening. "I understand you're angry with me. But if I do that for you I have to do it for everybody, and then our classroom would be a mess. I'm not trying to hurt you. You know I like you."

He looked at the floor.

"Don't you?" She tried to make eye contact. He didn't respond.

"Don't you think it bothered me to have to call your mom? I didn't want to suspend you. I'm doing this to help you."

He mumbled at the floor. "Some help."

She could barely hear him. She remembers her thought at the time — that he looked like a five year-old, pouting. Hannah smiled at him and twisted her head to make eye contact. He jerked his head farther away. She twisted hers closer. Creases spread across his cheeks as he struggled to keep from laughing.

In the weeks that followed she started to see that encounter as a possible turning point. She allowed her students to choose between *The Adventures of Tom Sawyer* or *Adventures of Huckleberry Finn.* Usually, once they read one for class, they read the other on their own. Anthony had refused, despite testing high on reading skills the first week of school. He said he didn't feel like reading and nobody could make him. After his suspension was over, Hannah gave him a copy of *Lord of the Flies.* As part of his consequence he had to stay after school every day for a week.

"Might as well read something," she told him. "You have to sit here, anyway."

Once he finally sat still long enough to read a few pages, he read a few more. But he completed his after-school detention before he finished the book. The following week he showed up after school. He wanted to talk about *Lord of the Flies*, and he wanted something else to read.

"Are you ready for some Mark Twain?" Hannah asked.

He shuffled his feet and looked at the floor. "I don't like reading that ancient history stuff."

Hannah suppressed a laugh. "The nineteenth century isn't exactly ancient, Anthony."

"Whatever." He turned to leave.

"How about something about a boy growing up in Oregon in the Fifties and Sixties?"

He allowed as how "That might be cool."

Anthony devoured *Ricochet River*,. in less than a week, even more eager for the next book. She knew he was hooked. When she told him *Adventures of Huckleberry Finn* and *The Adventures of Tom Sawyer* were like *Ricochet River*, he finally relented. Not that Hannah even cared about Anthony reading Mark Twain anymore. He was reading, and loving it. He still wouldn't raise his hand in class, but he wanted to talk to Hannah about the books. Every time he finished a book he came in after school, bubbling about the book.

Reading and being enthusiastic didn't necessarily equate to a complete turn-around, but he had come farther than she had imagined. And his smile was growing more winsome with each visit.

The image brings a brief twinkle to her eyes. She walks back to the window and eyes the waving maple. She spaces out for a moment, looking at the leaves and branches without focusing on them. The sun comes out from behind the clouds, casting an emerald sheen on the big multi-pointed leaves. She fixes on the leaves again, blinks, and gasps.

Across the street, red-tinted eyes glare back between the up-and-down motion of the branches in the breeze.

This is no illusion from her imagination and fear. The boy from the courthouse is alone on the corner, smiling at her, laughing.

5

Prior to the trial's fourth day Robert Hanson holds a press briefing in a park across the street from the federal courthouse. Fil leans against a mailbox a few feet from the corner, waiting for the drama to unfold. This guy is too much, Fil thinks. Hanson ought to keep his mouth shut instead of blabbing to the media.

The tall statue of a bearded, uniformed man dominates the middle of the square. A double row of buttons protrudes from his military tunic, and a broad-brimmed cavalry hat tops his head. The solitary, metallic sentinel is gray and green, faded by his long exposure to the Oregon rain. Curved walkways, lined with benches, intersect in the middle of the park. Towering oaks and alders shade a deep green, well-kept lawn.

Two of Hanson's men carry a portable wooden platform and place it on the grass next to the sidewalk. Another man hops out of a white van with the letters KMTV on the side, and begins unwinding a thick black cord along the ground. Fil decides he better move closer. He hustles along the walkway and takes up a spot near the platform. A stubble-faced man in baggy pants and a rumpled jacket slouching on a bench, opens his eyes, glances at the sudden flurry of activity, and closes his eyes. Two prone, curled bodies occupy other benches. Several pigeons peck at the ground nearby.

Fil nods at a man with a note pad who walks up and stands next to him. One of Hanson's men gives Fil a hard look. Fil looks away, then glances back to find the man still fixing his hard glare on him. He takes a deep breath. The musty scent of molding, cut grass lingers in the damp, morning air.

A swarm of journalists suddenly arrives, some taking up positions with tape decks and microphones while others stand ready with pens and note pads. Hanson, clean shaven and smelling of Aqua Velva, mounts his portable platform. Three television crews hurry in and set up directly in front of him. Fil cranes his neck around and steals a peak behind the gathering press.

Drivers accelerate their cars to make the next traffic-light, or stop suddenly, on the busy, one-way street that separates the park from the courthouse. Pedestrians, wrapped in rain coats, sweaters, or suits, scurry toward jobs and errands. They clench their jaws, rivet their eyes straight ahead. Few stop. But some are unable to resist the show, and a small crowd begins to gather.

No Nazi uniforms are present today. Hanson is adorned in a dark blue pinstripe suit. His brown, thinning hair is combed straight back. His bodyguards wear sports coats; a few followers choose suits, too. The big man appears confident, authoritative.

"I don't have a statement to read, I'm just here to answer your questions." His invitation is pleasant, but a strident, sarcastic tone seeps through, giving the impression he would sound slightly shrill ordering a cheeseburger.

A man in the back, holding a pad and pencil gives a casual, half-wave of his hand. “Anthony Jones’ family, on the advice of their legal counsel, aren’t talking to the press. Why did you decide to make yourself available to us in the middle of the trial?”

A few reporters turn to see who’s asking the question. Fil shakes his head.

“If you like, I’ll leave right now.” Hanson smiles, and his entourage laughs. A few people in the crowd chuckle. “I know the conventional wisdom is that I ought to keep a low profile until after the trial, but I have nothing to hide, and quite frankly, you nice people are going to help me get the word out.”

“Is it your position that Blacks and Jews and other minorities are inferior to the White race?” a young, blond-haired man standing next to a television camera asks.

Hanson smiles.

He eats this stuff up, Fil thinks. Half the local news stories on Hanson are about him and his separatist philosophy, instead of the trial.

“We think the evidence speaks for itself,” Hanson pauses. “Read the scientific information on differences between the races. We don’t discriminate. Jews can have their rights. Blacks can have their rights.” He pauses again. “Even homosexuals.” He takes another pause.

Fil recalls an aunt who would take her foot off the gas pedal as she drove on the freeway, give a shot of gas, then take her foot off again, then back on — making him nauseous nearly to the point of vomiting. This guy is going to make him puke, Fil thinks, if he doesn't get on with it. Or if he does. Fil smiles.

"But we have our rights, too," Hanson resumes. "We have the right not to have to live or work or go to school with Jews and Blacks and queers. We believe the races should be kept separate. White Nation is just that — a movement for a white nation."

Several reporters continue to scribble. Others look at each other. A woman in a dark pantsuit confers with her camera operator, then turns to Hanson. "What about reports that members of your organization met with the skinheads who killed Anthony Jones just hours before the murder?"

"That's totally false." Hanson attempts to maintain a pleasant tone, but his stridency penetrates, creating a sound that resembles a bad sweet-and-sour sauce, a smooth sugary sweetness followed by the sour bite of too much vinegar. "My people never met with them. Someone is trying to muddy the water. There's absolutely no evidence at all we were ever even in Portland, let alone met with these people. We've driven by here on the freeway, but we've never even stopped."

"We understand that they have a witness who is a former member of your organization?" the same reporter asks quickly.

"He's perjured himself in his affidavit. The First Amendment protects us from most of their claims. Everything else is just hearsay."

"It sounds like you're not worried?" The reporter's statement, posed as a question, comes from the man in the back who asked the first query. He's wearing a gray sport coat and a blue shirt that's open at the neck. His sandy hair curls behind his ear.

"I'm not worried about the evidence. If the jury looks at just the evidence, we'll be fine. If they buy into this nonsensical, roundabout crazy pattern that the plaintiffs are going to somehow try to draw — that somehow we had some way of controlling these people magically, that we had some way of guiding them around the country to do people in — then we could be in trouble."

Hanson's pace accelerates, forcing his attempts at an even, melodic tone into an occasional screech. "We didn't pay salaries to anybody. These people were not members of our organization. They did not pay dues to us. I think the jury, if they are at all on the ball, are going to see right through that."

Hanson pauses for a breath. Before another reporter can fire a question, he raises his hand, signaling he isn't done.

"Unfortunately," he continues, "We are forced to defend ourselves because we lack the funds to hire high-priced attorneys, so that will be tough."

Fil waves his hand in an effort to get Hanson's attention. One of Hanson's bodyguards glares at Fil, but he fends off the eye contact, staring straight at Hanson, who's playing to the gathering crowd.

"We're growing and learning from this hardship and strain, this persecution." He continues over the clicking of cameras. "Young people are seeing us, and they are coming to us because we speak to their concerns."

"Then you don't deny that you recruit skinheads into your organization?" Fil exploits the opening. He feels his pulse quicken.

Hanson shoots a disdainful look at Fil. "We influence skinheads." Hanson lets the word "influence" drip out as he stares at

Fil. He turns back to the crowd. "We don't have members, or cards, or dues; we have a lot of friends and associates around the country and some of them are skinheads."

He pauses. A reporter starts to ask another question, but again Hanson raises his hand to silence the query, and then continues. "They usually come to us because they are a little tired of a lot of the activity they've been involved in, which is sometimes a little bit knee-jerk; and they see we do produce a newspaper that goes all around the country, and they want to get involved with that and find there's another way of going about things than just getting in fights on the street. Of course, there's a lot of them who gradually get out of the skinhead mode and become professional with us, wearing suits and growing their hair. We don't spend our time on skinheads. We spend our time on youth. So the inference that this is some kind of skinhead deal is simply not true."

Fil grabs another chance. "Would you say the bulk of the youth you appeal to are working class, white kids?"

Hanson tightens. His bodyguards lean forward, muscles tensed. Hanson puts forth his most pleasant voice.

"Yes, we generally appeal to working class white youth and since there are skinheads involved in that group of people, obviously, they're welcome, too. We were one of the first associations that said, hey, these guys are okay and just because they want to shave their heads and so forth, they're still okay with us. We don't care if they're Left or Heavy Metal, we know they're young and have problems. We welcome everyone."

Everyone who is white, Fil thinks. Before anyone can fire out another question, one of Hanson's associates steps up and says they've run out of time, they have to get to the courtroom.

News crews begin a rapid breakdown of equipment and cords, and the scurrying off begins. Fil finds himself face-to-face with the reporter in the gray sport coat. As their eyes meet, Fil starts to say something when one of Hanson's burly associates bumps him hard, nearly knocking Fil off his feet. Hanson's man doesn't look back, but the action brings a wry smile to the reporter's face.

"Better watch your step, Fil."

Fil shakes his head and grins. "You should talk, David. Your first question practically ended the press conference before it got started."

"Hanson wasn't going to walk away from this. The guy can't keep his mouth shut."

"We can always hope." They laugh.

"What about you, Fil? Get anything helpful out of this?"

"Not much, but I appreciate you letting me know about the press briefing. You never know when something useful might turn up. I think it's interesting that Hanson sees his appeal as broad-based."

"You don't think it is?" David and Fil take a couple steps off the sidewalk and on to the grass as a camera operator pulls his microphone cord by their feet.

"He may be putting out the message to a broad base," Fil says. "But I think it's a fairly narrow group that hears it."

"It might be broader than you think. I'm working on a feature piece on a kid from a fairly wealthy family who joined the Aryan Brigade."

"The Aryan Brigade. What do you know about them? How are they different from White Nation?"

"I don't know a lot about them. Both groups have staked out the Pacific Northwest as the region for their homeland. But the Brigade has more of a militia feel to it. They're more into rules and regimentation."

"I would really like to interview somebody from the Aryan Brigade. Can you turn me on to somebody?"

"You're nuts, Fil. They would just as soon string you up as look at you." David runs his hand through his hair. Then he twirls a curl of hair behind his ear. "I interviewed one kid who quit because he got tired of their crap. He'd be cool. Devin Nelson. He lives in Springfield. I'll get his number to you."

"Terrific."

"I won't say you owe me one. I'm not sure I'm doing you a favor."

"That reminds me, I may have someone for you. I met the neighbor of Tommy Larson's grandmother. Her take on the kid might be an angle for a story for you. The old man is a great source."

"You got his name?"

"Earl. I didn't get his last name. Lives next door to the kid's grandmother. You'll have to knock on two doors, at most."

David laughs. "I gotta' go, Fil. My deadline's calling." He takes a step, then turns back. He fingers the curl behind his ear again. "Look, maybe it's none of my business, but some of these kids who follow Hanson don't always think real clear. They go to prison for murdering you, but you're still dead."

"I appreciate your advice, but I figure as long as I'm in broad daylight with lots of people around, I'm okay."

David stares at Fil, raises his voice. "You don't think these people are capable of tracking you down, Fil?"

"Yeah, I know." Fil looks down and away.

David puts out his hand and they shake. His hand is worn and thin, but the grasp is strong. He gives Fil a warm smile.

Fil watches him walk away. He sighs. He's glad he's leaving Portland. After he gives Hannah a call.

6

Joe spots a couple skinheads cut across the street, and head toward him. He looks at Hulk. "We're gonna' miss the start if Billy doesn't get here soon."

"Where the fuck is he?" Hulk flings his cigarette at the concrete wall. Cinders and ash bounce back.

"He had to go by his sister's. He said he would be here."

"His sister's? That's twice in three days. I thought he doesn't have nothing to do with her anymore. And the plan was to meet at my place, not here."

"He said her old man had done something for him. He had to return the favor. That's all I know." Joe shrugs his shoulders.

"Was he still in his mood?"

"No. Not really. He seemed jacked up about Hanson."

"If he was so jacked, why isn't he here?" Hulk raises his voice.

"Geez, man, don't blame me. I'm here."

"I ain't blamin' you, Joe." Hulk leans toward Joe, then tilts back on his heels. "The meeting's gonna' start any second. I'm ready to go in without him. That's what I'm sayin'."

"Let's give him another five. Okay?"

The two approaching skinheads nod at Joe and Hulk as they enter the building, a two-story motel that's been converted into apartments. Paint peels from its walls. Stray patches of weeds break up the dirt yard.

"I'm gonna' take a leak." Hulk walks around the side of the building.

The dirt yard reminds Joe of a vacant lot he used to hang at after school. Fist-fights broke out there nearly every day. Joe wasn't a fighter. Kids at school called him nerd because he was skinny and liked to read. But outcasts intrigued him. He liked neo-Nazi literature and thought the skinhead crowd might be cool. At the lot one day, trying to prove his toughness, he picked a fight with a kid who he thought he could handle. He held his own, too, until the kid's older brother stepped in. Joe was battered, bloodied, on the verge of submitting, when Billy entered the fray.

Joe had heard of Billy, seen him around, but hadn't met him. Billy must have been watching the fight, waiting for the perfect moment. Joe figured Billy didn't care about him. He saw an excuse to kick the crap out of somebody. Still, he wound up saving Joe's ass.

"What's funny?" Hulk walks up.

"Nothing." Joe pauses. "I was just thinking about the first time I met Billy."

"The time he kicked the shit out of that guy? You think that's funny now, huh?" Hulk snickers.

"Funnier than getting the shit kicked out of me." They laugh.

"You ready to meet the man?" Hulk asks.

"For sure. But I wonder why Hanson is holding this meeting now."

"What do you mean?"

"The heats on, dude."

"Yeah, balls ass move. Typical Hanson." Hulk juts out his jaw.

"I'm not sure it's that smart. They're trying to prove he's connected to skins. Seems like he's asking for it."

"Shit, Joe, he can't let them intimidate him."

"I don't know," Joe looks down, kicks at the dirt. "If I were him I'd be worried about informants and shit like that." He looks up. "You know, lay low until after the trial."

"You read too many spy books, Joe. Informants? Shit." Hulk shakes his head back and forth. "Now's the time to make contact with the troops. Man, I'm jacked to meet the man."

"I'm jacked to meet him, too. But the number one witness against him is a skin that's blabbin'. That's all I'm saying."

Hulk leans forward and back, then shifts his weight from one foot to the other. Joe looks down the street. No sign of Billy. A car pulls over the curb and parks in the dirt yard. Three skinheads get out. They exchange nods with Hulk and Joe as they enter the building. Hulk takes out his cigarettes, pops one in his mouth and lights up.

That morning Joe tried to run his doubts about Hanson by his mother, but she used it as an excuse to condemn Hulk and Billy. He told her she shouldn't put down his friends, and stomped off. It seems like a waste of time to get Hulk's views on Hanson. Joe glances back at him.

"You ever talk to your mom about Hanson and White Nation?" He asks him, anyway.

"Damn straight."

"Really? What does she say?"

"She's been fucked over by Jew landlords and Jew bosses her whole life. She says, 'Right on.'"

"Your mom is tough — a real working class heroine."

Joe shoots his fist in the air.

"What the fuck is that supposed to mean? We're not working class. I got a good paying job at Smith's warehouse."

Joe shakes his head. "I just meant your mom is on the front line — a real white woman."

"You got that right."

"You're lucky, Hulk. My mom hassles me about Hanson."

"No shit?"

"Yeah."

"Well, you can't have everything, Joe. At least your mom's a fox." He grins.

Joe pictures his mom in one of her nice outfits, on her way to show a house, her thick, dark hair pulled back. He never thought of her as bad looking, but it hadn't occurred to him she was attractive. He pictures Hulk's mom. Overweight, rumpled. "A night with the bottle," Hulk calls it when his mom is hung-over, looking like a wreck. And then there's Billy. Joe can't imagine what it would be like to lose his mother. He wonders if Billy's mom was more like his mom, or Hulk's. He kicks the dirt. Hulk lights another cigarette, exhales a big puff of smoke.

"I guess you never met Billy's mom," Joe says.

Hulk shakes his head. "Nope. Never did."

"It's gotta' be rough for Billy, his mom killing herself."

"She didn't kill herself." Hulk sounds irritated. "She got drunk and crashed into a tree."

"Where did you hear that?"

"From Billy. Where else?"

"He told me she killed herself by driving her car into a tree."

"What difference does it make? Dead is dead."

"Seems to me it could make a big difference."

"Seems to me you read too many books, Joe." He raises his voice again. "How the fuck could Billy know? Getting drunk and drivin' into a tree is the same as killin' yourself. Ain't it?"

"I guess so."

Two more skinheads come around the corner, nod at Hulk and Joe, and enter the building.

"I give Billy five more fuckin' minutes, and I'm goin' in."

#

Billy scans the room as he crams into a spot on the floor amongst several other skinheads. Bare patches in brown, thin-grained carpet reveal hard concrete underneath. Three skins hog a long couch that could fit four. Another dozen use folding chairs. Two bottles of tequila head in opposite directions. A swig is taken and the bottle is passed along. Everyone is drinking beer. Billy holds a cold bottle against his eye for a few seconds, then presses the beer to the other eye. Hulk and Joe claim some space next to Billy.

Most of the skins are wearing black boots with red shoelaces — a Nazi signal — jeans, T-shirts with suspenders and some leather.

Spiders compete with swastikas for the most popular tattoo.

Billy leans his back against the corner of a second, smaller couch seating two people and glances down at the boots next to him. Green shoelaces. He spies a quick peek at the guy behind him, a mean, tough-looking skinhead; older, maybe twenty-five or so. Billy doesn't recognize this guy, nor three or four others. The rest he either knows directly or has seen around and knows who they are.

Billy elbows Joe and nods at the skinhead with the green laces. Joe shrugs his shoulders. Billy gives Joe a jacking-off motion with his hand, and grins. Joe laughs and nods his head.

"Green laces," Billy whispers to Joe and rolls his eyes toward the boots.

Joe raises an eyebrow. "Yeah?"

"Green laces mean you beat up a queer."

Joe takes a longer look at the guy, then back at Billy.

Billy whispers again. "I think this guy is some kind of Christian Nazi. I might have to kick his ass." He laughs. "Probably secretly fucked the faggot first."

Hanson clears his throat and the group quiets down. He faces the gathering, sitting on a straight-backed chair. He smells of soap and aftershave, a sharp contrast to the unwashed smell of the skins. Wafts of Aqua Velva mix with the fumes of Cuervo Gold.

Billy whispers in Joe's ear. "Look at Hanson. Suit. Tie. Any other clown shows up looking like him wouldn't last ten seconds with this crowd."

Joe shakes his head. Billy tries to keep his voice down, but he gets excited.

"He'd be raw meat, dude. Not fucking Hanson. He has these bones in the palm of his hand." Billy laughs.

"Shush." Several skins stare at Billy.

He glares back, then returns his gaze toward Hanson.

Hanson smiles. "Have you ever asked yourself why sanctimonious people at every level of society treat racial separatists the way they do?" The shifting of a chair scraping against the floor and a couple coughs break the quiet.

Hanson pauses, looking around the room, making eye contact one by one. "I've gotten a big kick out of all these interviews with the media. They all come at me with the conclusion already in their heads that I am wrong. They have the moral high ground. These self-righteous fools assume everyone is created equal, that all racial groups are equal. That's what you're taught in school since day one, right?"

Some heads nod, a few voices mumble affirmation.

"Think about it; it is obviously false. Everyone is not equal. That belief is a mental disease suffered by millions of people."

The room is quiet.

Billy marvels at Hanson, how he asks a question no one could answer, then answers it himself. Now he's in control, Billy thinks.

Hanson continues. "The latest scam of the Jewish conspiracy is this hate crime baloney. Soon, the courts will be so jammed it will take five years for a traffic ticket to go to trial."

"Maybe that's not too bad, after all." He laughs, and half the skins hoot and holler and laugh with him. Others chuckle.

"Now, remember if you find yourself defending your life against a nonwhite or Jew, and you punch him in the nose, for

God's sake, don't call him a nasty name."

The room erupts in laughter, hoots and applause.

"Fuck hymie," one guy shouts.

"Right on," another amens.

The popping sound of opening beer cans combines with the murmur. The green-laced skinhead hands a bottle of Cuervo down to Billy, who doesn't look up as he grabs it, takes a swig and passes it on to Joe. The tequila warms Billy's throat.

"Listen up, guys," Hanson's tone is hushed. "Anything I say to you can and will be used against me, so I'm not going to encourage you to do anything you're not already doing. What I am going to do, however, is to encourage some of you to do it somewhere else."

A few react with puzzled expressions. Most stare, blankly, at Hanson.

"We've had a lot of success here in Portland and other cities around the country: Detroit, Chicago, Seattle, Atlanta. But our studies show there are a lot of people sympathetic to our view all around the rest of Oregon. Grants Pass and Elk Hill are particularly hot spots. I know a lot of your families come from rural places. If you still got cousins and friends back there, don't forget 'em, pay 'em a visit. Just 'cause they're not on the front line fighting against the non-whites and the Jews like we in the cities are doing doesn't mean they don't care and don't have a role to play in White Nation."

A big rawboned kid with a Mohawk raises his hand.

"Yes."

"I don't hear you talkin about faggots any. We got faggots

causin' more problems than anything in this state."

Billy looks up and back at the skinhead with the green laces. The guy looks down at Billy with a fuck you stare. He stares back.

Hanson resumes. "Anybody who is a Jew, a non-white or a non-Christian is our foe. White Nation is a white Anglo-Saxon Christian organization."

"See what he's doin', Joe?" Billy whispers. "He's including as many skins as he can."

Joe nods.

"The Jews have recruited the queers along with the niggers and their numbers are growing. We have to deal with them all."

"And the goddamn SHARPs!" someone shouts.

This generates a new round of several voices at once, people shouting right on, and fuck the SHARPs. After several seconds Hanson's handlers shush the room and everyone quiets down.

"Can anybody here tell me what SHARPs stands for?" Hanson raises his hand like a teacher looking for an answer.

Somebody shouts, "SkinHeads Against Racism and Prejudice."

A chorus of hisses and boos follows. Then laughter.

"Well," Hanson intones, "talk about a bunch of Hymie-controlled faggots —"

Before he can finish, the place goes wild again. Everybody hoots and hollers approval.

"Anybody who calls themselves SkinHeads Against Racism and Prejudice is obviously a tool of the Jew, and anybody with a name that queer has got to be a fag."

"Yeah, but I still want to know what we're gonna' do about them." Says a big burly skinhead who shouted the first SHARP question. He sounds more charged and angry.

Another skin answers him before Hanson has to. "We outnumber the SHARPs ten to one. Who cares? When you see them, rat pack them."

There's a couple right on's and yeah's but the burly man won't let it go. "Bullshit. There's gettin' to be hundreds of these SHARPs, and we better be prepared."

People start shouting at each other, but Hanson quiets them with upraised arms.

"Our best estimates, and we make it our business to know these things, are that there aren't more than a couple dozen of these dupes in Portland. Now again, I'm not here to tell you what to do, but I know I wouldn't want these phony skins giving my town a bad name."

Everybody hollers again, but the burly skin remains upset, shaking his head and talking to the guy next to him.

"Let's hang out for a while and get to know each other. We've got some of our literature here and we'll be glad to talk with you about our newspaper and how you can get involved. There's plenty of brew."

A big cheer goes up and people start talking to the people next to them, mostly the guys they came in with.

Billy watches Green Laces. He's talking to the burly skin and the guy next to him. Then the three cross the room and head for the door.

"H, Joe, let's blow." Billy races to the door.

Several other skinheads leave right away, too. Hulk and Joe follow Billy.

Billy reaches the bottom of the concrete stairs, his adrenaline pumping. Green Laces and the other skins are part way across the dirt yard. Billy directs his shout at them. "Hey, did you fuck that fag before you kicked his ass?"

Green Laces turns around looking a little confused. When he sees Billy, he smirks. Hulk and Joe catch up to Billy, and the six face off. Size-wise they look even. Hulk is bigger than the burly skin, but the burly one has a harder look. Green Laces is especially mean-looking. He turns to walk away.

"Hey I'm talking to you. I wanna' know if you fuck fags?"

"Why?" He turns and steps toward Billy. "Do you want me to fuck you in the ass or do you just wanna' suck my dick?"

Green Laces' buddies crack up along with four other skinheads who have come out of the apartment and are watching.

Billy's face turns pink. His neck tightens. He tenses his muscles and moves closer to the older skin, edging to within an arm's length. "I wanna' know if you're one of those Jesus lickers or if you're a real Nazi?"

Green Laces looks at the burly skin and rolls his eyes.

"Fuck you." Billy spits it out.

"Fuck you." Green Laces whispers his rejoinder with a hard, daring edge.

They jump at each other, swinging, but Billy ducks down low and comes up hard, smashing the top of his head on Green Laces' chin. Billy's awareness heightens. He senses everything, from Green Laces' breath, to the friends and foes at his flanks.

Hulk and the burly skin look at each other, but neither advances. The burly kid looks from Hulk to the fight and back to

Hulk again. Hulk does the same, looking back and forth, from the fight to his potential foe. Joe and the other skin remain tensed, but they stay put. The group of gathering skinheads encircles the two, cheering and hollering.

Billy should be no match for Green Laces, who is older, tightly muscled, and a seasoned street fighter. But Billy is a whirlwind of fists and head butts. Relentless. He connects a blow to Lace's gut, follows with a smack to his face, lands a left roundhouse to Laces' ear and a right uppercut to his chin. Green Laces lands a couple blows to Billy's head. The two break apart, but Billy doesn't allow Laces to catch his wind or center himself. In less than a second, Billy resumes his disciplined flailing; swinging both his fists, butting with his head, attacking. Green Laces manages to break free from the assault again, but Billy is on him, punching at his gut while keeping his own head down. Billy absorbs a couple more roundhouse blows to the side of his head, but he counters with a direct hit to Laces's nose. He sees his foe reel back for a second. Billy lands another blow to the face, a roundhouse to the ear, and catches the nose again. The older skin is getting the worst of it. On the third break, Green Laces backpedals long enough to pull out a knife.

Hanson and the remaining skinheads rush down the stairs.

Billy hears them approach as he pulls out his knife. With the stakes suddenly higher, the two keep their distance, dancing around each other. The crowd is shouting, some yell advice, but the two focus total concentration on each other, watching every flinch. Neither attacks the other. They jab and feint, waiting.

Hanson shouts. "Back off, we don't need to fight each —"

In the split-second Green Laces takes a side glance toward Hanson, Billy strikes. He thrusts the knife, coming up low and ripping upwards. He sticks Green Laces deep in his belly, right above the belt, and yanks the blade up into a rib and out. Laces slashes back too late, nicking Billy on his arm.

Police sirens wail in the distance, the crowd freezes for a second, then everyone scrambles. Hanson's lieutenants rush him into their car and speed off; Billy, Hulk and Joe are into the night in an instant.

Green Laces' two buddies help him into a car and by the time the police arrive, moments later, the lot is empty.

Part Two

7

Hannah looks up from her weeding and sees wafts of smoke, etching streaks of gray and charcoal across the horizon. Waves of heat rise from the slopes surrounding Max and Gretchen's land, lifting, then realigning the broad, smoke-induced strokes in the sky. She searches the distance for the blaze, but it's too far off. She imagines firefighters, clad in yellow, bent, scraping the earth with axes and shovels.

She knows their look, and how they feel, from five summers fighting wildfires — three as a temporary hire with a state crew, followed by two more on the elite Bear Hollow Hotshots. It was Max's crew, and he got her on, but her first year turned out to be his last. He had been fighting wildfires for ten years, and his bad back was making it impossible to carry on.

"Everybody thinks hotshot work is glamorous," he said. "Our crew battles closer to the flames, we're sent into more precarious terrain, we take up more dangerous points on the fireline; but mostly it's the same damn drudgery of digging hard ground in suffocating heat. And more of it."

"Pace yourself," he cautioned her. And it remained her mantra long after he had quit.

But pacing was nearly impossible at the Silver Woods fire. It was early September, and firefighters throughout the West thought they would be winding down. Many college students among them had already left for school. Crews were spread thin. Then, what had been an average summer for fires, suddenly changed. Temperatures soared above one hundred. Thunder storms rolled across Oregon and Idaho. Night after night, thousands of dry lightening strikes touched off dozens of new blazes.

The Bear Hollow Hotshots jumped on the Owl Creek blaze before it could gain any momentum, making short work of what might have otherwise turned into a terrible blow-up. The all-out effort left them drained, and they should have had a few days off when fire command rushed them in to stem a losing battle at Silver Woods.

All wildfires produce smoke, but strong, downward air pressure served as a lid above Silver Woods Canyon, trapping the smoke and shoving it down their throats. As the crew wound its way along the jagged, narrow trail to the fire's edge, Hannah peered into the surreal, smoke-shrouded stands of fir, attempting to get her bearings. She had hiked Silver Woods once, and recalled steep canyon walls, but she couldn't locate them through the haze. Once they got within a few yards of the fire, updrafts lifted the smoke, clearing the area directly in front of the conflagration.

Yellow flames consumed the dry undergrowth, crackling and hissing. Hannah took up a position between Rick Manning, one of two rookies on the twenty-person crew, and Daryl Brown, a six-year hotshot veteran. Tom Clevenger, the crew leader, was on the other side of Rick. Despite their uniform dress — brown pants, yellow shirts and bright orange hard hats — and even with their faces turned away, she could easily distinguish one from the other. Daryl was lanky. Tom was bullish. And Rick still moved with a rookie's uncertainty.

She swung her pulaski at a foot-high Douglas fir seedling, whacking the little tree, roots and all, from the forest floor. She preferred the wooden-handled tool with its ax-head on one side and thick hoe on the other. Before she ever wielded her first shovel against a wildfire, Max advised her to vary her tools. "Repetitive motion will get you," he warned. The digging motion put upward pressures on her wrists and back, while swinging the pulaski placed a downward pressure on her back and elbows. After a couple hours she would swap tools with Rick or Daryl. She repeated her motion, swinging the pulaski over her right shoulder, sliding her right hand along the handle as she kept her left grip firm, whacking down hard at the combustible forest growth.

Except for short breaks to rest and eat, they dug fireline hour after hour, well past sunset, the fire providing all the light they needed. Hannah kept pushing back her exhaustion, willing herself to keep working. She glanced down the line at Tom who was bent over, but still digging; and at Rick, who had to stop to rest more and more often. She noticed Daryl moving his long arms in and out as he shoveled, revealing the fatigue in his muscles. It was time to quit, but they fought on. Around midnight they headed back to base camp, where Hannah collapsed in her tent, figuring she might get five hours sleep before the sun rousted her for round two.

She was awakened before dawn by the buzzing and whirring of axes and shovels, one after the other, grinding against the sharpening wheel. Once awake, the scent of pancakes and fried potatoes drew her from her tent and into the smoky darkness. By five a.m., the time she thought she would be waking, she was already on the line, swinging her pulaski, the taste of smoke overpowering her tongue.

She began her second day on Silver Woods like she would any other firefight, slowly working the concrete from her muscles, as she warmed to the task. The flames gnawed at the forest floor, burning grasses and shrubs, moving from their right to their left as they dug fireline to keep the blaze from turning a corner. The rest of that day and the next became a giant blur — of whacking and scraping at the hard clay with pulaskis and axes, shoveling the forest debris aside, Hannah muttering under her breath, "Pace yourself," over and over again.

On the third night they didn't even return to base camp, sleeping for a few hours in the fireline they had dug. The morning of the fourth day, Hannah wanted to slowly move into the battle, loosening her aching muscles and joints. But the fire hadn't slept. They were behind again. The tips of the yellow flames glowed red and orange. Tom scrambled to the line and dug in. Despite his weariness, he was unrelenting, putting his back to his shovel, extending the line in a focused race against the fire. No one complained. Everyone followed his lead. Hannah peeked over her shoulder at Rick. He was panting, but working hard. He would be okay, but she needed to keep an eye on him. If anything out of the ordinary struck, the rookie might need help, and Tom would have his hands full taking responsibility for the entire crew. In an emergency, he expected Hannah to look after Rick.

It was only a couple hours later when she felt her own fatigue. "Push through your exhaustion," Max had told her. "It's like the wall in a marathon. You have to push through to the other side." But this wall felt different from others. She doubted her reserve. No matter how deep a breath she tried to summon, her lungs felt empty. She looked down the line again. Tom's hands were on his knees. He was panting, trying to get in more air. Rick was on one knee, leaning on his shovel handle for support. Already, Daryl was displaying his odd shoveling hitch.

Hannah sucked in a deep breath, tasting smoke more than air. She imagined it floating in her lungs the same way it hung in the woods. She could feel it clinging to her hair and skin. Three straight days and nights of eating, sleeping and breathing smoke was getting to everyone, but fire command believed containment of the blaze was at hand. It was no time to let up. Silver Woods was winnable. The crew raced to connect their fire line with a natural rock outcrop. Another hotshot crew and a state crew were coming from the other side, battling to converge with Hannah's crew and encircle the blaze. They could do it, if they could only push themselves a little longer.

Hannah felt something in the air — something different, but she couldn't place it. She scraped her pulaski along the ground, dragging another small pile of debris away from the fire's path. She sensed the change in the atmosphere again, and paused. The wind had stopped. The air felt heavier. She stood still and listened. A quiet enveloped her.

She had heard talk of the eerie silence. But it was all second hand. Folklore. A drop in the wind, the calming of a wildfire — before it blew. Despite having never heard it before, she knew it. She looked up the fireline. Tom was looking back at her. He felt it, too. The others were still digging and hacking. But he knew it was time to get out.

Later, they would learn what caused the blow-up. One air system had created the downward pressure, forcing a ceiling on the fire, trapping it between the steep canyon walls that bordered Silver Woods. That morning, a fierce wind blew in from the opposite direction, blowing the lid off the box. It was like opening the flu on a simmering fire in a wood heater. Once unleashed, the fire exploded. It came straight at them, moving fast, driving thick clouds of smoke, roaring.

Tom raced along the line, pulling the entire crew together. He had to shout over the sudden din to be heard.

"We've got to get out. Everybody remain calm." Tom seemed excited, but showed no signs of panic. The wide eyes on nearly everyone else troubled Hannah.

Max told her she could fight wildfires for ten years and never face imminent death, but if a fire ever blew up, she had to remain calm. "Your natural tendency is to bolt. You've got to center yourself first. No matter how much your body tells you to run. Survey the terrain, the wind and the fire. Then move with a purpose."

And that's what Tom seemed to be doing. Flames attacked the forest to their left, storming through thickets of brush and vines. But he took the time to look at everyone, gauging their state. "Stay in contact with the person in front of you and behind you," he reminded them. "Now, let's go."

He motioned with his arm and took the lead back along the fireline. They hadn't gone more than a hundred yards when they saw the fire crowning — leaping from tree top to tree top. Trees were exploding. Below the fire raced through the grasses and ferns of the forest floor. Their fireline had been breached. Hannah could see Tom turn and shout something to Bill Woodsen, who was right behind him, but she couldn't make out his words. He was pointing away from the fireline. She couldn't see what he was pointing out. The swirling smoke made it hard for her to see beyond a few yards.

Tom led, and the crew followed. Soon, they were on a trail. The path steepened. She pushed on, panting to catch her breath, her muscles aching. She saw Bill teeter before he caught himself and continued. Hannah glanced back when the path zigzagged, but she only saw Sam Capaletti and Hal Brown. The rest of the crew had disappeared into the smoke-filled terrain. She could hear the flames cracking and popping on her flanks. A tree exploded fifty yards to her left, lighting up the woods, but the blinding smoke quickly engulfed her, obliterating whatever brief view the flames revealed.

When she turned her gaze back toward the front, the path was gone. Rick, Marcia Reilly, Bill and Tom had all vanished in the thick haze. The wind was pushing the smoke into them, reducing visibility to less than an arm's length.

Hannah heard Rick hacking and gasping. "I can't see," he wailed, "I can't see the trail."

She caught a glimpse of his yellow jacket as he stumbled to the ground. He had sucked in too much smoke after expending his air shouting. Tom, Marcia and Bill were in front of her, somewhere. The rest of the crew trailed. Hannah tried to center herself. But taking a deep breath would have felt like ingesting the enemy. She closed her eyes, instead. Any step into the thick smoke could be a misstep. She opened them. For a second, the swirling winds revealed a glimpse of the terrain. An open space was adjacent to the trail, with a barren rocky area just beyond. Less fuel for the fire. She grabbed Rick by both his arms and put her face within inches of his.

"Get out your fire tent and get in it."

Sam drew even with Bill and Hannah. "What are you guys doing?" he panted.

Sam had the same look as Rick. His eyes were wide, his face pale. Their bodies looked like they were held up with slack strings. Again, she told herself to be calm.

By then Tom had come back toward Hannah with Marcia and Bill at his elbow. "What the hell are you guys doing?" Tom's voice sounded higher, edgy. "We've got to stay close."

"Look." Hannah pointed into the thick, dark haze. "We can't see two feet. Our only hope is to let this thing pass over us."

The fire's roar surrounded them. Beneath it the snapping of fresh kindling hissed. A thick ball of flame suddenly shot out of the smoke, whizzing over their heads like a Roman candle, exploding and sending a shower of glowing coals in every direction.

Betty Robertson and Hal Brown caught up to them. The wind swirled the smoke and ash, creating visual openings, only to seal them off. In seconds, gusting winds had turned the blaze into a storm of whirling, burning embers. Hannah turned back to Tom and the others. Frozen eyes stared back. Even Tom held the dazed, wide-eyed look. He had endured a cracked elbow and a dozen bee stings on the Saddle Fire, without uttering a word of complaint. And he had been chased by wildfire blow-ups before. But this was a new terror — the feeling of being blindfolded in the middle of a fire storm.

Hannah calmly touched Sam on his arm. "Dig like hell, then get out your fire tent and get in."

She yanked Rick's shovel from his pack and shoved it into his hands. "Dig!"

Once again, the swirling winds revealed a brief opening in the smoke. She grabbed Tom and pointed to the nearby stretch of barren rock. "Look!"

He emerged from his daze, nodding. "Hannah's right. Let's do it."

He raced a few paces off the trail, threw down his pack, and with three massive strokes of his pulaski, cleared a patch of earth. He straightened up, looked at his crew, ripped his shelter from his belt, and held it up for everyone to see before he unfurled it.

Adrenaline trumped fatigue as the firefighters frantically followed his lead, tossing their packs to the side, scraping at the ground, digging fuel-free patches of dirt. They unfurled their tents and began a mad scramble to get safely beneath their individual fire shelters. All had practiced the maneuver in training. None of them had ever used them in a fire. Hannah was concerned about the others, especially Rick, but in the swirling smoke, she could barely see. And she had to prepare her own patch of ground. She dropped to her knees, scraping down to dirt and rock with her pulaski. She bounced back up, ready to unfurl her tent, and paused.

The fire detonated trees on both her flanks. The wind screamed like a hundred sirens at once. Then, with a sudden fury, the full force of the blaze came straight at them, blowing away everything in its path, including the smoke. She saw the panorama clearly. Her brown and yellow-clad comrades unfurling their thin, silver foil tents, with the red, glowing monster surrounding them. A serenity engulfed her. Most of her crew were safely beneath their tents, struggling to hold down the flaps with their hands, knees and elbows; others were diving to the ground, pulling the tents around them. Then she unfurled her tent. The wind ripped at it. She struggled to hold on. Her heart leapt to her throat. She couldn't deploy the tent. She had waited too long. The heat was searing. Embers flew by her. She dove to the ground. The wind, still strong, lessened closer to the forest floor. She allowed her tent to ripple and wave above her before it slackened for a second. Quickly, she hooked her boots into the shelter's foot straps, pulling and wrapping the fire tent around her. The fire roared over her. She fumbled for her canteen and soaked herself in water.

Beneath the scorching heat and bellowing scream of the conflagration, Hannah could hear the cries and moans of the crew. She found it difficult to distinguish one voice from another, or to make out any words; but, occasionally one person's cries were clear and isolated from the others. Rick hollered that he was on fire. She heard Tom yell back to stay calm, to stay put, before their voices disappeared again under the roar of the fire storm.

She felt alone in her shelter and knew her friends were undergoing the same terrifying isolation. The temperature in her tent was soaring. Smoke found its way in under the edges. She felt like she was breathing dirt and smoke more than air. The wind grabbed at her tent, lifting it. She held on. An orange-yellow finger of fire snaked into her shelter and shot past her cheek. She rolled on it, suffocating the flame. Her deep sigh led to the ingestion of more smoke. Marcia's scream cut through the roar, but Hannah couldn't make out any words. She could only hope no one would panic, throw off their shelter and run. It was the worst thing to do, and still she had to fight off the urge to bolt.

She heard her own groans, and wondered how long she had been moaning, when she realized the smoke had left her tent. The wind still whistled, but the fire's bellow had diminished. Her shelter remained hot to the touch. Slowly, she lifted the edge and peered out. The fire had ravaged this patch of woods and moved on.

The Bear Hollow Hotshots crawled out of their shelters into a charred forest. The smoke had lifted. Spot fires still licked at stumps and standing, burned trees. Hannah looked around at the crew. Dazed, blackened faces stared back. They counted each other. Everyone had made it, but John Harris remained on the ground, moaning. Several people rushed to him. His legs were badly burned. Marcia scrambled around, looking for her pack, found it and raced back with salve and gauze for John's burns. Others had minor burns, and they started fumbling for tubes of salve and containers of aloe vera. Everyone was covered with soot and dirt.

"It may take an hour or two before help arrives," Tom said. "Look for your packs, gather your things, and try to relax."

Less than half a mile ahead of them, smoke funneled upward, blackening the sky. They heard the blaze, like a train in the distance, moving on down the line. Nearby, spot fires still burned, thickets smoldered.

Marcia remained with John, holding his hand, comforting him. Others tried to busy themselves. Hannah looked at Tom. He managed a weak smile. She pursed her lips. Somberness slowly gave way to increasingly animated survival tales — of their individual struggles deploying their shelters, of brushes with flames and the suffocating agony of the smoke and unbearable heat in their tents.

Fire Command would offer them a week off. But, other than John, all were back on the line twenty-four hours later, choosing to protect Silver Woods.

#

Hannah looks at the tips of her fingernails, black with Max's rich garden soil, then stretches her arms skyward. She's been using muscles she hasn't used since she quit fire fighting eight years ago.

"Damn," she mutters to herself. Why can't she feel this way in the city? Even with aching muscles.

She starts toward the house, hears the water running and remembers the shitakes. She jogs to the side of the house, turns off the faucet and ambles to the front porch, where Max is planted in his beat-up old rocking chair.

"How's the weeding?" he asks.

"I won't run out anytime soon."

He chuckles as she settles into one of his newer rocking chairs. He had planned to extend the deck into a wraparound structure, but he's put it off for years. With his latest injury, Hannah doubts it will ever get done. At least Max fixed the overhang roof last summer. It provides some extra shade in the heat, and she figures her brother will be spending a lot of time under the protection when the rains come.

The front of the house is shaded by several tall trees. Two forty-foot firs and a giant old cedar on the left, two spreading maples on the right, an alder and a sequoia directly in front of the porch. With the temperatures nearing one hundred degrees, and the sun baking everything, the porch is cooled to below ninety by the trees and a breeze from the creek.

Despite a wetter-than-usual June, the earth is parched and thirsty. It's the fifth year of drought, and the ground quickly sucks up the water, leaving the terrain cracked and dusty. Weeds and thistle that bolted with the nourishment of the heavy spring rains are bone-dry kindling. Moisture is hidden away like treasure in the trunks of the giant Douglas firs, but Hannah knows if these woods go up in flame, they, too, can burn. The creek, roaring in January and still bubbling with enthusiasm in June, barely whispers now.

"We're lucky it was never this dry when we were fighting fires," she says. "Although I suppose we would have gotten into it."

"We would have loved the torture. Like chili peppers," Max adds with a slight Mexican accent.

"Yeah, your peppers and tomatoes are eating it up, but I'm

afraid the rest of your conifer paradise is turning into a desert, Max." She nods up the hillside. The tall, green firs glisten in the sun.

"Aside from the creek, you're right, this place is scorched. Well, that low spot near the spring is as mucky as ever. It'll never dry out."

The site of Max's accident, not far from the spring, is out of her view. She visualizes it and shudders. Sitting on the porch where Gretchen was raped is even more disquieting. But most disturbing is the helplessness she feels for Gretchen.

Max reaches for a big, glass pitcher and pours a tall drink for Hannah. Ice cubes clink against the glass as he sets the pitcher back on the deck by his side. He's already working on his own drink. She takes a sip and recognizes their childhood drink of lemons, oranges, a lot of water and a little sugar.

"You're using honey instead of sugar?"

"Of course."

Her throat is parched, and she can't resist gulping the cold, orange liquid. She glances at Max's foot. It's no longer heavily bandaged. In the several weeks since the accident, he's progressed from crutches to a cane. He still doesn't move around much, spending most of his time on the porch.

"How's the foot today? Any better?" she asks.

"It only hurts when I walk on it. But it feels fine propped up like this, said the three-toed sloth."

She laughs. "When do you see the doctor again?"

He finishes swallowing a long gulp of the drink and wipes his mouth with the back of his forearm. Ice-cubes clink against the bottom of the glass as he sets it back down. "I didn't make another appointment. I'm going to see how it goes for a while, see how much it improves on its own."

"Does the doctor think that's a good idea?"

"Who knows? He says the foot's use is permanently limited. Like I couldn't figure that out. I'll learn to live with another limitation. I'm just worried about God dropping the other shoe — so to speak."

Hannah grimaces. "This isn't your fault at all, huh, Max? This is all God trying to get you?"

"He didn't try. He got me."

Hannah shoots Max a skeptical frown. "It seems like the only time you believe in God is when something goes wrong."

"You know what I believe."

"Shit happens?"

"It's a little more complicated than that."

"But there's nothing you can do to stop things, or make the world better?"

"You got it. Watch the tube, read the paper, but stay out of it."

"Watching the tube is cheating. You have to participate, too."

"That's your rationale for attending the Hanson trial?" Max suddenly raises his voice. "You would be cheating the cosmos if you didn't make yourself a target for some neo-Nazi nut case?"

Hannah doesn't respond. She recalls a thought she had after the courthouse hallway encounter. Fear of falling, sometimes, is really a fear of jumping. She finishes the drink in her glass. The last remnant of an ice cube pings the bottom of the glass as she sets it back down.

"Hey, sorry," Max says. "But I'm allowed to worry about my kid-sister."

"That's okay." She smiles.

They're quiet for a moment.

"Hey, did I tell you about this great stretch of woods I discovered?" Max asks.

"No. Before your accident?"

"Yeah. An old growth forest that hasn't been logged. It feels totally primeval."

"Near here?"

"It's off Foster Road."

Hannah wrinkles her brow.

You know Harlan Road. Off 262?" Max asks.

"Sure."

"Foster is off Harlan. There's some logged units in there, but once I got past them, it was virgin woods."

Hannah hears young voices faintly, skipping just ahead of the girls. By the time she can make out the definition of the words, she sees Heather, Michelle and Michelle's friend, Polly, rounding the bend.

"The Jews really control the blacks, Michelle."

"That's crazy, I know it's crazy cause my Dad is Jewish."

Hannah looks at Max.

"What on earth are you talking about?" he asks his daughter and her friend.

"Some dumb boy told Polly that —"

"Let me tell it," Polly interrupts, "This boy —"

"Carl Edwards," Michelle interjects.

"Right, Carl Edwards. He told me Jews control Blacks and make them riot and Jews control most of the world through banks, too."

Max and Hannah look at each other with dumbfounded expressions. Hannah is glad she isn't in Max's shoes and wonders how he could possibly explain this to eleven-year-olds.

"It isn't true, is it Dad?" Michelle asks earnestly with Polly waiting expectantly and Heather looking bored.

"It's definitely not true," Max says. "There are people who hate Jews and Blacks who make up that kind of stuff."

Hannah figures Max wants to go into greater detail about who controls the banks and what their interests are, but her brother knows better than to attempt that explanation. She smiles as he quickly settles on another approach.

"Let me tell you a story."

"Howard the Magnificent Teddy Bear!" Heather shouts excitedly, jumping up and down.

"No, sweety, a true story."

"Howard is true." Heather says as she crosses her arms.

Michelle rolls her eyes.

"I know, Heather, I mean this is a story that happened to me when I was a kid. In fact, I was just about Michelle's age, maybe a year younger."

Michelle and Heather sit down on the steps, looking up. Polly follows their lead.

"Remember your Great Aunt Sophie, Michelle?" She nods her head affirmatively. "Heather, she died when you were just one, and Great Uncle Joseph died before either of you were born.

Well, when I was nine or ten years old, I went to visit them one summer, not where they lived, but where they were vacationing, in a small town in Iowa called Storm Lake. My Mom and Dad put me on a Greyhound bus, and Aunt Sophie and Uncle Joseph met me at the bus depot there. It was the first time I took a trip on my own like that, and I was really excited.

"They were staying at a motel that had little log cabins — probably imitation log cabins, looking back, but I didn't notice then."

Max looks at Hannah as he makes this remark. She knows of the trip, but she doesn't know where Max is going with his story.

"Well, the people who ran the motel where Aunt Sophie and Uncle Joseph stayed had a little boy a year or two younger than me. Naturally, they hooked us up to play together. There wasn't much to do and we had to stay near the house. One day, when we were hanging out in this sideyard, tossing marbles or something —"

The girls look at each other with quizzical expressions.

Max continues, "The little boy, I don't remember his name or what he looked like anymore, but I remember he had Jewish people and African American people mixed up, although we called African Americans, Negroes then."

Polly looks at Michelle and mouths the word, barely uttering a whisper, "Negroes?"

Michelle shakes her head up and down.

"The boy said, `We've got both in this town, two Jew families and one nigger family.' I didn't say a thing. I didn't say I was Jewish. I just stood there, and he didn't say anything else. A bit later, we were still playing in that sideyard when a car drove by and the little boy pointed and said, `Look, there they are.'

"I looked at the car where the boy was pointing, but I didn't know what it was I was supposed to see.

"`The Jews. Don't you see?' he said to me. But the people in the car were black. The little boy had learned his parents' prejudices, but he got them mixed up.

"Although I was Jewish and swastikas had been painted on our synagogue, and neighbor kids who were Catholic had said some mean things to me about being Jewish, I never thought much about it compared to the prejudice against Negroes. I had seen news stories of police with dogs attacking Negroes who were just sitting in the street. Anyway, when that kid made that mistake, lumping us together that way, I realized for the first time how really stupid prejudice was."

The kids are silent for a few moments. Finally, Heather speaks up. "Can we hear Howard the Magnificent Teddy Bear now?"

Max laughs, "Later, sweetheart. Why don't you girls go play for a while now?" They all get up and run into the house.

"I never knew that story," Hannah says. "I just remember being mad because I didn't get to go, too."

"Yeah, it really had an impact on me. Well, I think the prejudice all around me was having an impact. But this kid's confusion made me wonder about it in a different way. He didn't even know who he was supposed to hate, let alone why."

8

Joe knows the look. His mother's working on a big sale. She's on the phone, in one of her nicer suits — the dark blue knit — pacing back and forth in a tight little space in front of her desk. Her back is to him, but he can see her fiddling with one of several pens jutting out of a ceramic cup on the back edge of her desk. A couple legal pads and a sticky pad are next to the cup, on the other side of the telephone base. A wooden-framed picture of Joe occupies the far corner. It's a posed, studio photograph of him she had taken on his fourth birthday. He's wearing a cowboy hat and a big smile. But, when he looks at the photo, he remembers the tantrum he threw when he had to leave the hat — a studio prop — behind.

She finally pulls the pen, jots something down, and finishes her conversation. "I'm sorry, Joey," she says, turning to face him. "Now where were we?"

"It's all right, Mom. You're busy. We can talk later."

"I've got to a show a house, but I've got a minute. What is it?"

"Have you been following the latest news about Robert Hanson?"

"I know he lost."

"Because he doesn't know what he's doing." Joe shakes his head, disgustedly.

His mother smiles. "If you're telling me you're through with that business, you know I couldn't be happier. The sooner you quit hanging out with Billy and Larry, the better."

"That's not what I said." He turns, takes a step, then raises his voice as he turns back. "Geez, Mom, that's why I can't talk to you about stuff like this. And his name isn't Larry. It's Hulk."

"I'm sorry."

"It's Hanson that's bothering me, not Billy and Hulk. Okay?"

"Okay."

"I'm admitting you were right about Hanson. I'm trying to figure out what to do about it."

"How do your friends feel about Hanson?"

He looks at the floor, then back up. "I haven't brought it up to them. That's the problem. They wouldn't understand."

She raises her eyebrows.

"I don't know what to do. The more I see of Hanson the more I think he's full of it. An all-white homeland here in Oregon and a couple other states?" He shakes his head.

She looks at her watch, then sits down at her desk chair. He takes a couple steps back and leans against the door frame.

"Don't get mad, Joey."

He sighs, looks at the floor, then back at her.

"You ask my advice. Then you get mad at me when you know all along what I'm going to say, anyway."

He grins, then looks down. She smiles back.

"I think you really do want to break away from those two."

He looks at the floor, then slumps, his back sliding down the door frame.

"If you quit hanging out with them, you'll make new friends. You know they scare me."

"You got Hulk all wrong. Everybody does because he's so big. But he's not like that." Joe straightens up. "One time Hulk showed me these Nazi cartoons he had sketched. I couldn't believe he could draw. When I told him how good they were he pulled out these other sketches — ducks and geese by ponds and streams."

"You see the good in everybody. But these boys are headed for trouble."

He stares at the floor.

"You brought it up, Joey."

"I know, but it's like I said, it's not Hulk and Billy. It's Hanson."

#

"Is this fucked-up or what?" Joe mumbles to himself as he limps down the back stairs from Billy's apartment building. He feels like Quasimodo, burdened and slouched to his right from the weight of Billy's television. The rickety wood stairs work their way down to a landing, where Joe makes a u-turn, sets the tube down, and takes a breather. He pulls a cigarette out, lights it, and sits down on top of the television. He looks out at the gravel parking lot. Hulk would have come along to help out, but he had to work. Joe would rather get Billy his television than face him without it.

He shakes his head at the thought of Billy hiding out. Somebody's been watching Billy's place. He's sure of that. It could be the police or the guy Billy cut and his friends. The thought gives him a sudden start.

"Creepy shit, dude," he says aloud, as if the sound of his own voice might soothe his rattled nerves.

He convinced Billy to hide out. Hulk said Joe had gone spy-nuts. Billy bought into Joe's concern, but doesn't like holing up, and he's been threatening to leave his hideout, a vacant, run-down old building next door to the warehouse where Hulk works. Joe shakes his head in disgust. He also created more work for himself. Billy made Joe his gopher, ordering him to get things from his apartment. Usually little things.

The television seems a bit much to Joe. His mother might be right about making new friends. But the time isn't right to break off from Billy and Hulk. How would it look? Joe asks himself. Right when Billy needs him.

Joe is startled from his thoughts by a noise from beneath him. His heart jumps up and kicks in at a faster pace. He puts the cigarette out and stands, listening. He sees a cat bolt across the gravel parking lot behind the apartment house. Joe sighs, chuckles, and picks up the tube again. Maybe they'll settle for him if they can't find Billy. He slides the heavy old-model television over one step at a time, then hefts it up onto his hip when he reaches the bottom. The stairs empty out on the side of the house. Hulk's car is parked in the back. Joe scoots for about ten yards and sets the tube down one last time. He mumbles and grumbles to himself as he gets ready to lift the set for the final ten yards to the back gravel and Hulk's car. He hefts it back up and begins a series of quick little steps toward the car. He looks down at the ground and at the tube, then back up at the car. He doesn't see the bat coming.

The impact smashes the picture tube and sends Joe sprawling, backward. He starts to scramble to his feet and stops, still on one knee. Green Laces towers over him, bat in hand, a sneer on his face. Joe sees at least three more skins on his flanks, two on one side, one on the other. He can sense at least one more behind him.

"You're gonna' tell us where your cock-sucking chum is, but first, give us your boots," Green Laces demands. Joe knows it's considered a supreme sign of weakness to give up your boots. If you're not willing to fight to keep them, you don't deserve to be called a skin.

"Fuck you." Joe spits it out. Unconvincingly. Green Laces laughs. Joe sees eye movement from a skin to his left and realizes he is reacting to something behind Joe, but the realization is too late. He feels an explosion at the back of his head. The big bonehead behind him has put the full force of his leg into his steel-toed boot. Joe goes flying forward, toward the pavement. Before his face hits Green Laces brings his steel toe upward smack into Joe's chin, crumpling his jaw. Joe screams in agony but remains conscious as they set upon him with their boots. He curls into a fetal position, trying to protect his groin and face with his hands and his curved position. One of his attackers keeps kicking him on the spine, as if it will pry him open, but Joe hangs in with his defensive posture. Several blows break through his hands and fingers and smash his forehead and eyes. He manages to block a slam from the bat with his forearm. He feels his bone shatter. He screams.

The skinheads reach down and yank Joe's bloody body up, one on each arm and one on each leg.

Green Laces takes Joe's face in his hands. "You're my little girl friend, now, aren't you?"

In a daze, Joe hears the other skins laughing. Green Laces puts his mouth within an inch of Joe's lips, and smiles. Joe's eyes are already beginning to swell shut from the kicks. He tries to turn his face away, but Green Laces holds him firmly. Joe pulls his eyes to the side — a weak, reflexive substitute for turning his head. Despite his anguish, he can't stop himself from squinting back through the swollen slits at his tormentor. Green Laces purses his lips, moving in as if he were about to kiss Joe on the mouth. Joe sees Green Laces's gray eyes. They look seductive, almost kind.

Green Laces opens his mouth wide and clomps down hard, grinding his teeth deep into Joe's nose. Joe shrieks. His eyes water. He hears and feels the crunching of cartilage. He labors to take a breath. Joe hears his own mournful wail like some distant siren. Green Laces is a wild dog, tearing at a piece of meat, yanking his and Joe's heads back and forth. Finally, he releases his penetrating grip and leaps back. Dizzy, Joe gasps for air. He feels like he's sucking mud through a straw, barely getting enough air to keep breathing. He can't even cry. He shakes his head once and sees Green Laces smiling again, swinging a bat like a batter warming up. Joe hears the other skins laughing and hooting. Their voices and figures appear in a nightmarish haze.

"Batter up," someone shouts. They all laugh louder.

Green Laces swings the bat into Joe's groin. His body limp, the thugs drop him, and resume kicking. Green Laces takes out his knife, runs it up the laces of Joe's boots, rips the boots off, and holds them up high. The gang of five cheers. They head off, laughing.

Joe vomits and goes black.

9

The Springfield City Council building isn't what Fil expected. Several massive planters contain huge ferns, stretching and reaching for giant skylights that saturate the spacious hallway with natural light. The walls are tan, the floor covered with polished, dark-brown tiles. Big green pillars, three feet in circumference, run from floor to ceiling, breaking up the space like trees in an otherwise open meadow.

He's right inside the doorway, fifty yards down the hall from the Council chambers. The door opens behind him and he quickly pivots. When his friend, Bradford Townsend, a KVAL camera operator walks in, Fil's face lights up.

"Hey, Brad."

"What's happening, Fil?" Brad's tone is even.

"Cold." Fil laughs. "They got this air-conditioning cranked up like a freezer." He shifts his weight from one leg to the other.

"So go back outside."

Fil looks away. He never knows how to respond to Brad's terse demeanor.

"No thanks," He laughs his short bursts of laughter. "I'll take this over ninety-nine anytime."

Bradford's gaze pierces him. Fil reminds himself not to take it personally. Brad behaves this way with everybody.

The black man is big in height and heft, and looks more like a bouncer than a camera operator. He holds his camera and tripod like little toys. Fil wonders why Brad feels a need to intimidate people. He reminds him of his Uncle Herman — his father's brother. Fil was raised by his mother and grandmother. He never met his father or any of his father's relatives, except for Uncle Herman, and he and his mother only ran into Uncle Herman by accident. Because his mother's brothers were so playful with him, he immediately expected any uncle to act the same way. But the big man wouldn't even make eye contact with Fil. He left the impression that nodding good-bye took an effort. After that encounter at age six, Fil always imagined his father to be the same way.

"What kind of entertainment do you think they've got in store for us, tonight, Brad?"

"Beats me." Brad looks around and lowers his voice. "These fuckin' Fundamentalists." He shakes his head back and forth and cracks a slight smile. "They make for great sound bites, though."

"I guess there's that." Fil grins and shifts his weight again.

"What's got you so antsy, Filbert?"

The use of his full name startles Fil. Nobody calls him Filbert, other than his mother. "I don't want to miss this, but I've got a meeting with a former Aryan Brigade member one hour from now."

"A former Aryan what? Shit, Fil, you are one dumb nigger."

Fil frowns. "Somebody's got to document these groups. Connect the dotted lines."

Individual people, and groups of two and three, open the door and pass by Fil and Brad. Occasionally, a person stops part way down the hall and looks at some framed acrylic paintings on the wall. Fil wonders if they're really looking at the paintings or eavesdropping on him. The paintings are uninspired renditions of flowers with titles like, "Mixed Bouquet" and "Poppies and Daises." Most of the people don't acknowledge Fil and Brad at all. A few exchange nods. Fil knows he appears slovenly next to his well-groomed companion. Brad's muscular build is obvious despite his loose-fitting, tan silk shirt. His brown pants are creased, his wing-tips polished. Brad not only matches the building's well-kept interior, he's color-coordinated with the decor as well. Fil's faded black cotton t-shirt is rumpled and ragged, his white tennis shoes dirty and worn. Brad carries a slick new television camera, Fil cradles an old Sony cassette deck held together with a wide swatch of duct tape.

"So tell me about these dotted lines, Fil."

"Unfortunately, I don't have them connected yet. But some of these fascist groups and Christian groups might be related."

"Seriously?"

"Hard to say for sure. Ask me again in a month."

Two women in their mid-twenties walk by. Both seem overdressed for the hot summer night. They don't acknowledge Brad or Fil, keeping their eyes focused on each other as they surround themselves with a protective layer of unbroken conversation. Fil follows them with his gaze, then glances back at Brad, who cocks an eyebrow at Fil, and grins.

"Whatever happened with that Jewish chick in Portland?"

Fil frowns again, looks away and mumbles, "Nothing."

"Nothing? That's all you have to say for yourself?"

Fil shifts his weight. "I called her, but I got her machine. I didn't know what to say." He pauses. Brad is staring at him, waiting. "I called back several days later, and her phone was disconnected."

"That's ugly."

"Yeah. Guess I blew it."

Brad glances at his watch. "We better get in there. They always start a little late, but it's already past seven."

"Go ahead." Fil says. "You better get your stuff set up. I'll be right there."

#

Bad-vibe gauntlet, Fil thinks, as he makes his way toward a seat in the front row of the packed City Council chambers. Then again, these fundamentalist freaks might actually treat a black man okay as proof of their tolerance. They're becoming worse than liberals. He laughs.

Several people stare at Fil with stern, scolding expressions, and he realizes he was laughing out loud for a second. As he takes his seat, he glances back apologetically.

The mayor is still addressing opening city-business items, and Fil is relieved to discover he hasn't missed any of the ballot-measure testimony, the reason he came. A state-wide fundamentalist group, the CFV, Citizens for Family Values, has targeted Springfield with a ballot measure that would declare homosexuality perverse and prevent equal protection for gays and lesbians. The group has collected the required number of signatures to place the measure on the ballot, but one of the two quasi-liberal City Councilors is attempting to maneuver to keep it off the ballot on technical grounds.

Facing the crowd, the mayor and the five City Councilors sit behind a long half-moon table, each with his or her own microphone. The council table is on a platform raised a couple feet higher than the rest of the seating. Between the table and the front row are two television camera operators, including Brad. They've set up off to the side, and because Fil came late and sits on the end, they block his view of half the council. That's not a problem. He wants to get the audience testimony for his research, and the public microphone, placed on a single podium facing the City Council, is unblocked.

The American flag and the Oregon state flag hang from six-foot, gold-colored poles off to the side of the council table. Inside the council chambers, the brown tiles of the hallway floor give way to a dark green carpet. Several rows of wooden benches provide the bulk of the seating. Like pews.

It's hard for Fil to tell because nearly everyone is white, and men from both sides are likely to sport beards and long hair, but he thinks he spies a segregation of camps.

The mayor finishes his remarks and the testimony begins. A man who looks to be about thirty, wearing a tan sport coat with an open shirt, makes his way to the aisle. As he walks to the podium, Fil gets a good look at his face. The man is clean shaven with intense, beady eyes. Fil smiles. This guy is gonna' let Jesus out, he'd bet the farm on that.

"I speak God's word. Ezekiel, thirty-three, six, explains that the watchman on the wall is required to tell the people in the town of the trouble that is headed their way." The man speaks with a certain stiffness, but it doesn't appear to be nervousness or awkwardness. Fil figures it's an intentional style.

"Proverbs nine and ten say fear of God is the beginning of wisdom. We are afraid of what our fellow man thinks when we should be in fear of the Lord. Every tongue will wag, every head shall bow."

Brad turns around, looks at Fil and raises an eyebrow. Fil shrugs his shoulders. The mayor warns the speaker he has thirty seconds left. It takes the beady-eyed man that long to tell the throng to pray for each other, to pray for the sinners in their city. As he finishes his plea, a little beeping alarm goes off. The mayor thanks him and calls the next speaker.

"In the scriptures in psalm twelve, verse eight, it says the wicked freely strut about when what is vile is honored among men." The phrase strikes Fil as funny, but he squelches a laugh. The self-conscious feeling that the crowd is watching him reminds him of getting in trouble with his cousins during church services when they were kids. The thought makes him want to laugh even more.

Fil wonders where the gay rights supporters are, as one speaker after another seems to support the CFV cause. The mayor calls for another speaker. A woman who looks to be about thirty makes her way to the podium. She's nice-looking with dark, shoulder length hair, but Fil thinks she looks uncomfortable in her well-pressed skirt and blouse, as if she's not used to wearing them.

"If the Christian way is to be good and caring to the innocent, then I beg you to understand two things. If you hear nothing else I say, hear these two things. One, I am innocent, and two, you are hurting me. I have committed no crime, and I hurt no one. I have chosen another woman as my mate. We are both adults. We love each other, and we choose to be together, but if this ordinance is passed, we could be forced to leave the house we've rented for the last six years. We could be fired from our jobs. Is this what Jesus would want if he were here? Someone please answer me that."

"Sinner!" someone shouts.

"Blasphemer!" another person attacks.

The mayor brings his gavel down. "Order." But he's drowned out.

"You goddamn fascists," a woman screams, standing up and lurching forward. Her feet stay planted, but her upper body maintains a threatening posture. "We didn't interrupt you. Let her speak — you hate-mongering hypocrites."

"I don't hate you. I hate perversion," the beady-eyed man responds, still in his seat.

The mayor smacks his gavel repeatedly, raising his voice in the process. "I will have order. Everyone shut up and sit down." The room is suddenly quiet, except for the echo of the pounding gavel. The mayor calls the next speaker.

"I would like to talk about statistics," a man in his thirties, wearing a plain, light-blue sweater says, after he settles into a spot in front of the podium. "In 1962 prayer was taken out of the schools. Now listen to this. Divorce — from 1962 has increased two hundred and fifty percent. In 1962 there were four hundred thousand cases of sexually transmitted diseases reported. In 1980 that rose to one million, one hundred thousand. Look at Rome. Look at France. What happens to a country after the morals decline? I ask you all not to allow our country's morals to decline..."

Fil realizes he's wandered from the litany. He's not sure how much he's missed. He's been looking at a large white banner strung across the wall behind the Council table. A big green fir tree adorns the center of the banner and blue and green letters proclaim: Tree City USA. He looks at the door. A bright red fire extinguisher is next to the wooden framed, glass door. A red pull lever is directly above the extinguisher, the round, red alarm several feet above that, near the ceiling. He would like to go yank on the lever, but his prankish mood has faded.

He glances at his watch. 8:03. He was supposed to meet the former Aryan Brigade member at 8:00, at a park by the Willamette River. It's only a few minutes from the city council meeting. When the speaker finishes and another is making her way to the podium, Fil gets up, walks back along the front row and heads for the door.

"We do not discriminate," he hears the next speaker say as he approaches the door. "What we do say is homosexuality is a sin and we should not have to live and work next to these sinners, or have to send our children to schools where homosexuals are allowed to expose our children to their sins."

Fil pushes on the metal bar that opens the door, and heads out. The door swings back, closing quickly.

The hallway is quiet. He lets out a big sigh. He gets about

halfway down the hallway when he hears the door open and release the noises of the crowded room into the hallway again. Then it closes.

"Say!" The call, though loud, doesn't seem unfriendly.

He turns around and sees a woman approaching him.

"Sorry. You're Fil Childs, aren't you?"

"Yes?"

"I'm Patty Happy, a friend of Jamie Holland. She told me about you." Patty Happy? Fil thinks. Like Gary Gay? He almost says something about the name, like is it real or made up, then decides not to.

"Oh yeah, Jamie." He isn't sure what to say.

"She said you're documenting all the hate crimes in Oregon, and some friends of mine are getting pretty severely harassed and want someone to know."

"I'm not really documenting anything." He says it pleasantly, but he's feeling a little irritated. "Certainly not all the hate crimes in the state. Your friends should let the police know — or there's a hotline in Portland they can call."

"They've already called the hotline, but that just lists numbers, you know, like 520 incidents so far this year. They live in a remote rural area in Douglas County. They don't want to tell the cops. They're afraid one of the cops could be doing it or be the cousin of somebody doing it or at least know them or something. You know?"

"Yeah, I know, but you've got the wrong guy. I'm doing research about different hate groups and their connections, like right-wing Christians' connections to neo-Nazi types. Is there any connection between the CFV and White Nation? That sort of thing. I'm not documenting specific incidents."

"I thought you were looking into the office break-in of that anti-CFV group."

"The 'No on Seven Committee.' Yeah, but I'm not investigating it like the police. I just chase down things like that because — well, like I said, it may lead to more information about right-wing Christian groups or neo-Nazi groups." He's feeling antsy. He's late to meet Devin, and too many people know about his business.

"I think that's why Jamie thought this incident would be important to you," the woman continues. "For just that reason. My friends are a group of lesbians who live together on a piece of land. They're not political, you know, active or anything. They started getting these nasty notes with swastikas on them, but signed Warriors for Christ."

"Warriors for Christ? I've never heard of them before. What else? I mean what else did the notes say?"

"There's been four or five different notes. I haven't seen them, I was just told about them, but they say things like 'you will die, dyke' or 'death to the Christ-killers'".

"Christ-killers?"

"One of the women is Jewish. It really scares them that whoever is sending the notes knows that — since they keep completely to themselves, you know?"

"Yeah, I am curious about this, but there isn't much I can do for your friends. I can't go tracking any of this down, although you can be sure I'll keep my eye open for any other mention of this group. As far as your friends are concerned, they should report this to somebody, some alternative newspaper, at least, if not the main media people."

"I agree with you. That's what I've been telling them, but they don't want any more attention drawn to them."

"That's the problem, isn't it? As long as everybody is silent, nobody knows how widespread this stuff is." He hears the resignation in his voice. He's tired. He's late. He needs to go.

"I'm sure they would agree with you, but they moved there to hide away. Like I said, they're not activists, they're into being left alone and leaving everybody else alone. Sure, they also think people need to know this kind of thing is going on. But they're scared."

"They ought to be scared. Where did you say they are?"

"Douglas County. The nearest town is Elk Hill."

"Elk Hill? I don't know it."

"It's off Highway 262."

"Sure, 262. There's some great scenery along there, but it goes clear to the coast. That covers a lot of territory."

"Elk Hill is east of I-5, away from the coast. They're pretty isolated — on a little side road off Harlan Road, which is the main road around there. Any time they go anywhere they have to take Harlan. After a while, in an area like that, I think everybody knows your business."

"Everybody knows your business no matter where you are." Fil shakes his head. "Give me their number and I'll give them a call for what it's worth — which isn't much." Fil laughs his halting laugh.

"I don't think they want me giving their number to anybody. I was thinking of having them call you."

He pauses. He would like to have some buffer from this craziness himself, like being able to call them but not the other way around.

He scratches his name and number on a piece of paper in his notebook, rips the corner off and hands it to the woman. "I'm hard to get hold of. Tell them to keep trying."

#

The park by the Willamette River turns out to be about half a mile from the city council building, maybe a little more. Fil figures he's fifteen minutes late. He rushes down several concrete steps and around a tall laurel hedge, to the area Devin Nelson described. Several towering maples create a high canopy above the long, narrow lawn that runs along the river. A breeze off the water doesn't make much of a dent in the hot summer evening, and only a few people occupy the benches along the sidewalk.

At a glance, no one looks like a former Aryan Brigade member. Two elderly men sit on a bench facing each other. A young man shuffles slowly along, with his toddler hanging on his hand. Three teenage girls, huddling on a bench, glance up at Fil, then resume their conversation. Another man sits alone. His thin mustache and wire-rims make him look more like a Bolshevik than an ex-racist. His brown hair sticks out just above his ears.

But he studies Fil with an intense, scrutinizing gaze.

"Fil?" he shouts from several yards away.

"Devin?" They approach each other and shake hands.

"You're late." Fil can't tell if Devin is upset. He was friendly on the phone.

"Yeah, sorry, I had trouble pulling myself out of this meeting. Then someone stopped me. Thanks for waiting."

"I don't have a lot of time."

"Okay, then let's get started." Fil still can't read him. His tone seems more neutral than angry. Fil takes a couple steps and sits down on a bench. Devin follows.

"Why did you leave the Aryan Brigade? Hey you don't mind if I record this, do you?" Fil sets his recorder between them, pushes down on his record and play buttons and balances his microphone on top of his deck, pointing toward Devin.

"I had a lot of reasons."

"How about one."

Devin stares straight ahead, then turns toward Fil. "Stupid-ass rules." He laughs. "Like the Aryan Brigade code. We had a poster on the wall with the ten codes listed. And we were expected to memorize them and practice them."

"What were they?"

"Number one: the leader is always right. Number two: never violate discipline. Get the idea? Stupid stuff."

"Not what you expected, I guess. What made you join in the first place?"

"That's a tough question." He stares straight ahead, again. Fil glances around the park. The two older men he noticed earlier are tossing handfuls of something on the lawn. More than a dozen pigeons peck at the ground, near their feet. The teenage girls are gone. "It's not like I ever set out to join," Devin turns back to Fil. "I was just hangin' with some guys at work. They were into Aryan Brigade stuff and they turned me on to it." He shrugs his shoulders.

Fil opens his mouth, then closes it. He wants to say how that's a flimsy reason to join a group as hateful as the Aryan Brigade, then searches for a question, instead.

"Listen, man," Devin says. "We got started late. I gotta' go."

"You're kidding me."

"No. I'm not *kidding* you." This time the tone is clear. Fil wonders if being late angered Devin that much, or if he didn't need much to get mad at a black guy.

"Tell me one more thing. Okay? You ever heard of a group called — Warriors for Christ?"

"No. Never heard of them."

"How about anybody operating around Elk Hill?"

Devin laughs. "Now you're the one who's kidding, right?"

Fil gives him a blank stare.

"Elk Hill is like the vortex, man. You gotta' check it out."

"Really? I had no idea. I hadn't even heard of Elk Hill before a few minutes ago."

"On second thought, I don't know about you." He shakes his head.

"What do you mean?"

"If I were doing a thing on neo-Nazis and militias I would head for Elk Hill. But I ain't a black guy. If I were, I wouldn't go anywhere near that neck of the woods."

"You think it's that much worse than here in Springfield?"

"Shit, man, you tell me. You're the black guy." Devin laughs.

Fil doesn't know what to say. He gives him a quizzical look.

Devin gets up. "I gotta' go man." He puts out his hand. Fil responds with a firm shake, then watches as Devin quickly steps along the sidewalk, turns and disappears behind the big laurel hedge. Fil reaches down, hits the stop button on his recorder, then rewind for a second. He hits play to make sure his recording worked, hears it, and hits stop again.

He glances back toward the park and the river beyond. The swift waters rush over the rocks, grabbing twigs and branches and dragging them into the deeper current. The two older men are gone, but half a dozen pigeons still peck at the ground, nearby. The father is sitting on the lawn, keeping an eye on his young son, who looks like he started walking on his own within the last few days. The boy balances himself by sticking out his belly to counter the weight of his butt. He lifts one leg high up in the air, as if he's pulling it out of thick mud, clomps it back down, lifts the other leg in the same manner and locates the earth beneath him before planting it firmly in place, propelling himself toward the pigeons. As he gains momentum he looks like he's going to either fall flat on his face or take off in flight. The pigeons scatter, but the tumbling boy keeps moving forward, apparently unable to stop or change directions.

10

The puny hands in front of Billy hold a snugly little stuffed bear. He smiles at the back of the soft, fluffy head. He feels happy — an elation that soars so high it scares him. He senses something dreadful, too. But its form eludes him. Tiny arms extend from him. They're his arms, and they make the stuffed animal dance back and forth, from side to side.

Suddenly the little bear goes flying. Billy's mother is in front of him, sitting on a couch, a drink in one hand, a cigarette in the other. Her face is gaunt; her hair wiry and disheveled. She's rocking back and forth, laughing hard. She starts coughing. He smells liquor — on him, soaking him, stinging his eyes. The laughter engulfs him. He hears someone whimpering beneath the hysterics. It's him. A long, skinny arm flies out, smacking him hard across the face. A cigarette burns his cheek, and sparks fly about his eyes. He screams. But the hand smacks him again, aborting his scream. He muffles his agony. A loud knocking reverberates behind him. The hand is raised again. He sees his mother's eyes. Fierce eyes warning him to be silent. The laughter again. The knocking is accompanied by an authoritative voice, but he can't make out the words.

"Let me the fuck in."

Billy hears pounding, a heavy thumping sound. Awake now, he sits up, covered in sweat.

"Fucking shit, Billy, I know you're in there. Open up the goddamn door already, will ya?"

Billy gets up, walks to the door and opens it. He doesn't even look at Hulk. He just turns and walks away.

"Fuck you," Hulk spits it out.

"This is bullshit." He turns back around and glares at Hulk. Then Billy looks down at the deserted warehouse floor. He tries to grab on to the dream images before he loses them, but they're already gone. He looks back up at Hulk. "I'm not afraid of some goddamn bone and his chums. He ought to be hiding from me."

Hulk looks directly at Billy, unflinching. "You're not hiding from this guy, Kid. Nobody says you are. But you gotta' worry about the pigs, too. You gotta' lay low. That's all, man."

"Laying low is for pussies." The bleak, dingy warehouse has been his hideout for more than a month. Bare wooden floors have gaps allowing frequent views of the ground floor below. Old concrete pillars, two feet square, break up the long, wide room. The walls are a pasty concrete. Spiders have strung their webs from pillar to ceiling to piles of boards and broken glass. A couple missing window panes and a tiny mesh screen let a little outside air into the cavernous space. "Pussies, shit. I feel like some goddamn rat in here. Nobody can bust me for anything. Let 'em try."

Billy tucks his chin into his underarm and takes a deep breath.

His odor is sticky-sweet, a nauseating smell of unwashed socks.

Hulk pulls out an unopened pack of cigarettes, opens it, takes one out and hands the pack to Billy. "Here." As Billy pulls out a cigarette, Hulk lights his, then Billy's.

Hulk's size and demeanor present the false image of a big, stupid oaf. Billy knows better. When Hulk wants to, he can be smooth and diplomatic. Billy knows the rap is coming.

"Jesus, Billy, you haven't been on the street. That cop, Skinner, fucked with me just last night."

"Skinner? Who the fuck is Skinner, and who the fuck cares?"

"You remember Sergeant Skinner, the fat pig. He's hassled us plenty before. Last night he's actin' like he's my best friend. He wants to know why he hasn't seen you around lately. He asks real loosey goosey — like me and him was buddies and it was an inside joke between us that you was hidin' out."

"Yeah, I know who you mean, but since when do pigs have names?"

"Duh. Like it helps to identify them — just like Porky." Hulk seems surprised by his own wit, and they both laugh.

"Oink, oink, Porky baby." Hulk holds his nose.

Billy cracks up. The image of his huge friend holding his nose, oinking, is too much for him. He can't stop laughing.

"And this little piggy squealed all the way home," Billy finally says as he runs around in a little circle, giggling.

"Oink, oink." Hulk says. Billy laughs.

"Oink, oink," Hulk says it again before Billy can stop and catch his breath. They fall into uncontrollable laughter, cackling and howling.

Billy finally catches his breath. "Man, I wish Joe was here." His mention of Joe sneaks up on him. Billy sees Joe beat half to death and lying in a hospital bed. He feels a sudden twinge of sorrow. Then anger. His face toughens.

"No kidding. The little dude would love this pig shit."

"Pig shit?" Billy barely gets out the words and they both howl again.

But the image of Joe won't go away. "How is Joe?"

"He's in a bad way, Billy. But he's gonna' pull through."

Billy turns hard. "What about that goddamn, cock-sucking bone. I can't let him fuck Joe like that. Let him try to fuck with me. I'll finish what I started." He pauses for a long time. Hulk doesn't say anything, and Billy sets his jaw and gives his hard glare. "I'm going to even the score for Joe."

"*We* are going to even the score, but now isn't the time, man. We have to lay low, increase our numbers, let Joe recover. These guys aren't going anywhere. We will get them, I promise you that."

"Bullshit."

"Look at Hanson, Billy. He's layin' low now, too."

"Hanson ain't layin' low. Hanson is fucked."

"He'll be back. He owes the nigger family several million dollars of which he has about five cents." Hulk smirks. "Big deal. I heard he's just squirlin' money away with cousins and such."

"I'm going fuckin' squirrelly in this rat hole. And what about that fuckin' cunt?" Billy recalls the look of the woman in her window, and smiles. He turns, walks toward the far wall, and tosses his cigarette on the wooden warehouse floor. He was on top of things enough to get her license number when she left the courthouse, and his sister's boyfriend tracked her address from there in exchange for some pot. Tracking her down was a regular James Bond move, Billy thinks.

He turns around and paces back toward Hulk.

"You don't have to stay here, Billy."

Here it finally comes, Billy thinks as Hulk keeps talking.

"You know that —"

"Fuck this goddamn country rap shit —"

"Goddamn it, listen. Just for a little while."

Billy looks at him.

"My uncle's place is perfect, man. This time of year it'll be great. We can get fucked up all day and all night. Nobody's around for miles to mess with us."

"Shit, man. Boring. Sit around in the middle of nowhere and piss on crickets. Fuck that."

"There is important stuff to do in southern Oregon, too. Remember what Hanson said, Billy. There's work to do in rural areas. And he mentioned Elk Hill. My uncle's place is near there. Man, we could be the vanguard —"

"You are fucked up. One minute you're saying we can just kick back, the next we're out recruiting for the Nation."

"That's exactly right," Hulk says excitedly. "For ourselves, too. We need troops, man. We can do both. We can have a good time, and that's exactly what will appeal to kids."

Billy doesn't say anything. He maintains his disinterested frown, but Hulk may be on to something. Recruiting troops.

Hulk continues. "Man, what have you got to lose? You can always come back to this rat hole — or face the cops or this guy,

Matthews. Let's just give it a week and see how it feels."

"Look," Billy softens his tone. "I hate niggers and kikes and queers as much as the next guy, but I don't know if I buy all this Hanson shit. Organizing. Look where it got him. Broke. Him and his fuckin' newspaper is shit out of luck now, dude. Fire-bomb the mothers and rat pack 'em, that's what I say."

"Look, Billy, Hanson may be off on some things, but he's right that we need more troops on our side. Besides, the two go hand in hand. That's how Hitler came to power. He not only spread his word, but he gave his followers some real action. We can do both."

Billy doesn't say anything.

"Hey, Billy, the country air may even help your eyes."

"My eyes? You are fucked up H. How the fuck is movin' to the country gonna' help my goddamn eyes?"

"Fresh air, Billy. Ever hear of pollution?"

He doesn't say anything. Hulk is acting like Billy's goddamn sister, or some juvenile hall counselor. Billy walks away, toward the far end of the cavernous room. His black jeans are heavy with sweat and grime. He hasn't bathed or washed his clothes in weeks. Joe's in the hospital, fucked up. Billy walks right up to within inches of the windowless wall and stares at nothing. He kicks at a pile of round metal sheeting. It echoes like thunder in the cavernous space. Sections of duct work still hang from the ceiling. The pile looks like some of the missing sections. Wires run everywhere, and fluorescent light fixtures, with missing tubes.

Hulk's plan could really work, Billy thinks. But he's gotta' get Green Laces, first. He had him. If the cops hadn't showed, he would have finished him right there. "Fucking cops," He mutters. Are they really on to him? There's something else nagging at him. He squeezes his head between his hands as if he could pressure his brain into recalling it. He can't remember, but something makes him think of his mother. He sees her sitting on the couch. She was always sitting on that goddamn couch, he thinks.

Billy finally turns around and heads back toward Hulk. He gets within a few feet of him and turns around and starts back the other way. Could they really recruit new troops? How do they make contact out in the middle of nowhere? He walks all the way to the wall and turns around again, pacing back and forth like a rat in a cage. Hulk watches him. Billy stops and rubs his sore, red eyes with dirty, unwashed fingers. The rubbing makes the itching worse. He walks toward Hulk again, comes to within a foot of him and stops.

"You can still get a big stash of speed?"

Hulk brightens. "For sure, man. As much as you want."

"As much as we can afford, you mean. I don't want to go to the middle of nowhere without a sizable stash, you know?"

"This guy owes me. We can get plenty."

"So what the fuck is your uncle like? Is he an Aryan Nation dude or Militia or what?"

"No, he's kind of down on Nazi stuff, but he's cool. He just thinks belonging to any kind of organization stinks, that's all. You guys'll get along, believe me. He's done hard time, Billy. You'll like him."

Billy lights another cigarette, inhales and exhales. "What did he do time for?"

"I've never really been sure. Something to do with beating his ex half to death, I think."

"So what?"

"So nothing. You asked what he did time for."

Billy doesn't say anything.

"Somebody's gotta' go by your place, Billy, and get your CD player and your CD's. My uncle's just got some old piece-of-shit turntable."

"Goddamn, you act like an old lady. I'll go by my place and get whatever I want."

"I tell you, Billy, your place is still being watched. That guy Matthews has got half a dozen guys, and he wants you for cutting him. Getting Joe didn't satisfy him. Why take a chance? Let me go by with some of my old football buddies. Nobody'll mess with me then. They'll just watch us and wonder what the fuck is going on."

"I don't want those straightlaced fuckers in my place. I'll go."

"Shit man, this being cooped up has you more jacked up than I've ever seen. Chill out, okay? I'll just go by there with a crowd for safety, but I'll go in by myself. Okay?"

Billy looks at the floor.

"I'm tired of being a goddamn rat in a hole. Look at me." Billy looks down at his body. His clothes could stand up without him. "I gotta' get outa' here. I don't give a shit how you want to do it. Let's just make this happen."

#

Billy looks out through a dust-covered window. He lights

another cigarette. As Hulk grows smaller and smaller, he pictures Joe in the hospital with tubes running in and out, bandages everywhere.

11

The girls bolt out of the house with Michelle talking rapidly. "Polly and I want to go up to my secret place in the woods without having to take Heather."

Hannah feels for her brother. Lately it seems like nearly every kid request takes on Solomonesque proportions. Max furrows his brow, hesitating. Hannah jumps in. "Why don't you stay here with me, Ms. Heather the feather? You can help me can tomato sauce today."

"Okay." She stands, waiting, as if her aunt were supposed to spring into immediate action. The older girls don't wait for Dad's confirmation. They take off, running up the road.

Max gives Hannah a relieved and grateful smile. "Michelle is becoming a teenager ahead of schedule."

"It's not too early for hormones, Max."

"No doubt that's part of it. But how much of her behavior has to do with the way her mother's been?"

"No way of telling. But I think time will take care of both."

"I hope you're right."

"Aunt Hannah, what about the sauce?"

Hannah gets up. "Okay, sweetheart, it's sauce time in Heatherville."

Heather laughs.

"The kitchen will be an oven," Max says.

"I know, but what do you usually do? A lot of tomatoes are ready now."

"Some years, I try to hold off and make more hot sauce in late September, but you're right, a lot of tomatoes are ready now. I think it's great, but I wanted to warn you. The kitchen'll be a sauna."

"We'll get into it, I was thinking I might bake some c-o-o-k-i-e-s as long as the stove is cranking, but I realized I would have my hands full with the sauce, the bottles and all the other canning stuff."

"Cookies?" Heather beams.

"You little smarty, you aren't supposed to be able to spell cookies, yet."

"She can't, really," Max says. "She's heard us spell it so many times, it's almost like another pronunciation."

Hannah laughs, and Heather gives her fake pouty face.

Hannah cranks the wood stove up with lots of little strips of fir and oak, and soon the tomatoes are liquefying and turning into sauce while the big kettle of water begins to warm. The clanging appears to rouse Gretchen, who wanders out from her bedroom to see what's going on.

"Looks like you're determined to burn us out, huh, Hannah?"

"Oh, God, Gretchen, I'm sorry. I didn't think to ask you. Max thought it was a good idea."

Gretchen walks over to Hannah, peeks at the pots on the stove, and takes in a big whiff of the tomatoes breaking down.

"I didn't mean it that way," she says. "I think it's great. The tomatoes need canning. I'll help, I could use a sauna." She laughs.

Hannah can't read her sister-in-law. Gretchen is wearing an old housedress, wrinkled and unwashed — the same one she's worn for days. Hannah reaches out and gently touches Gretchen's arm. "I don't want to be in the way. I want to help."

"You are, Hannah." She laughs. "Helping, I mean." Gretchen gives Hannah a direct gaze. But her chin starts to quiver and she looks away. Hannah puts her arm around Gretchen's shoulder and squeezes.

Heather looks up at them. "Mom, as long as Aunt Hannah has the stove going, you and me could make cookies."

"You and I," Gretchen pauses, stressing the correction, "could make cookies."

"Yeah!" Heather jumps up and down. The women laugh.

Gretchen grabs her daughter's cheeks and squeezes them. Heather breaks loose, runs over and grabs a chair and moves it in front of the cupboards where the mixing bowls are kept. She climbs up to get them, but Gretchen intercepts the potential disaster.

"Sweety, let me get the big bowls down. How about if you get the chocolate chips, the butter, the sugar and the flour. You know where all those things are, don't you?"

"I can't reach the chips." She says it with a you-know-that lilt.

Hannah watches, as mother and daughter break into a practiced routine. When she first heard the details of the rape, she thought Gretchen had done everything right and wouldn't have any of the typical self-blame. She fought back when many people would have felt overwhelmed. Now Hannah is rethinking her view — maybe it was that audacious attitude that betrayed her. To have fought back so ferociously and still be subjected to the horror, the invasion and humiliation, was a lot to overcome.

It was a question that had torn at Hannah before. When she took her self-defense class, the instructor insisted fighting back was the only alternative, but Hannah was familiar with other women who had said different situations called for different responses.

"Mom, don't forget to put walnuts in this time." Heather is pouring sugar in the biggest mixing bowl. Her mother has already poured the correct amount into the measuring cup.

"Okay, but walnuts go in only half the cookies."

"Seventy-five percent."

"Where does she get stuff like that?" Hannah laughs and pokes Heather in her belly. "You're not supposed to know things like seventy-five percent."

Heather squirms and giggles. "She picks up everything," Gretchen says. "She may not understand what seventy-five percent is, but she knows it's more than half."

"Howard tells me 'cause I'm special," Heather says the word, special, with no hint of braggadocio.

"Who is Howard?" Hannah asks.

Heather looks at her with complete exasperation. "Howard the Magnificent Teddy Bear."

"I'm sorry, Heather, but you'll have to tell me about Howard. I really don't know about him. Maybe it's from living in Portland."

Heather scrunches up her forehead. "Yeah, probably too many vibrations in the city, Aunt Hannah." Hannah and Gretchen look at each other with raised eyebrows and grin. "Too much vibration can really mess up mentriloquism."

"Mentriloquism?"

Gretchen rolls her eyes toward the front porch and Hannah gets the message. A Max story. But Heather has her Dad's rap down pat. "Ventriloquism is when you throw your voice." The little girl looks at her aunt to make sure she knows what ventriloquism is. Hannah nods an affirmation to the serious adult expression on the five-year-old face. "Mentriloquism is where you throw your thoughts. Only people can't do it. Only Teddy Bears. That's how Teddy Bears are going to save the world some day. But my Dad says they still have a lot of work to do to get the kinks out."

"To get through the city vibrations, probably."

"Probably, and getting around mountains can be hard, too."

Hannah tosses another piece of oak on the fire. The stove has heated up, and the big pot of water reaches a boil. She feels her hair sticking to the back of her neck and a bead of sweat running down her side. She moves away from the stove and takes a big swallow of water from a quart jar sitting on the table. Gretchen and Heather are at the far end of the table, as far away as they can get from the direct heat of the stove.

"Where are you at, Hannah? I'll have a first pan of cookies ready to go in about five more minutes, but I can put them in anytime. I don't want to get in your way."

"I'm probably about five away from dipping these jars in the boiling water, but I think I need a break. Maybe I'll wait till you're done with the cookies and then do the whole shot."

"If you like. I'll do a couple trays and check with you. Why don't you hang out with Max for a bit?"

Heather looks at Hannah. "You're all wet."

Hannah laughs. "You're not the first person who's said that to me."

Gretchen has been dropping dabs of chocolate chip cookie dough on the baking pan and is ready to stick the tray in the oven. Heather is eyeing the bowl and the spoon. "Can I lick it, Mom?"

"Not till we're done. Are you ready to open the oven for me? Get the hot pad, first."

Heather is already reaching for the pad and rolls her eyes. "I know, Mom, do you think I'm a baby or something?"

She opens the oven and the heat pours out as Gretchen shoves the pans of dough inside. Heather closes it back up and runs after her aunt.

#

Hannah smiles. There's a joyful feel for the first time in a long while. It's amazing what a batch of chocolate chip cookies can do for the spirit.

Overheated kitchen or not, in summer, Max, Gretchen and the girls almost always eat outside around the picnic table. At dusk the mosquitoes begin to buzz. Michelle and Heather fight over whose turn it is to light the citronella torches. Short, thick bamboo poles support little metal containers that hold wicks dipped in citronella oil. The flames provide bug repellent as well as light.

"I still don't understand," Heather suddenly pipes up. "Why do moths kill themselves in flames?"

"They're attracted to the light," her father explains.

"I know that, Dad, but why do they do it so it kills them?"

"It's a mystery to me."

Hannah takes a poke at Heather's belly and says, "The flame is irresistible, like chocolate chip cookies. If you didn't have your Mom and Dad telling you to stop, you would eat cookies until you burst, right?"

Heather giggles and squirms.

"It's time for bed," Max announces.

"Don't I get a story?" Heather asks.

"You always get a story, don't you?"

"Just making sure."

Everyone laughs.

"Do I have to go to bed now, too, Dad?" Michelle asks.

Hannah jumps in. "I'll let each of you pick a story if you both get ready now."

"But her stories are for little kids," Michelle counters, a slight whine in her voice.

"So why don't you stay out here with Mom and me, sweetheart, while Aunt Hannah reads the first story to Heather, then you can join them for your story?"

"Sounds like a plan," Hannah says.

Hannah observes Michelle's reluctance to give in to her Dad. But, apparently, her aunt-approval rating still holds some value.

Michelle says, "Okay, I'll wait for the second story, but I'm going to go up to my secret place in the meantime."

"Not after dark, honey," Gretchen says.

"Mom," Michelle tenses her voice. "It's not that dark, and I have my flashlight. Besides, I've been there after dark before."

"You have?" Max demands. "When?"

"I don't know. One time a couple weeks ago when Polly spent the night, we went up there—and other times, too."

Max and Gretchen look at each other, then give Michelle hard stares.

"I don't know what the big deal is. We're just right up there." Michelle points up and off the road toward some thickets in the woods, then swivels her hips and shoulders into a defiant posture.

Hannah watches her brother and sister-in-law. Max seems unsure. Gretchen doesn't appear to be weighing the possibilities.

"No," Gretchen says firmly. "I don't care what you did before. You're not going up there after dark anymore."

Michelle loses her defiance for a moment, tucking her shoulders, slouching.

"Okay, okay. Jeez." Michelle turns and walks back to the house, gradually regaining a willful strut.

Gretchen and Max raise their eyebrows and look at each other. Heather grabs her aunt's hand and pulls her away.

#

The wall between the kitchen and a spacious front room, the family's main hangout, stops halfway, creating a huge open space. The doorway to Max and Gretchen's room is straight back, the entryway to the girls' room off to the right, with the only bathroom in between. A small alcove just off the entry-way to the family room could be used as a breakfast nook, but Max snatched it for a place to keep a desk and a few bookshelves. He envisioned doing some writing there, but it mostly became the bill-paying and tax-laboring corner. With a sleeping pad and a modicum of privacy, the cubbyhole has become Hannah's sleeping quarters during her visit.

As Heather and Hannah by-pass the alcove entryway and head across the family room toward the girls' bedroom, Hannah notices Michelle curled up on the sleeping pad, reading. She smiles at Michelle, but Michelle doesn't look up.

"So, what story are we going to read tonight, Ms. Feather?" Hannah asks as they enter the girls' room.

"I don't want a read story. I want you to tell me a story."

"I don't have good stories like your Dad, I'm afraid — let me think for a minute."

Heather takes her teddy bear off the bed, pulls her covers back and jumps into her bed. "Didn't you and Dad hear the same stories when you were little?" She holds her teddy bear in a big hug.

"I think we did. Mostly, the same stories, but your Dad —" Hannah catches herself. She was about to say makes up better stories, and then thinks better of it. "Your Dad learned more stories after he was already grown up, I think."

"I can tell you a story if you want, Aunt Hannah."

"Really? Can you tell me about the Teddy Bear and his mental ventriloquism?"

"Not mental ventriloquism. Mentriloquism. Starring Howard the Magnificent Teddy Bear." Heather looks down at her little bear. "But I don't know all of it."

Hannah laughs. "Okay, I guess we'll have to get your Dad to tell it some other night. Know any other stories?"

"The girl who cried fox."

"Is that anything like the boy who cried wolf?" Hannah asks.

"I don't know that one," Heather says.

Hannah laughs. "So how does this one start?"

"Once upon a time," Heather says seriously.

Hannah laughs and slips under the covers, and they both curl up on Heather's bed, facing each other. Heather pulls her teddy bear close.

"His name is Charles," Heather says, looking at her bear.

"Charles and Cinderella were very close, so Charles is sad a lot of the time now and needs lots of loving."

"Cinderella? Your cat?" Hannah hasn't seen Heather's cat this visit, but she kept forgetting to ask Max about it. "Did something happen to Cinderella?"

"She disdapeared. Everybody thinks she died."

Heather is quiet. Hannah isn't sure what to say. She figures Heather doesn't really understand what it means for her cat to be dead, but she must know it's bad. And maybe she knows it means she'll never see her cat again. Hannah runs her hand over the top of her niece's head and down her back.

"I think maybe she got lost," Heather finally says. "Do you think if she's lost she'll ventually figure out how to get back here?"

"You know what, honey?"

"What?"

"I had a friend who had a cat that used to go away for a month at a time and just come home for a week or so. He figured his cat had several places he visited. Gray Boy's great circle route, he called it. Gray Boy was the cat's name. Well, this friend of mine lived in a house he rented that was in the middle of a peach orchard; and the house was real old. One day, the man who owned the house decided to tear it down and put in more peach trees, and my friend had to move out. He took a long time to move out, packing up everything and making several trips to his new place, but when the last day came, Gray Boy was off on one of his journeys. And you know what happened?"

"No." Heather's eyes are big.

"The man tore the house down. My friend figured one day Gray Boy came back like he always did and the house was just gone. It must have been quite a shock to the cat."

Heather has a puzzled and troubled look on her face. Hannah realizes this story, which always elicited laughter from adults, wasn't received in the same way by a five year-old.

"What happened to Gray Boy, Aunt Hannah?"

"My friend never saw him again, but he figured he just kept on his great circle route. Gray Boy must have had lots of other friends, lots of other places to stay."

Heather still looks troubled. Hannah wishes she hadn't jumped into the Gray Boy story. "Heather, if Gray Boy could go away for so long and still come back, so could Cinderella."

"Aunt Hannah," Heather scrunches up her forehead. "Could we have to leave our house for it to be torn down?"

Hannah laughs, "Oh, no, honey. Your Mom and Dad are buying this house. Someone else owned my friend's house. The man who owned it could do what he wanted with it. This is your house.

Nobody can make you leave."

Heather seems to accept the explanation, although Hannah doubts she understands it. Heather fusses with Charles for a minute to get him all settled down for the story. Then the little girl's eyes get big and she begins. "Once upon a time there was a little girl..."

#

Hannah steps out to the front porch. Max is back in his rocking chair perch, watching the night descend. Gretchen is gone. "I love those kids of yours, Max."

Max's studied frown breaks into a big smile. He turns to Hannah, beaming. "I know you do."

"The little girl who cried fox?"

He laughs. "I keep telling her it's a wolf, but she got fox in her head and that's that. So you didn't get to hear about Howard the Bear and Maurice the Mouse, huh?"

"She doesn't remember all of it. You're still on deck for that one."

"I think she purposefully forgets the sad parts."

"A sad fairy tale, Max?"

"Well, it's only sad in parts. It ends happily ever after like any good fairy tale." He pauses. "It's just that one of the mice kids is mean to his brothers and sisters. Heather doesn't like that."

"Well, don't give the story away. I still have to hear the whole thing one of these nights before I go."

Max and Hannah watch the night. The quiet sits comfortably between them. Crickets and the low murmur of the creek accompany their reverie. After a while, something reminds Hannah of an earlier question. "Do you remember when the girls came home the other day and Michelle said, `My dad is Jewish'? Why did she put it that way?"

"Instead of, `we're Jewish?'" Hannah nods.

"I think I kind of blew it when she was younger. We celebrated Chanukah and Christmas, but I told her Jewish kids didn't get Christmas presents. She opted for the presents."

"So, can't you change the rules, now, God?"

"Well, I sort of did, for Heather. I tried to for Michelle, but some of that early stuff sticks in ways you can't change."

The citronella torches cast a bright light. Max gets up, hobbles over and snuffs them. He prefers the darkness, and the mosquitoes won't be a problem this late. He hobbles back to his chair.

"I wouldn't think raising kids with two different religions would be nearly as hard as two different races." Hannah offers.

"Still thinking about that black prince of yours?" Max grins.

Hannah feels her face flush, but Max can't see her in the dark. "Prince is a little strong."

"You're still thinking about him."

"He didn't call. It's been two months. Do you think we could talk about something besides my non-existent love life?"

"Sure. What would you like?"

She doesn't respond right away and Max is quiet, too.

"I was hoping Gretchen would hang out with us, tonight," Hannah says, after a while.

"Why? Because she made cookies today?"

"Yeah, and she seemed to be opening up. I mean really coming out of it."

"She goes up and down. I think she's coming back, but it's two steps forward, one or two back. It's slow."

Max speaks in a low monotone, which isn't like him. She looks at him. He's staring out at the horizon or the darkened sky and doesn't see her stare. It's as if she can peer into his psyche if she just looks long enough or hard enough without his knowing.

Her brother needs his soul mate, she decides. He's not just sad for Gretchen. He's lonely, too. Hannah considers the pattern of her sister-in-law. Gretchen emerges from her shell during the light of day and in the company of the girls, withdraws at night and is probably closed to Max. He just takes it as a reasonable reaction to her trauma and is giving Gretchen all the space and time she needs, but Hannah wonders how long Max can go without his own emotional nourishment.

"Max?" she asks softly. "If you don't mind my asking, how rough are things between you and Gretchen?"

Max stares straight ahead. He doesn't look at his sister or acknowledge he even heard the question. The creek whispers beneath the crickets.

After a while, Max finally speaks, but he continues to stare straight ahead as if the words will be found on some distant spot on the blackened sky. "I don't know what to say. I thought my instincts would have been to be physically comforting, to hug and hold and draw her to me. But Gretchen has a wall up. I'm really lost."

The last words trail off and Max stares into the darkness, leaving the image of still more words out there somewhere to be found. Hannah wants to ask him how he's doing, she wants to know what else she can do for him, but she realizes she's already doing as much as can be done, by being there.

"Has she talked to you about it, at all?" Hannah asks.

"When she was interviewed by the sheriff. I was there. I think she was still in shock then. Her description may be helpful to the sheriff, but I don't think it did her any good — in the sense of a release or coming to grips or anything."

"But she has had some counseling, right?"

"There isn't anybody near here. We drove up to Roseburg, but she wasn't happy with the counselor there. She talks on the phone with a woman therapist in Eugene once a week. I'm sure it helps some, but — you know, the phone doesn't cut it."

"Yeah." Hannah spaces out for a few seconds. "What about the sheriff? Do they have any leads? Do they think these guys are from around here?"

"I don't know. It's like a needle in a haystack, I think. I'm not optimistic. I guess the manly thing to feel is some irrepressible urge for revenge, but I just want Gretch to be okay."

Max pauses and stares out at the night, then starts again. "That's not true, Hannah. I want to find them and stomp them into the ground. Make them hurt before they die." His voice is rising and Max stops, suddenly. He appears to regain control, lowers his voice, "If I hadn't been so out-of-control angry when I discovered the madrone — so fucking impatient — maybe none of this would have happened."

Hannah is shocked. She's about to tell him not to blame himself when he starts in again.

"I guess I don't know what I feel. Sometimes I want to find those guys and rip them apart. Then I think I don't care about them at all — well, obviously, I want them stopped from hurting anyone else, but we want all rapists stopped, don't we? What does it matter if they catch these particular guys and not thousands of others?"

"Gretchen must feel especially unsafe knowing these particular guys are out there. Having them locked up won't ease the agony, but it will give her a little security again."

"Maybe. Like I said I just don't know. Well, sure, that would help Gretch — some, but not nearly enough. God, Hannah, talking about this just makes me realize how fucked up I am over it all. It makes me feel guilty to even talk about how it's affected me. And what about the girls? They don't know what happened, but they know their mother is changed. I think they know she's hurting. When I think of how badly this whole thing has affected me, I can't even begin to imagine how Gretch must feel. How can anyone expect her to be even one tenth okay? I hate them. They raped Gretchen. They ruined our lives. We'll never be the same." Max's voice keeps rising and falling.

He pauses and shifts his weight, moving his bad foot down and back up to circulate the blood. His voice is low and calm, again. "I think she has one image she can't shake — like a nightmare. When she talked to the sheriff, she kept talking about this blackened tooth right next to this gap tooth. The sheriff would ask for other features, and she would say one thing or another but she kept coming back to the black tooth. I thought that kind of specific would be very helpful, but the sheriff didn't seem too enthused by it."

Max and Hannah sit in silence for a long time. Finally, Hannah says softly, "You just have to keep reminding yourself the worst is over, Max."

He responds instantly, as if he had heard her words before she spoke them. "If there's one thing I've learned, it's that the worst is never over."

12

"Goddamn it H, I've never seen you act like such a big fuckin' pussy. I just wanna' go by the bitch's place."

Billy snorts hard. He catches a glimpse of Hulk, who jerks his head around at the harsh sound. Billy laughs, wets the tip of his little finger and sticks it in the silver film canister again. He pauses and sneers at Hulk, sticks the tip of his finger up his nostril and snorts again.

"Take it easy, Billy. I'm headed there now. It would be one stupid move to get busted tonight. We got this rig loaded with meth. We would get pusher-level shit if they snatch us now."

"Bawk, bawk," Billy sticks out his elbows and flaps his arms up and down.

Hulk turns off Hawthorne. "Man, I can't help it. I gotta' bad feeling. Main streets are making me goosey and side streets are making me goosey. We're all set to blow town and you gotta' do one more deal."

"That's right. That's fuckin' right." Billy smiles, and rocks his head back and forth, then he sways his whole torso from side to side. "I gotta' do one more deal. I gotta' rat somebody, first, then we blow town."

Billy feels giddy, like a caged animal that's been set free. He lights two more cigarettes, hands one to Hulk.

"This is it!" Billy screams. "Turn here. Right. Right."

Billy bounces off his seat like a little kid arriving at the circus. "Pull over, H."

Hulk is already pulling over to the curb as Billy says it. They look up at the apartment window.

"Nobody's there, man. I been checkin' it out just like you asked. Nobody's been there for weeks."

Billy gets out and stands by the car. He throws his cigarette on the sidewalk and stares up at the darkened windows. "I could break in and trash it. I could torch the dump."

"What did you say?" Hulk leans over and shouts through Billy's opened window. Billy spots a "For Rent" sign in the front door window. Maybe Hulk is right. The apartment looks deserted.

Billy leans down, his enthusiasm diminished. "I said I could torch her dump."

"Get in, man. This deal ain't happenin' tonight."

Hulk seems surprised when Billy gets in, like he expected him to put up a fight. Billy laughs, then stares straight ahead. Hulk had kept the engine running. He pulls away from the curb.

"We're on our way, dude." Hulk says.

Billy turns and looks at him. "I said I gotta' rat somebody before we blow town." His voice has an icy edge.

"Oh man, Billy," Hulk sounds shrill, whiny. Billy smiles.

"Turn right here," Billy calmly orders. He directs Hulk north, then east. The two skinheads cruise in silence for a few minutes.

"We're really askin' for it," Hulk says.

Billy grins. "Nigger huntin'."

"We got a car full of speed, dude."

"Slow down," Billy says. "Let's go around this block."

Hulk obeys. He knows the drill. Drive-by speed. They glance up and down the street looking for a potential victim.

"Let's turn here," Billy says.

The dark side streets are deserted. It takes longer to find a target, but the victim has less recourse. They go around the block, spotting no one.

"Let's go deeper," Billy speaks in a low monotone. "It's safari time, H."

"Goddamn it, Billy. Why can't you be happy with a fuckin' queer or a drunk Indian or something? You gotta' go to god-damn Africa."

"The hunters are the hunted," Billy says, maintaining his ee-rie monotone. He lights up another cigarette. He bounces up and down. His eyes dart back and forth. After a while he tosses the cigarette on the floor, picks up a chunk of metal pipe, and caresses the weapon. He drops the pipe on the floor. He smiles at Hulk, reaches down again and lifts up a length of chain.

"Piece of chain, Hulk?" Billy leans over and twists his head around until he's nearly in front of Hulk, blocking his view. "Piece of chain?"

Hulk doesn't say anything. He looks past Billy's ear, keeping his eye on the street. Billy sees a person alone in the dark, walking slowly. Hulk keeps driving. Billy knows Hulk sees the figure, too.

"What the fuck, H. Let's rumble."

Hulk doesn't slow down. "It's an old lady, Billy. Look at her, she can barely move."

They turn their heads and check out the old woman as they pull along side her.

"She's a white woman, Billy. She's a white woman, a grandmother or some fuckin' thing."

A silence engulfs the car for a second. Then Billy explodes.

"I don't give a flying fuck!" He screams at the top of his lungs. He can feel his veins throb, his face turns flush. He's off his seat, smashing his head and shoulder into the car's ceiling. He feels like he can push himself right into the metal and break through it.

"I don't give a fucking — fucking — fuck!" Billy spits out the words. He's still pressed against the ceiling. But he doesn't open the door.

The woman cowers when she hears the shrieks from the passing auto. Hulk cringes, too. He keeps the car moving, though. Billy is shaking. He gulps for air, takes in a huge breath, wraps his arms around himself, slumps back in the seat, and curls into a ball.

13

Hannah is walking in a parking lot filled with people. She's walking at a comfortable pace, and the people are spread far apart. Her arms dangle freely at her sides. Her gait is easy, relaxed; her smile expansive. Her pace is picking up, though, and the concrete parking expanse is becoming a broad avenue with more and more people walking faster and faster. She begins to feel the space around her shrinking, the buffers between her and others disappearing. As the avenue narrows to a thin sidewalk and the crowd jams in, she feels as though she can barely breathe. She starts taking deep breaths, trying to keep from gasping; for a second she's outside herself, above the crowd. From that vantage she sees the funneling of the crowd like cattle into a chute; then she's back in the herd, suffocating. She awakens, short of breath, soaking wet.

The worst effect of the tomato canning and cookie bash is not the sweatshop, but the lingering heat the house holds. Hannah has been tossing and turning all night, sleeping off and on through fitful dreams. She reaches over to the side of her sleeping pad and looks at her watch. 3:15. She goes over the dream in her mind so she'll remember it in the morning, then realizes she's already forgotten an earlier dream. She tries to recall it but can't. She rolls over on the pad in the alcove, pulling the thin white sheet over her.

#

"Aunt Hannah, the fat hand is on the eight and the skinny hand is on the six." Heather rubs her eyes. She's standing over Hannah's sleeping pad. Hannah takes a second to register the words, then translate them.

"Shit." She grabs for her watch.

"We overslept, didn't we?" Heather asks.

Max's morning rhythms have changed, only in part because of Gretchen; also because he stays up late watching the night from his perch, and because moving into the start of a new day has become more difficult.

Hannah volunteered to become the designated kid-starter. Max protested, but Hannah insisted. "If that's not one of the main reasons you asked me to come, it's certainly one of the main reasons why I wanted to come."

So Hannah rises before Max and Gretchen, wakes the girls and gets them off in time to catch the day-camp bus.

"The bus is probably at the end of the road right now, sweetie, I'm afraid we did oversleep."

"How do Michelle and me get to day-camp, then?" Heather puts her palms out in a shrug.

Hannah resists grammatical correction. "I think you girls'll just stay home today."

Heather's chin goes into a quiver and her voice rises, "I can't miss today. We're going up to the lake to have a picnic and swim."

Hannah is having trouble waking herself and focusing on parent crisis behavior. She lets out an exasperated sigh. Heather fights back a full-fledged cry. A couple tears escape down the little girl's round cheek. Hannah would like to wake Max and let him handle the kid crisis. Unconsciously, she puts her hands inside her t-shirt and stretches it. Hannah has never liked pajamas or nightgowns, preferring to sleep in the nude. At Max and Gretchen's she's been more comfortable sleeping in her underpants and an oversized t-shirt.

"Hmmm," Hannah puts an upbeat lilt in her voice. "I've got an idea."

"What?" Heather brightens.

"Maybe we could take our time getting up, have breakfast and all, then I'll drive you up to the lake and you can join everybody there."

Heather jumps onto her, and Hannah catches her in a big hug. "You are the best aunt in the whole wide world. You really, really are."

#

The girls bolt from the car once they spot their friends. Hannah watches them for a moment, then looks down at Heather's stuffed bear.

What now, Charles? She thinks. Would a bear like to go for a hike in the woods? Heather insisted she take him along in case she gets lost on the way back.

Max and Gretchen could use some time alone with each other, and a little forest time sounds wonderful to Hannah. She could finally check out that great stretch of old growth woods Max had told her about. When she fought forest fires she practically lived in the woods. Since then she's been lucky to average one back-packing trip a year.

She heads back from the lake on Oregon Highway 262, then turns on to Harlan Road. After several miles she passes a sign for Foster Road. That's it, she remembers, pulls off, turns around, goes back and turns on to Foster. She passes a couple more side roads before Foster turns from blacktop to gravel. A combination of fenced pasture and stretches of tall firs gives way to forest. After a while it turns into a narrow dirt road. The woods are crisscrossed with old logging roads. Most of her women friends would think she is nuts to do this alone, but Hannah's firefighting sojourns left her feeling safer on logging roads than on city streets. She takes one.

Soon the ruts in the road become too deep. She's looking for a good place to turn around when a low-lying marshy spot brings her to a stop. She gets out. Hannah is afraid she could get stuck, but doesn't see any easy place to turn around on the narrow, rutted road. She gets back in, backs up a little, and speeds up to get through the wet spot. She spins out, slightly, but otherwise cruises through with ease. About a half-mile down the road, she comes to a landing where logs had been loaded several years earlier. She turns the car around, pointing back the way she came, and gets out to explore.

The landing itself looks like an old crime scene, still revealing the signs of the logging operation: scattered limbs, ends of trunks, a couple whole logs that apparently weren't usable, and a long, inch-thick piece of cable. Logging has pillaged the area straight ahead and to her right. Stumps, piles of slash, and an occasional single, thin tree dot an otherwise barren landscape. Hannah has seen a lot of clear-cuts fighting fires and backpacking, but the despoiled terrain still bothers her. It always will, she thinks.

Gazing out at the ravaged ground makes her think of Gretchen, and she starts to cry. Soon, the tears come in torrents. After a while, she stops, pulls her t-shirt out and wipes her eyes.

To Hannah's left, a young forest still flourishes. She wipes at her eyes again, turns away from the clear-cut, and climbs over a big mound of earth. She discovers two wide ruts, remnants of a deserted logging road. Within five minutes she's in another world, completely out of sight of the clear-cut's devastation. Where the woods reclaim their turf, the old road disappears. Young fir trees, ranging from ankle high to waist high, occupy what was once the middle of the road; ferns sprout up everywhere, and grasses and blackberry vines fight for space.

Hannah steps lightly over several fallen trees, ducks under small limbs, no thicker than her wrist. Straight ahead stand young Douglas fir trees, about twenty feet tall, their lower branches, alive and spreading. The even spacing between the trees makes Hannah think of a Christmas tree farm. She follows what's left of the old road, but the trees get taller and closer together, leaving the terrain less passable. Even where the land slopes away, her view is obstructed. The trees stand, like classmates posing for a photo, the taller ones in the back.

She stumbles across a piece of rubber that looks like a car's floor mat. A few steps farther, she sees a pile of junk: plastic jugs, a rusted muffler, a black, tar-covered five-gallon container, and several unidentifiable items. She decides to leave the road and winds her way into the thickness.

Fine, lacy strands of gold-green moss mingle with leaves, needles, and the decomposing wood of long dead trees. Together, they join the red clay of the forest floor to form a lush, spongy carpet. Sometimes the density of the woods gives way to an open space where the light shines, casting an emerald glow on a field of ferns. Then the forest closes up under the shadow of tall, crowding trees and appears as night in the middle of the day. Here, moss clings to trunks and stumps, avoiding the light. Chinquapin, madrone and oak appear individually, and in clusters, but Douglas fir still dominates.

A quick sound startles Hannah. She turns just in time to see the tail of a deer scrambling deeper into the woods. The forest becomes darker, the firs taller, ranging to seventy feet in height; they appear to be much closer together, too. Nearly all their lower branches have fallen away, and they stand tall and straight, like sentinels. She picks her way around fallen logs, working her way deeper into the woods. The forest floor spreads out in front of her again with hundreds of tall ferns reaching toward the sky. A huge and knotty Douglas fir towers over its companions. The last stand of trees seemed like a land of giants, but they appear like saplings compared to this great one. Hannah lingers in front of the grand old being, thinking it a rare colossus.

But as she continues, the forest stretches before her with dozens of giant firs of similar girth and height. The canopy of the towering giants creates a cave-like world, the trunks of the trees appearing as enormous stalagmites. Hannah imagines she's the first person ever to set foot on this piece of ground. She knows virgin forests can have that effect, but her mood is quickly spoiled when she comes upon a pile of beer cans and plastic wrappers. If she had an empty backpack she would haul the junk out. She curses the anonymous culprits who left their garbage and moves on.

She arrives at a precipice overlooking a steep sloping stand of younger trees. She would hike farther still, but the rougher, uneven ground would make short work of her tennis shoes. The forest carpet and the old road's red clay have already taken their toll. She scouts for a comfortable tree to lean her back against and spots an unbelievable tree.

This can't be, she tells herself. The trunk is clearly that of a fir tree, but as she looks up, she sees hundreds of tiny little maple leaves dangling from the branches. She blinks and looks again, stunned by this apparent freak of nature. Then she realizes it's a trick of nature. The maple leaves only appear to be coming from the fir. The long, dainty, maple branches have twisted around from the opposite side of the fir. Different kinds of trees don't intermarry, she reminds herself, conjuring up a thought of Fil. She laughs at herself. Was he really that special from one meeting, or is her life that void of interesting men? She looks the tree up and down, enjoying the illusion one more time, and pats the trunk with her hand.

"Well, I think you're special enough to hang out with awhile," she tells the tree, settling down with her back against her new friend. "Even if you are a fake." She crosses her legs and scoots her butt forward, creating a slight recline for herself, and peers out at the forest view.

#

Hannah falters on a dark and narrow path. Reddish, twisted, witch-like yews grab at her with long hairy arms. She picks up her pace. She feels the presence of unknown forces. She turns quickly to catch a glimpse. There's no one there. A hard calloused hand, bigger than a baseball mitt, rubs against her back. She jerks forward, looks back. Again, nothing is there. She attempts to walk faster. Her legs seem heavy, growing heavier with each step as if they are stuck in a quagmire. She strains to lift each leg out of the heavy muck and place it back down. She hears screeching. Has it always been here? She wonders. The screeching grows louder, coming at her from every direction. She's terrified. Something is chasing her. She knows it, but she doesn't know what it is. She knows she has to go faster. She can't. She can't move at all.

An inner voice counters the panic and calms her. Relax. She moves slowly forward, and the path begins to broaden, unfolding into a green and golden field. The sun envelops her with warmth. Birds sing to her.

Hannah awakens with a start, forgets where she is, then focuses. The rich, explosive warbles of dozens of little wrens are real. The sleepless night had caught up with her. She was dreaming, still propped up against the fir. Fully awake now, she sees the tiny brown birds hopping about. She smiles and stretches.

Despite the cool, forested spot, she's been sweating. Her blue jeans and t-shirt cling to her. She pulls the shirt slightly away, letting air in, then looks at her watch, looks again, startled. 3:00. She shrugs and gets up.

#

In her car, heading out, Hannah notices that the road slopes slightly upward. On the way in, it seemed level. As she approaches the wet, muddy spot, it appears steeper than she remembered and there's a large rock protruding on one side. She had completely missed seeing the boulder, or hitting it, on the way in. She figures she can navigate around it on the way out, too. She revs up her speed a bit as she hits the mud. Her wheels spin out and toss her into the rock. It's not a damaging hit, but her momentum slows and her wheels spin. She gives it more gas, before realizing she's digging ruts. "Damn", she mutters aloud.

She gets out to assess the predicament. "Goddamn," She curses the road. "Goddamn it."

She circles around her vehicle studying the mess. Her assessment isn't good. Any effort to get out will dig her in deeper, and if she wastes too much time and doesn't get her car moving, she could lose the daylight before she gets out of the woods. It's still fairly early, though, so Hannah decides to give it one good shot. She looks around for some flat pieces of wood to wedge under the tires and comes up with several skinny fir branches with lots of needles, but as she creates a bed under the rear wheels for traction, she shakes her head again. The car looks like it's sinking deeper in the muck. She feels like crying, but takes a deep breath, steadies herself and pushes on.

Hannah gets in the car, puts it into drive and gives it some gas. The wheels spin. She slams it into reverse and floors it. The wheels spin. She shoves the car back into drive and floors it again. More spinning. She shuts it down. Heather's stuffed bear, Charles, stares at her. I don't suppose you can use your mentriloquism to get us some help, can you? He just stares back. She imagines he might be thinking something like, I'm still too young to be any good at mentriloquism, and I'm going to be very scared if you leave me here in these woods all alone. Some bear, she thinks back at him and laughs at her dialogue with the stuffed animal, but she can't help moving him safely under the seat, for Heather's sake, at least.

Hannah thought she was going on a short daytime jaunt when she left the house hours earlier and didn't bring any water. It's a hot day, and she's thirsty, but she doubts a lack of water will become a problem. She locks the car up, city reflexes still in command, and starts up the road.

#

Hannah has been walking for an hour and a half when she comes to a private road twisting out of sight up a wooded hillside. A sign reads, PRIVATE DRIVE.

If someone is there, she'll have found help, but if it leads nowhere or nobody's around, she'll have wasted all that time and energy for nothing. She decides to go for it and begins the upward trek.

The view keeps changing as the road winds and twists. Sometimes the woods are thick, dark; where the trees give way to mostly low-lying brush, the space lightens. The steep climb forces her to stop and catch her breath.

She reaches the top of the rise. The road and land slope away to her right. She sees some sheds and a trailer down in the flats, an old pick-up parked in the midst of junk and debris. The hood is open. It could easily be a vehicle that doesn't run. Perhaps nobody is around, but having come this far, it's worth the rest of the trek, she reasons.

Near the bottom of the road a fence begins, though it's in disrepair with numerous gaps. A pasture stretches out on the other side of the fence, on the same side of the road as the trailer and outbuildings. On the opposite side, to her left, Hannah views a thin forest of skinny young alders and spreading viny maple. In August, the colors are just beginning to turn. In a couple more months, this little patch will be ablaze with fire red; now the alder and maple are still mostly light green with splotches of yellow and hints of orange and red. Hannah, feeling worn from her long trek, gets a shot of renewed vigor as she turns off the road up a long driveway to the trailer.

She passes a huge pile of junk: rusting metal, beams and pipes, beer cans and bottles, boards with nails, tree limbs, a car door and broken sheets of glass. She sees the pick-up she spotted from the road — an early fifties, red Dodge. She's still thirty yards from the trailer door when she hears a dog begin to bark wildly from inside. It gives her a start, but she continues, passing a rusting axle and several tires. As she nears, within several yards of the trailer, she hears a man's voice quieting the dog. The door opens, the man is bent with one hand on the door handle, the other grasping the dog by its collar.

"Don't worry. We don't get much company, so she's all excited. She won't bite or nothin'." Hannah can hear the man as she moves to within a few feet of him, but his head is still turned away because of the grip on the dog. She thinks she smells alcohol, even from a few feet away. He releases the mutt, and it bounds toward her. The dog has quit barking and seems to be seeking nothing more than a pet and some attention. She quickly obliges. Bent down, petting the dog, she feels the man approach, the stench of alcohol now undeniable. Hannah straightens to shake hands and introduce herself, finally coming face to face with her potential rescuer.

"I'm John Cooper," the scraggly man says as he puts out his hand. "Friends call me Jack."

He smiles, revealing a space where a tooth is missing. A blackened tooth is next to the gap.

14

"We gotta' do something about this light before we crash tonight," Billy mumbles through a mouthful of stale bread. He takes a sip of hot black coffee and looks at Hulk. It's six o'clock in the morning. Billy is often up at six if he hasn't gone to bed yet, but he never gets up this early.

Hulk's Uncle Kirk stares across the kitchen table at Billy. "What light?"

"The goddamn light. What other light is there?" Billy shakes his head like Kirk is too stupid to bother with. Kirk tenses his wiry frame. His torso leans forward, but his feet stay put.

"The sunlight?" Hulk asks.

Billy looks at him with disdain. "Yeah, the goddamn sunlight. What the hell do you think I'm talking about? I hate the goddamn light." Billy rubs his eyes with the backs of his hands.

"I never heard of anybody hating sunlight before," Kirk says evenly.

"Well, you've heard of it now. I hate that shit first thing in the morning. It makes me think of angels or some goddamn holy thing."

"Angels? You are some weird kid." Kirk looks at Hulk and shakes his head. He looks back at Billy. "Okay, tell you what. We'll get a blanket and you can put it over the window tonight — but, listen — don't treat me like shit in my own home or I'll run your ass out of here. Got it?"

"Yeah, I got it, dude."

Kirk stares at Billy. Billy glares back, with his hard, dark stare. Kirk's muscles tense again. His jaw tightens and juts. Billy readies himself.

"So what you got goin' today, Uncle Kirk?" Hulk asks.

Kirk and Billy stay locked. After a pause, Kirk responds to his nephew, but he keeps his gaze on Billy. "I got another couple days on a roofing job over to Roseburg. If you want to come along you can. I could use an extra hand. Jack and J.D. flaked out on me, again. Jack says his truck threw a rod or somethin' — he's just too bullshit drunk to get off his ass. You can ride with me or follow me in that piece of shit you call a car. It's up to you."

"I thought I would turn Billy on to that swimming hole off the Umpqua. If he can stand the sunlight," Hulk smiles.

Kirk laughs. Billy sneers. Kirk rocks back and forth from his heels to his toes. He's got his hands on his hips. After a few seconds he looks at his watch.

"I gotta' get going." He looks at Hulk. "Anything you need? There's food in the fridge. Only a couple beers left. You want more beer you gotta' go over to Pinkerton's Market."

"Way over to Pinkerton's?" Hulk whines. "What about Ricos?"

"They went under three or four years ago. Shit, BJ's was bigger than Ricos and they closed, too."

"What the fuck is going on?"

"Where you been, boy? Goddamn preservationists pulled the rug out from under the loggers. If there ain't no money to spend, the corner store bites the big one, too. Pinkerton's is the only place I know of, unless you want to go clear to Roseburg." He shakes his head, looks at his watch again.

"I gotta' get." He leaves the table to finish getting ready for work. Hulk looks at Billy, who stares at the retreating figure.

#

The hike to the top of the oak and alder-covered hill is long and arduous. Hulk likes feeling winded. He realizes he misses pushing his body like he did when he played football. But he senses Billy is becoming agitated. Billy's steel-toed boots work great in the concrete jungle, but he has trouble getting his footing on the uneven terrain. Hulk keeps getting ahead.

He turns around and looks at Billy. "Watch out for the poison oak, dude."

"You better not be serious. You know what poison oak will do to my fuckin' eyes."

"I am serious." Hulk points to a fiery red plant a few feet from Billy. "That's the shit right there."

"Fuck. How am I supposed to know this shit when I see it?"

"Just avoid anything that's red." Hulk laughs.

When they finally reach the top, Billy unlaces his boots and pulls them off. His black wardrobe serves as a solar-collector, too, and he's hot and grumpy. Hulk, wearing hiking boots, jeans and a faded yellow t-shirt, sprawls on the ground nearby, staring out at a series of rolling stands of young trees. From the crest they spot some other homes, trailers, barns and outbuildings, and a snaky road, but mostly more woods. Hulk pulls out his pack of cigarettes and lights up.

"This place of your uncle's ain't as isolated as I figured." Billy has to gulp air before he can say more.

"What are you worried about? Look out there. We can see everybody for miles around."

Billy pulls out his cigarettes, but he doesn't light up.

He's still fighting to catch his breath. "And they can see us."

Hulk looks at him, then twists his head around and looks back down at his uncle's trailer. "You gotta' point."

"Damn right, I do."

"Uncle Kirk's buddy Jack's got a place that's out in the middle of nowhere. He says if you don't want to be bothered you go to Jack's. That's why he's out there. But I don't think we could stay with him."

"I'm tired of your uncle's bullshit, that's all I know."

"If you would just ease up, you would like him, man. He's a major scammer."

"I don't see no scams, H. I just see a lame old dude bustin' his butt workin' for the man."

"That roofing stuff is just hit and miss. Him and Jack pull off a lotta' shit."

"Yeah, like what?"

"Like they got this deal where they cut firewood off people's land and then turn around and sell the suckers their own shit."

Hulk laughs. Billy stares at him.

"Ease up, already."

"Ease it up your ass. If this scam is so hot, why isn't he doin' it instead of this ball-breaking roofin' job?"

"Jack and this other guy — J.D. — messed up one time when Uncle Kirk wasn't there. I don't really know what happened. All I know is they gotta' lay low for a while. Anyway, you shouldn't push my uncle, Billy. He can be a hard dude."

"I been to prison, too." Billy spits back. "I'm not afraid of him just 'cause he's done time." Billy finally lights his cigarette.

"MacLaren ain't prison, man."

"The fuck it ain't. What would you know, jock strap?"

Hulk shakes his head. "Jesus, Billy, ease up."

"Quit being a goddamn pussy, then. You act like you're afraid of your fuckin' shadow."

Hulk doesn't say anything. He takes in the view and the quiet. He spent his early years on a farm. It seems like his mom was always baking something, filling the house with the scent of baking bread, or chocolate melting. And he was outside a lot, running with his dog, hiking. It's hard for him to remember many details. He was only six. He had a tree fort. Or maybe just a few boards nailed over a couple branches. He's not sure. He went there when his mom and dad fought. He was up there when she came to him and told him to pack his things because they were leaving. Her face was bruised and her eye was swelling.

He looks over at Billy, staring at the horizon.

"It musta' been rough, Billy. I mean your Mom dyin' and all." Hulk says it in a quiet, soothing voice. Billy just stares straight ahead and doesn't say a word. Hulk figures it's best to let him be.

After a long, quiet pause Billy, still staring straight ahead, speaks so softly Hulk can barely hear him. "She didn't die."

Hulk doesn't know what to say. His jaw drops and he stares at Billy, but he doesn't say anything. He wonders if he heard him correctly.

Still staring straight ahead, Billy raises his voice ever so slightly. "She didn't die, Hulk. My mom's not dead. At least as far as I know."

Hulk doesn't say anything.

The two have been quiet for a long time when Billy finally asks, "Whatever happened to recruiting the troops, H?" It's mid-afternoon and the night owl looks like he's ready to go back to sleep. He pulls his little silver film canister out of his front jean pocket, unscrews the lid and peeks inside.

"It's our second day here, man," Hulk responds. "I thought we would take it easy, you know. We can check out Roseburg tomorrow."

"I'm just not into this country shit, man. I wanna' do something." Billy wets the end of his finger, dips it in the canister, shoves his finger up his nose, snorts, repeats it with the other nostril. He hands the canister to Hulk.

"The thing is, Billy, you got to get to know the lay of the land here, just like in the city. Once you know the neighborhood, you know who is easy to jack up and where the best places are to rat somebody. We need to do some exploring. You never know what you may find." Hulk wets his finger, sticks it in the canister and snorts a couple times.

"Like what? Some goddamn squirrel?"

"Like a beaver, dude." Hulk jokes, but Billy doesn't laugh. Hulk scans the horizon, and Billy stares at the ground. A dark shadow passes over them, and they both flinch. Billy cranes his neck around, trying to spot the silent intruder.

"Shit man," he finally spots it. "It's a goddamn hawk."

Hulk laughs.

"What the fuck are you laughing at?"

Hulk shakes his head back and forth unable to stop from laughing for a few seconds. "It's not a hawk," he finally says. "It's a buzzard." He laughs again.

"A buzzard?" Billy looks at Hulk, then at the bird. Its big, dark wings are still. It rides the currents.

"Yeah, Billy," Hulk says, still smirking and shaking his head. "It's a goddamn vulture."

Billy watches the bird circling around and around, floating up and down on the breeze. After a while another buzzard joins the first one, and they glide back and forth. A third joins them.

Hulk stares straight ahead, letting his thoughts drift back to his mother again. He wishes she understood White Nation better. It's these goddamn niggers and bean-eaters and slant-eyed mothers that are leaving her with nothing but the shit jobs. In White Nation, his mom and women like her would have a good life. Hulk hears Billy say something, but he can't make it out. "What are you sayin' Billy?"

Billy stares at the ground, shaking his head back and forth, mumbling. Hulk slides closer, a little at a time, until he hears the barely audible murmur.

"Fuckin' bitch." Billy keeps repeating the phrase, like an unholy mantra.

15

Warnings to remain calm click off at rapid intervals. Although Hannah knows she revealed her shock, she reminds herself the black-toothed stranger isn't likely to equate her look with anything other than general nervousness. She doubts she can outrun him or out-fight him. She's in the middle of nowhere. She needs to stall and look for an out, for anything.

"My name's Hannah. My car got stuck a ways down the road."

"I didn't figure you were out for a Sunday stroll, honey."

Hannah wonders if he would seem so slimy if she didn't know who he was. She decides he probably would, no matter what the circumstances. She takes a deep breath to calm herself, but the reek of alcohol and body odor nauseates her. "Did you go to sleep at the wheel? Not too many places to get stuck this time of year."

"I managed to find a spot, somehow." She gives a slight laugh, trying to remain loose and appear relaxed.

"Well, come in and set a spell, then we'll get you outa' there."

"I guess I'm feeling anxious to get going, if you don't mind."

"Well, honey." The seedy inflection feels like bugs crawling on her skin. "I know you must be anxious, but I ain't movin that fast. So, come on in, have a seat. I'll be glad to help you out as soon as I'm ready."

She reconsiders bolting. He's probably too drunk to chase her, but where does she go? She's worn out already, and he can just get in his truck and come after her. She could insist on waiting for him outside, but she feels vulnerable just standing out in the open. She still holds some element of surprise. After all, he doesn't realize she's on to him. Perhaps she can spot a weapon or something. "All right, I appreciate any help you can give me."

The trailer is dirty and cluttered. A kitchen counter and sink overflow with mostly non-kitchen items: metal parts, screws, bolts, a screwdriver, a couple of wrenches. She makes a mental note of the screwdriver's location. A restaurant-booth style table is filled with more junk, including a nearly empty bottle of Jack Daniel's, and the benches on both sides are piled high with metal parts. She expects her scraggly host to still play out a semi-seduction scene, to clear a spot for her to sit at the table before he forces himself on her.

He turns to his left, past a narrow door, and takes three steps into another room. He motions for Hannah to follow. She takes one step; he's sitting down on a bed facing her. He makes an odd up and down motion with his shoulders. He pats the bed.

"C'mon, honey, sit here next to me."

She shakes her head, pulling back. "I don't think so —"

He grabs her wrist. Her watch scrapes at her skin as she yanks away. He's left with the watch as she turns to run. She can feel him behind her, but she's out the door ahead of him. The dog jumps up, barking. Hannah has no time to think. The pick-up truck is just steps away. She reaches it, still feeling him behind her, rips open the door, leaps inside and slams it shut. Before she can lock it, he's yanks it open. She scrambles across the seat and out the other side. He rushes after her, but she feels more distance between them, perhaps as much as a few feet as she runs toward the nearest haven, a small, dilapidated shed. She takes a deep breath, imagining an unleashed pack of wild dogs, and swings the shed door open, revealing a dirt floor and a few tools in a six by four foot space. Hannah rushes in, pulling the wooden door behind her. Black tooth has reached the door. He yanks it. There's a knob of some kind on the inside and she holds on to it, bracing her legs and putting everything into what she perceives as a life and death tug of war.

"Hey, come on, honey, I'm not going to hurt you." He pleads, his voice slurred.

He's got to be kidding, she thinks, but his slurred voice gives her more confidence. She glances around and sees a long loop of wire hanging down near the door.

"Come on, you don't want to stay in there. Come on out, I just want to talk."

As he continues to babble, Hannah feels the tension on the door release for a second. She takes a chance. Still holding as strongly as she can with her left hand, she grabs the wire with her right and yanks down hard toward the knob, pulls the wire past the knob and jerks it up and over, and back down, surrounding the knob with the wire and pulling it tight. Then she wraps it around again and with both hands yanks it back toward the nail where the wire begins. She lets out a big sigh, stands there staring at it, ready to resume the battle in an instant, if need be.

Black tooth has quit pleading and pulling. She listens for him, but doesn't hear anything except the panting of the dog. Her adrenaline still rushing, she assesses her predicament. Despite being locked in a shed, she feels exhilarated. She looks around the shed again. Shovels and an ax lean against a wall: weapons, should the barrier give way. She still doesn't hear anything outside, except the panting and stirring of the dog. Could he have gone back to the trailer? Any sense of time has escaped her. She glances at her watch for a reality check, and remembers it's gone. Her hand is scratched and bloody. Small price to pay, she tells herself.

It must be late afternoon, perhaps early evening, Hannah reasons. Black tooth has been drinking, probably heavily. Maybe he's passed out. Whatever, she can't just stay here. She's got to make a move eventually. She hears Heather's little voice say "ventually" — and smiles.

If she waits until dark she could be in a much worse way. No one knows where she is. She looks over the tools and grabs a short handled ax. She can wield it better than a shovel. She holds it ready in her right hand and begins to slowly unwind the wire with her left.

When she cracks the door open, the dog barks. She quickly bends down to touch the dog and quiet her. The door swings back. Hannah jumps up, startled, but ready. The rapist is nowhere in sight. She pets the dog and quietly orders her to stay.

She steadies herself and moves out. In the quiet, she moves around the pick-up, her head turned around staring at the trailer door. She takes a quick glance inside the old vehicle. No keys. She should have let Max teach her how to hot-wire, she jokingly scolds herself. Never really figured it would come in handy. Hannah keeps moving away from the trailer, still looking back at the door, but glancing all about, alert. She picks up her pace and half-jogs past the rusting pile of junk. The dog, which has remained quiet except for constant panting and tail-wagging, stops at the pile and begins barking. She squats down and pets the dog.

"You go back and lie down," Hannah whispers in a soothing voice. "That's a good dog. Lie down and be quiet." The dog gives a short bark and settles down again.

Hannah walks backward, keeping her eye on the dog and the trailer. After twenty yards, she turns and picks up her pace again, jogging the final one hundred yards to the private road that led to the rapist's trailer, and begins walking back the way she had come. It feels hot and muggy but she walks briskly, continually glancing back to see if anyone is coming. She wants to run, but decides she needs to pace herself for the long haul. The uphill climb reminds her she's operating on empty. She hasn't had anything to eat or drink since early morning.

When she reaches the top of the rise, she looks back. Nothing is stirring below. She feels some relief, but he could be on her in a matter of minutes. She pushes on, down the hill this time. When she reaches the juncture of the private road and the road her car is stuck on, she feels a wave of exhaustion, a mental letdown. She knows it's unlikely anybody will come along this road except the rapist, and heads away from her car, toward the more traveled road.

Suddenly, Hannah hears a motor and dashes toward the brush before realizing the sound is a small, low-flying aircraft. Her heart quiets as she resumes her trek.

Finally, she hits the juncture for Harlan Road and turns toward the way she came. Now she figures a friendly vehicle could come along as well as danger. It's difficult to track time. She doesn't know if she's been walking for an hour-and-a-half or three hours. She spots the junction sign. She'll hit 262 soon. As she rounds another curve, Hannah sees the highway up ahead and hears a car. She realizes it's coming from behind her. Again she heads for the cover of brush off the road. But she hears it late, and before she can get out of the line of sight she sees the vehicle — an old Volkswagen van straight out of the sixties. Hannah makes out the passenger first — a bald head, or very short hair. The driver's head is blocked by a dangling sun visor. As the vehicle pulls up and stops, Hannah's pounding heart begins to slow; two women occupy the front seat.

"You look like you could use a ride," the woman in the passenger seat says, leaning slightly out the window. Hannah can tell she's a big woman, even with most of her body blocked by the door. Her shoulders and upper body appear large and strong; her hair is extremely short, nearly shaved. Hannah guesses she's in her mid-thirties. A younger woman with dark shoulder-length hair is behind the wheel. They smile. Hannah feels overwhelmed by the warmth.

"God, could I ever!" She reaches for the rear side door, but the big woman opens her door first.

"That door is busticated," she says, grinning. "Come on, we'll squeeze you in." The woman slides over, her large breasts jiggling, and Hannah climbs in.

"My name is Madeline," the big woman says, then changes her voice to an imitation of highbrow British, "but everyone calls me Mad." She laughs a halting little laugh and then bursts into a full laugh, giving Hannah the feeling she knows her from somewhere.

"This is Peggy." Mad points at the driver, who acknowledges Hannah with a smile and a nod.

"I'm Hannah." She sees them staring at her hand, and she realizes she's till carrying the ax. "Oh, God, sorry." She laughs nervously and awkwardly reaches down to place it on the floor.

"You look like you've been through the ringer, sister," the bigger woman says.

The driver looks back in the mirror and pulls slowly back on to the road.

"I hardly know where to begin, but the most important thing is we need to get the police as soon as possible."

Peggy says, "We can get you to a phone at a store up here in less than ten minutes, maybe five."

"So, what's happening? Why the police?" Mad asks.

"My sister-in-law was raped by two men several weeks ago, and I just ran into one of them. We need to get the sheriff over to this guy's place while he's still passed out."

"Passed out? You knocked this guy out?" Mad asks.

"No, I think he's passed out drunk. I just think we ought to get the police on this guy as soon as we can."

Peggy steps on it, figuring getting stopped would be fine under the circumstance. "So, this guy lives out here somewhere?" Peggy asks. "I don't get it, you were tracking him on your own or something?"

"I was out on a Sunday drive — on a Tuesday," Hannah laughs. "It was totally by chance I happened upon this guy's place."

"You were out for a drive?" Peggy pauses waiting for a response and when she doesn't get one, continues. "Like in your car?"

"Oh God, my car. I forgot about my car. I need to get my car, too."

Peggy and Mad crack up, laughing. Mad asks, "How did you lose your car, honey? Sounds like you left in one hell of a hurry."

"No, that happened earlier. I got stuck in a muddy spot in the road."

"Mud?" Mad laughs again. "You found mud this time of year. That is an accomplishment!"

Hannah laughs, "That was the easy part. The question is: can I find my car now?" They all laugh.

"First things first," Mad says. "Let's get the cops on this guy, then we'll figure out how to get your car."

The reality of all that has happened suddenly sinks in, and Hannah feels physically drained. She takes a deep breath and sighs.

Mad puts her arm around Hannah. "You're okay now. We'll have the cops out there in minutes. We've been having some problems, and the local sheriff has been real good. No help, but real good." Mad laughs a full laugh.

"Hey, Mad," Peggy asks, "you don't suppose this guy — the

rapist — could be one of the guys that shot at us?"

"Who knows? Could be. He could be one of these goons, I suppose."

"You got shot at?" Hannah asks. "What did the guy look like?"

"Oh, we didn't see him," Mad says. "Somebody shot up our house in the middle of the night. There's a group of us who have a piece of land on a little side road back off the road you were walking on. We've been receiving threats and hate-notes. We figure it's more than one guy, maybe some neo-Nazi group or something."

"The notes have swastikas on them." Peggy adds.

"Why are they bothering you?" Hannah asks. She looks them both over more carefully, noticing for the first time how pretty Peggy is. Her face has a natural healthy blush. It's not just the suntan, Hannah thinks, this woman has a real glow. Mad's features are strong, practically chiseled. Hannah feels drawn to the big woman's self-confidence and exuberance. Neither looks the least bit Jewish to Hannah.

Mad says. "The notes call us Jew Dykes." She laughs a couple short laughs. "We're all a bunch of dykes. Six of us share this place. Just one of us, Sarah, is Jewish."

"There used to be six of us," Peggy corrects Mad. "Two left because they were scared. The rest of us are staying no matter what."

"You said the cops were helpful?" Hannah asks.

"I said they were good." Mad says. "I mean after we finally called them. They were nice to us, not like we expected. Well, the state police were a minor drag. Cold, you know. The county sheriff was nice, like a good old boy — only we were treated like we were part of the good old boys' club. Like he wasn't the least bit uptight about a bunch of dykie women. Still, nobody's been really helpful. I mean nobody's been caught or identified."

"You didn't call the police right away?"

"Not after we got the notes," Peggy says.

Mad continues. "We didn't trust them. But friends up in Eugene and Portland kept telling us to involve the cops anyway. We were thinking about it when the house got shot up. We called them right away."

"We were freaked." Peggy says.

"We still are." Mad says.

"We were hesitant to let the media know," Peggy says. "But we changed our minds about that, too."

Again, Mad picks up Peggy's line. "We've got a guy staying with us right now who documents this kind of stuff for an anti-hate coalition out of Eugene. He's not a reporter or anything, but he's got it all down, now. He's actually done with his work, I think. We just can't get rid of the guy."

They both laugh. Hannah doesn't get it. She gives them a puzzled look.

"Just kidding," Mad responds. "The guy's a real sweetheart. We hit it off, and he asked if he could hang out for a couple weeks." Mad puts her highbrow accent back on. "Enjoy the country life." She pauses, then continues, still with the highbrow accent. "It's not like we need a man around the house or anything."

"I met a black guy who documents hate crimes, but he was a student at the University of Oregon," Hannah says.

"This guy's a student at Oregon, too. He's black," Peggy says.

Hannah wonders if it could possibly be Fil, then rejects the notion. "What's this guy's name?

"Fil," Peggy says.

"Filbert the nut," Mad says, and they both laugh the same familiar, infectious laugh.

Part Three

16

Hannah fusses with her hair, glances at herself in the rear-view mirror. She likes the way she looks. Thin and tanned. Even her silver streaks appeal to her. But her stomach's in turmoil.

Mad told her to take the first gravel road to the right past the twelve-mile post. She spots it, turns right, then slows to accommodate the twisting, turning, bumpy gravel road. She comes to a long straight-away that climbs sharply. An embankment forms a steep wall on one side. The land drops off on the other. Blackberry vines run wild. An occasional oak or maple hangs a branch high over the road.

Other than the dead-end, around-the-bend location, Mad and Peggy's place is almost the exact opposite of Max and Gretchen's. Their land is open and exposed with a view that looks out on the world, while Max and Gretchen live at the bottom of a secluded little hollow. When Hannah comes around the bend at her brother's, a rushing creek and sloping hill-covered woods greet her. Here she looks at the stump-dotted terrain and sees tombstones. Mad had said they got the land cheap because it had been logged, but that warning fails to adequately prepare Hannah for the barren expanse. She wonders how they confront it every day.

After the initial shock wears off, however, she realizes it's not that bad. In this climate, some kind of green comes back everywhere, even if it's blackberry vines, morning glory and poison oak taking over the stumps. Some trees remain: an occasional madrone and a stand of alders, not far from the house.

Hannah pulls her Datsun into an open space between Peggy's van and a 1965 Pontiac, a big old yellow boat of a car. That's got to be Fil's, she thinks. Whatever dull sterility the logging has created, Mad and company have countered with vibrant colors, green-thumbing their noses at the unnatural defoliation. The old, white farmhouse with its wrap-around porch acts as the canvas. Directly to the front, Hannah sees layers of shades of pink: Martha Washington geraniums, carnations, dwarf snapdragons, and little frilly pink dianthus with darker pink centers. Several baskets with purple, white and pink fuchsias hang from the porch roof. Around to one side, stretching out of her view, Hannah spies an array of deep red roses.

Off to the other side, a fenced garden erupts with plants, heavily laden with plush, ripe vegetables. A dozen tomato plants, tied to tall stakes, climb seven and eight feet off the ground. They're loaded with green and red fruit, ranging from tiny, cherry and pear-shaped tomatoes to big, bulging beefsteaks. Nearby, shiny, purple eggplants crowd each other for space on their sagging green plants. The peppers offer greens, yellows, oranges and reds. Cucumber and squash vines climb trellises, fashioned from bamboo. Several bolting broccoli plants look like their best days are behind them. The flat, vegetable garden gives way to a mild slope, stacked with strawberry plants and blueberry bushes. If any ripe, red berries are still loitering in late summer, they're hidden beneath dark, green leaves. The blueberries are gone, but the bushes run their branches up and out, staking new turf for next year's bounty. Giant orange marigolds appear everywhere, like tiny psychedelic pompons. A cluster of towering sunflowers beam their approval from a far corner of the garden.

As Hannah approaches the house she sees four women and Fil, grinning and laughing. Her stomach churns. It's late Saturday morning, and the whole crew appears to be lingering on the front porch — reading the paper, talking, sipping coffee. One of the women has a guitar on her lap, but she isn't playing. The wide porch wraps clear around the house in both directions.

"Hi, Hannah," Mad greets her first, then Peggy.

"You didn't have any trouble finding us, did you?"

Before Hannah can answer, she sees Fil's jaw drop. His eyes get big, and he starts shaking his head back and forth. "Holy shit. Hannah?"

"Holy shit, yourself." Hannah sounds normal to herself, suppressing her nervousness quite well, she thinks, as she starts up the stairs. She had resolved to be no more than cordial when she saw him.

Fil gets up to hug her as if they really are old friends. That's what she told Mad and Peggy. She feels herself loosen as she moves toward him, and feels like giving him a big kiss, but the thought produces an awkwardness. She closes back up a little. When they hug, most of the clumsiness dissipates. But she can't shut down her internal dialogue. Is her yearning mutual? Or is he just a friendly, huggy guy?

They pull back, hold each other at the elbows and look at each other's faces.

"So, I guess that term paper or project of yours must have brought you here?" Her words feel cumbersome.

Fil lets out his short, jerky laugh. "You remember that?" He bursts into his full laugh. "Well, I sorta' got talked into this particular trip. Apparently, there's a fairly active group operating in this area that nobody's heard of before."

She remembers Fil as being calm in the courthouse hallway. Now, he seems speedy.

"They could provide a link between neo-Nazi groups and right-wing Christian groups, and these —"

"There's a difference?" One of the other two women, the one with a guitar on her lap, interjects.

Fil smiles at the woman who spoke. "Spoken like a true Jew, Sarah." Everyone laughs.

"So as I was saying before I was so rudely interrupted," Fil smiles, "I basically got drafted to check out —"

"Drafted?!" Peggy screams and fakes a choking fit.

"Woo, woo," Sarah croons.

"Poor Fil," Mad chimes in.

"Okay, okay," Fil shakes his head, blushing and laughing. "So I volunteered because I couldn't help myself."

"Then he volunteered to stay here and protect us —" Mad can barely get the words out without laughing, and the other three join her in laughter. As if on cue, some nearby crows kick up a big fuss.

"See what I have to put up with," Fil says to Hannah, smiling.

"I see how much you hate it."

"God, Fil, we invite Hannah over and you keep her there on the edge of the porch," Mad says. "Why don't you pull up a chair, Hannah? I'll get you a cup of coffee or something."

Fil jumps in before Hannah can respond. "Hey, before you get settled in — maybe — you would like a quick tour of the place, and I could get a break from their torture."

"You love it." Mad says. "You're not going to drag her off first thing. She just got here, and Dana and Sarah haven't even met her yet."

"Oh yeah," Fil says sheepishly and turns toward the other two women. "I guess you must already know Mad and Peggy. This is Sarah and Dana. This is Hannah."

Sarah and Dana have barely nodded their hellos, when Fil blurts out, "Jesus, Hannah, you're the one who nailed the rapist?"

Everyone laughs again, and Fil joins them, laughing at himself. The crows, hanging out in the nearby stand of alders, caw again, sounding like a bunch of rowdy teens. Fil glares up at them, like a middle-school kid attempting to quiet his friends with a hard look.

"I didn't really nail him. I escaped from him. The cops nailed him after we called them," Hannah says.

Fil grins. Hannah thinks she catches him staring at her with an admiring look. She feels her face turn flush, and looks down.

She looks back up, at Mad and Peggy, who are smiling at her.

She likes the relaxed camaraderie amongst Fil and the four women. She feels bonhomie she usually feels only with people she's known for a long time. But she feels torn. Should she settle in and hang out? Or find a way to spend some time alone with Fil?

"So, have a seat already," Mad says, scooting over to make room on the couch. "Maybe this guy can earn his keep and get you a cup of coffee."

Hannah slides in next to Mad, notices the big woman's lime green stretch pants, the ugliest pants Hannah has ever seen. They look like something women with beehive hairdos, shopping at K-Mart would wear, or maybe red-neck women on a bowling team. Then she imagines Mad bowling and decides it fits. Hannah realizes Fil is looking at her, waiting for a response. She looks back at him. "No, nothing for me, thanks."

"Maybe you would rather have tea?" Fil offers. "I already have a pot of chamomile going. I'll go get it." He takes off before she can answer.

The women laugh again. "Old friend, huh?" Mad razzes Hannah. "He looks like he just got bonked in the head with the moon."

"Well —" Hannah doesn't know what to say. She shakes her head and laughs, which makes the four women roar with laughter again.

Fil comes back out with a cup of tea, hands it to her and sits down on the porch ledge. Hannah's stomach still feels queasy. The tea seems like a good idea.

"Your sister-in-law must be relieved with that guy locked up." Peggy says.

"For about one second. Until she realized the other guy is

still out there."

"God, what a drag," Sarah says.

"And now Gretchen is freaked about maybe having to testify at a trial."

"Things are going to be rough for her for a long time." Mad says.

Everyone is quiet.

"Your garden looks great." Hannah says.

"The veggie garden is mostly Sarah's baby," Mad says. "We all help, but she'll whip those little plants if they don't grow — and they grow." Everybody laughs again. "Now, the flowers —" Mad lightly jabs Hannah in the ribs with her elbow, "tell me how much you like the flowers —"

"Oh, God, I love the flowers," Hannah quickly responds with total sincerity, and everybody laughs. The crows caw, too, as if they're in on all the good jokes.

"The flowers are my passion," Mad finishes.

"Pink passion," Sarah adds, raising her eyebrows.

Fil is sitting on the edge of the porch looking back at the five women who all face out, away from the house. He points behind Hannah's head. "Check this out, if you want passion." He says it coldly, and nobody laughs.

Hannah turns around, twisting her torso and craning her neck. About a foot away from a big picture window, the wood is splintered and has a small hole. She moves her eyes and spots two more similar gaps.

"Those three holes?"

"Bullet holes," Mad says. "The big window, there, was shattered. We replaced it right away."

"Either that, or have the house filled with flies and wasps," Peggy adds.

"WASPs?" Mad emphasizes and laughs. It takes a second for the others to get the double meaning. Then they all laugh. The crows are quiet.

"God," Hannah says, "it must have been scary."

"Look who's talking," Mad responds. "Ms. Locked-in-a-shed-and-I'll-bust-the-mother-fucker-anyway."

"Well, I wasn't exactly locked in the shed. I mean — I locked myself in the shed."

"Typical woman, lock yourself in a shed so the man won't have to," Mad says, and cracks up. The women, the crows and Fil join in the racket.

"Seriously," Hannah says when the laughter quiets down, "What's it like living with this constant harassment?"

"Oh, they weren't this mean to me until you got here," Fil quickly interjects. His joke is met with hissing.

"Honey," Mad says, responding to Hannah, "this ain't harassment. This is I'd-just-as-soon-kill-ya-as-look-at-ya. Harassment we can take. It's plain ol' vanilla harassment nearly every time we go to town."

"Not like this," Peggy says, nodding toward the bullet holes.

"Not anywhere near that intense," Dana says.

Hannah realizes Dana's been very quiet. She can't see her real well from where she's sitting and didn't get a good look at her before she sat down. Dana seems to be about thirty. She has short brown hair, her skin bronzed by the sun. On second glance, she appears to be wearing nothing more than a big beach towel.

"Yeah," Mad picks it up again, "When we go to town they just shoot nasty remarks at us."

"Really? All the time? I mean — like in Elk Hill, or in — what's the name of that little town — Clayton?"

"Everywhere, Hannah," Mad says. Everyone else nods.

"But not everybody," Sarah suddenly adds. "Really. Don't get the wrong impression. I think it's clearly a minority who give us shit. But even if it's a small minority, there are some number of shit-givers everywhere."

"It's been this way ever since you moved here — what did you say — more than five years ago?"

"Oh no." Mad responds. "There were always a few dirty looks or gawks — very rarely we might hear a nasty comment. But once the Citizens for Family Values started their anti-queer campaign, things got a lot worse."

"A whole lot worse." Dana and Sarah say it at the exact same time and look at each other, but they don't smile.

Everyone grows silent. Something disturbs the crows, or maybe they just get bored. The rowdy crowd suddenly takes off.

"Hatred in the name of God," Mad says after several seconds pass.

"That's what we get for letting them create God in man's image," Sarah says. No one laughs.

Hannah steals a glance at Fil, but he seems completely unfazed. She isn't sure if he saw her looking admiringly at him, but he has a little smile pursing his lips.

"So, what about you, Fil?" She asks, "Do you get harassed

when you go into Elk Hill or Clayton?"

"Hannah," Mad says, putting on a condescending voice, "Fil isn't a lesbian."

"Are you sure about that," Sarah says. They all laugh, and Fil shakes his head back and forth, laughing.

Hannah is looking right at Fil when Dana gets up, tosses her towel over her shoulder and walks, completely naked, back into the house. She notices that Fil's eyes don't follow Dana. For the first time, she considers another possibility: maybe Fil is gay.

After another couple seconds of silence, Fil asks her, "Ready for that tour of the grounds, yet?" He tries to look directly at Hannah, but his eyes dart around, apparently anticipating a hazing.

"Actually, I am a bit too antsy to sit on the porch for a long stretch, just yet. Maybe we could go for a walk, catch up — and keep you away from their abuse." Hannah smiles and rolls her eyes at the three women who respond with catcalls.

"Sure," Fil says, appearing like he's just been told yes for the first time at a junior high dance. The women exchange excited and knowing looks. Hannah thinks they're acting like grade school siblings who just caught their parents in a rare kiss.

"So, are we going?" Fil asks.

"Yeah, I'm ready." They turn and negotiate the three steps down and turn their heads back toward the group on the porch.

"Don't stay out too late, kids," Mad shouts. Everybody laughs.

Under the circumstances, the walk away from the house seems agonizingly long. Actually, it only takes a couple minutes for a winding path to them get past the stumps and openness, and into a stand of young alder.

"It looks kind of barren around their house, but it doesn't take long — you'll see — and the land gets pretty nice." Fil says.

"It looks nice to me, already," Hannah responds. She could probably squeeze her hand around the skinny young saplings, but the hundreds of little trees hold a pleasing open aesthetic for Hannah that the crowded, entangled woods lack.

They reach the top of a small rise and descend into a more thickly-forested area of young, spreading firs and cedars. Soon, they're climbing again, single-file, up a steep, narrow trail, bordered by low-lying thickets, blackberries and scotch broom. Occasionally, Fil lifts a blackberry vine out of the way and holds it until Hannah passes.

"You know, all this time I thought Fil was short for Philip."

Fil bursts out with his familiar short laugh. "That's what everybody thinks. My name is Filbert."

"So I learned. I thought maybe your parents might be fans of the great African middle distance star. Filbert — Bayi?"

Fil's face brightens. "Yeah. I mean his last name is Bayi. But I'm not named after him." He laughs, shaking his head with the pleasure of a child who never tires of telling the same knock-knock joke. "Oregonians are so track hip. But I'm not that young. I think I was about ten when he was doing his thing. My parents named me after the nut." He laughs again. "What's in a name anyway? A nut by any other name would still be a nut." He laughs his full blown infectious laugh and Hannah laughs, too, despite thinking the line isn't particularly funny.

The terrain opens up again. They follow a well-worn path

through a meadow covered with tall, dry grasses, wilting in the August heat. The ground gently rises. Hannah and Fil can walk side by side, slowly negotiating occasional obstacles of brush and branches.

"So how did your parents come by Filbert?"

"When my Mom was pregnant with me she would go for long walks including a trek through a filbert orchard. Pretty simple, huh?"

"A filbert orchard? Here in Oregon?"

"Yeah. There are native Oregonians who are black, too. We don't all come from LA." He says it pleasantly, but it strikes Hannah wrong.

"I'm sorry," she says, "I didn't mean anything —"

"No. I know you didn't. I didn't mean anything, either. People just assume I'm not from here, that's all."

They reach the top of the meadow, and the land slopes down again. A thick stand of trees and bushy growth narrows the way. Fil slips ahead of Hannah and walks sideways, looking back at her.

"Did you get teased for Filbert in school?" She realizes she's interviewing Fil with one question after another. She can't seem to stop. A way of avoiding a nervousness that silence brings.

"A little. Friends called me Fil the same way they might have if I had been named Philip. And it stuck. No big deal, you know."

He turns and resumes walking along the narrow path. She follows behind him. A more comfortable silence sits between them now. The path opens up and they walk side by side again. A field dotted with stumps spreads out to their right.

"You seem pretty tight with these folks here — Mad and Peggy and all — but I thought they said you just met?"

Fil laughs his short little bursts of sucking-in-air laughter. "Yeah. I met them a few weeks ago." As he laughs his full laugh Hannah feels like that one day at the courthouse could have been a whole childhood of memories; the laugh is so familiar it chills her and comforts her at once.

"It really is something, isn't it?" Fil asks. "I mean how close you can get to people in a really short time?"

Bingo. It's the opening she needs, but her stomach tightens at the thought of saying something, and she feels short of breath. She passes on the opportunity.

Fil continues. "Maybe it's Mad and Sarah. I mean, I know it's at least partly Mad and Sarah, and Peggy to a lessor extent." Fil stops walking and faces Hannah as he continues, "They're so open. It's partly me, too, I'm sure. I've always been able to get close to people quickly. But, I think it's mostly the intensity of danger. You know? You get thrown into some situation where you feel threatened, and you're suddenly friends for life. Know what I mean?" He turns and starts walking as he asks the question.

"Yeah." Hannah can't pass it up this time. She's slightly behind Fil, just off his shoulder. Her heart is pounding, but not too out of control. "Isn't that — at least in part — what happened to you and me? Well, maybe you didn't feel the danger I felt in the courthouse that day, but — well — for some reason I feel like we're old friends."

Fil stops and turns toward Hannah, his voice genuine. "We are." He touches the back of her upper arm with his hand and runs it lightly down to just above the elbow and holds it there. "I felt very connected to you back then. I feel connected now. I wanted to see you again."

She's comforted by his words, but she still isn't sure if he wants romance or friendship. She needs words, she tells herself — concrete, specific words. Or a kiss. She laughs. Then she wants to pull the laugh back. She realizes Fil just put himself on the line, emotionally, and he might misread the laugh. But he smiles back, with a questioning look.

She reaches her hand up to his cheek and touches it softly, pulling him toward her and reaching up at the same time. She gently touches her lips to his. Fil responds, tenderly. They pull apart, but not far enough to really look at each other; and bring their lips back for more, kissing delicately again. The kiss deepens. Fil pulls Hannah into his arms. She snuggles in tighter. His soft-looking frame hid his strength, and she feels secure despite her racing heart.

Finally, Hannah pulls back and looks at him, smiling. "Well, I guess you're not gay."

Fil laughs. "You thought I was gay!?"

"No, not really. You do have kind of a gay sound to your voice, sometimes."

"Moi?"

"Actually, it just occurred to me for a second back there when you didn't even take a peek at Dana's butt." Hannah can't believe she said that, but he doesn't give her the time to obsess over it.

"Well, that's exactly why I didn't. I knew I was being watched. And the truth is I am a butt-man. It took all my self-discipline to keep my eyes off her." He laughs, a little nervously, like he regretted letting that slip out so easily.

She wonders if he likes her butt. "Feel a little intimidated by the Mad-women, do you?"

Fil laughs. "Mad-women. I like that. Intimidated, though? Not me. I just don't want to risk having my dick cut off."

They both laugh, but the silence that follows makes her feel awkward. He seems uncomfortable, too, for a second, before he takes the lead, and they resume walking. She relaxes again and savors the moment.

"I'm trying to get to a particular path I discovered on a walk a few days earlier," Fil says. "But I'm not sure how I got there. Things look different, but I think I'm headed in the basic direction. Of course, a slightly wrong angle can take you farther and farther off course, and it can take a long time to get back on track." He comes to a halt, and looks around.

"So what do you think?" she asks.

"I'm not sure. I had a destination in mind, but I'm not sure how to get there."

"Sounds intriguing." Hannah smiles. "Are we talking metaphysically here?"

He laughs. "No, nothing too heavy. Just a light little meadow, actually."

"I'll follow. It sounds nice, but it doesn't really matter. I mean, it's a gorgeous day, we're in the woods; anything we run into out here will be wonderful — well, other than poison oak."

"Well, then." He puts out his arm and elbow, and imitates Mad's imitation highbrow accent, "M'lady?"

She puts her hand through his arm, laughs and smiles.

"Charmed, I'm sure."

They don't have to go far. Just beyond a thicket of viny maple and blackberries, a meadow spreads before them. Hundreds of tiny yellow wildflowers are scattered among the light green grasses. She watches the flight of a small dark bird — black, with a purplish tint. The bird has a distinct, yellow circle around its eye. When it lands among the wild flowers, Hannah notices that the color of the eye is identical to the color of the flowers. The bird's dark form is highlighted against the light green field. It seems unafraid as it pecks about for food among the grasses, as if the black bird believes its tiny yellow eye is enough to camouflage it among the flowers.

17

WHITE AMERICANS FOR A WHITE WORLD
WE ARE WORKING-CLASS WHITE YOUTH PROUD OF OUR RACIAL HERITAGE. WE WOULD PREFER TO SMASH THE PRESENT ANTI-WHITE ZIONIST (JEW), PUPPET-RUN GOVERNMENT. IF YOU ARE AGAINST RACE-MIXING AND ARE WILLING TO WORK FOR A NEW WHITE MAN'S ORDER, JOIN US TODAY. FOR MORE INFORMATION CALL 723-1189.
HAIL VICTORY

"Man, this is unbelievable." Hulk bubbles like a four year-old. "Where do you think these guys are coming from?"

Billy can barely believe their good fortune, either. Hulk's Uncle Kirk found the one-page flyer on his windshield after work, brought it home and dumped it in their laps. Hulk sits at the cluttered kitchen table, Billy standing at his shoulder. Several brown-colored plastic coffee cups, each with anywhere from a tablespoon to a half-cup of coffee, are scattered along the counter. Cigarette butts float in several of them. One cup overflows with butts and ash. The cramped trailer reeks of tobacco and beer.

Hulk takes a slice of plain white bread, smears it with peanut butter, and stuffs the whole thing into his mouth. Billy stabs his finger in the peanut butter jar and pulls out a big gob, pokes it in his mouth, and sucks on it.

Hulk swallows, twists his head around and looks back up at Billy. "So, what do you think, Kid?"

Billy uses his tongue to rub the sticky peanut butter off his teeth, moistens it with saliva and swallows. "How would I know who these guys are? They're white men, anyway."

"Sounds like an organized group, don't you think?"

"I've never heard of them," Billy says, "but at least they have enough balls to get this thing out and distribute it." Billy drags his little film canister out, licks his finger, and sticks it in. He shoves his fingertip up his nose and snorts. He repeats the same steps, and snorts the little white grains up his other nostril. He licks his finger and offers the canister to Hulk. "Speed, H?"

Hulk shakes his head. "Not right now. Think we ought to give these guys a call?"

"Fuck, yes. Shit, man, this is exactly what we've been waiting for." Billy slides around the table and reaches for the phone.

Hulk turns the flyer so Billy can read the numbers. Billy pushes the buttons. When the phone is answered, he asks, "Yeah, are you with the group that put out this white-man flyer?"

The voice that responds sounds young, cautious. "Yeah, who are you?"

"We're with White Nation." Billy says proudly. He looks at Hulk to see his reaction to this stretch of the truth. Hulk smiles enthusiastically, and Billy continues. "We're a couple of skins from Portland. We're cooling our heels down here for a while, and we saw your flyer."

"Cool."

Billy pictures a pimply, skinny kid, kind of gawky. He waits, impatiently. "So, you wanna' get together, or what?" He looks at Hulk, and motions with his hand and arm like he's waving traffic on.

"Yeah, definitely. Hey, what's gonna' happen to Hanson, anyway? The news says they put him outa' business."

"Fuck the hymie press," Billy says. "They fucked him up, but they can't keep him down. Hanson'll be back."

"He ain't gonna' have to go to jail?"

"That was never the problem. They sued him. What else would a Jew lawyer do for a bunch of monkeys?"

The kid laughs.

"Now he owes them a bunch of money he doesn't have. He's layin' low. But the troops are in the field, man. That's us."

"So, do you guys — like — work with Hanson?"

"Sure. We were at the trial, and we were with him plotting strategy later, too. That's why we're down here now. We're organizing white kids in rural Oregon." Billy looks at Hulk, a little embarrassed about his stretch of the truth. Hulk looks back, smiling.

18

Fil sees Hannah checking him out in her rearview mirror, making sure he's still on her tail. She has her turn-signal blinking, but she points to a store, anyway. As she pulls into the gravel lot, he pulls in alongside her. There aren't any other cars in the lot. She gets out and walks around to his window and bends down.

"I don't suppose you know the word, *mishpucha*.?"

He laughs. "No. You stopped to ask me that?"

"My brother's place is just a couple miles from here. I stopped to get ice cream for the girls. *Mishpucha* is the word for in-laws. I have that feeling — like I'm taking my new beau home to meet the family."

He grins. "You are."

She reaches through the window and gives him a peck on the cheek. "I'll just be a minute."

Hannah straightens, turns and walks away. Nice, Fil thinks, checking out her butt. She suddenly stops, turns back. "Hey, this place is really neat. Why don't you come in for a minute? They've got this battered old chest-style coke machine with floating chunks of ice, and big jars of candy behind the counter."

She doesn't get it, he thinks. Just walking in a store, together, could be a hassle. Particularly a neat little red-neck store. Then he chastises himself. Why get involved with her if he's not willing to deal with this shit?

"Okay." He opens the door and gets out.

A long wooden planter, filled with geraniums and primroses, along with the wilted stalks of several dead flowers, sits directly in front of the store. One wooden step leads up to a short, narrow wooden porch. The building looks old, but two modern-looking pay phones hang on the outside wall. A big, carved, wooden sign reads: Pinkerton's Market.

"You've got to check out this Coke machine," Hannah says excitedly as she pulls open the wooden-framed screen door. A thin piece of sheet metal, painted fire-engine red, runs across the middle of the door. The six-inch wide sign features a brown bear chased by a swarm of bees. It's faded and scratched, and parts of the bear are silver, revealing the gray metal underneath. The soda-pop machine, right inside the door, is also red; but it's a darker color, and the metal seems thicker, heavier. Hannah lifts the lid, exposing a grid of gray, metal rods. The tops of dozens of bottles of soda-pop stick up between the rods. The metal container is filled with water, including large chunks of ice. Hannah is bubbly, like a little kid showing off a new toy. She slides a bottle along the row to the end where one rod runs perpendicular to the rest.

Fil takes the machine and Hannah into his view, but his concentration is down a store aisle to a counter in the back. The wooden floors are worn, rutted, and the shelves appear to hold the usual corner-grocery-assortment of goods: canned items, boxes of cereal, cleansers, toilet paper. An old man with thick white hair, sits on a high stool, reading the paper. He glances up at Fil and Hannah, and cocks one of his bushy, white eyebrows when he spots them. Fil thinks it could be a judgmental reaction, or it could be the reaction the old man always gives, no matter who walks through the door. Fil doesn't see anyone else in the store and relaxes a bit. He notices an old white cooler with red letters that read: ice cream; but the machine is filled with frozen pizzas. A huge deer head with antlers is mounted on the wall above the cooler. Fil realizes Hannah has pulled the bottle down to the end and into a slot, and pulled it up.

"See?" she asks. "It catches here until you put money in." He reaches for some change in his pocket, but she already has a couple quarters and a dime out and sticks them in the slots on a box on the side of the chest. She pulls the bottle up again; this time it comes through and out. She pops off the bottle top on the opener on the side and hands the bottle to Fil. The ice-cold liquid invites him to drink, and he does, but he's distracted by an image in his head of a bunch of good ol' boys waltzing in the door and seeing a black guy with a white woman. He realizes Hannah is waiting for confirmation, and he smiles at her. It's not a typical Fil grin, though.

"What is it?" Hannah asks. "Is something wrong?"

"No, not —"

The screen door opens and a hefty man walks through. Fil hesitates. The man is wearing suspenders and a gray shirt with thin black and white lines. The long sleeves seem odd to Fil at first, but he notices the man's shirt is caked with dirt and grime, too. Fil figures he's been working in the woods, probably a logger. The man's eyes are cold, his facial expression hard. Fil looks at Hannah, who seems to barely notice the guy.

"It's complicated," Fil says to her, "I'll tell you about it later. Just get the ice-cream. I think I'll wait outside."

Hannah hesitates. "Okay. I'll just be a second."

Fil stops in the doorway for a second. He spots a magazine rack on the wall. Each slot is labeled with names like "Good Housekeeping" or "Women's Day," but the "Women's Day" slot is occupied with a "Hustler," the "Good Housekeeping" has a "Gallery" in it. Fil laughs and heads out the door, back to his car to wait.

#

Hulk is driving. Billy rides shotgun, navigating from the directions he wrote down, but his mind drifts. The towering Douglas fir that line the rural road remind Billy of a drive he took when he was eight years old. It must have been a short time after his mother left him. The school year was over, but his third grade teacher, Mrs. Johnson, called his sister and told her she had arranged to get Billy in a day camp. There wasn't any grass. Only dirt. And little cabins. Some of the kids must have stayed overnight. It seemed like they all knew each other.

His sister told him being the new kid could be scary, but it could be good, too. He could use day camp to make a new start, and to make new friends.

He remembers running really fast through the woods. It was

some kind of race. He didn't win, but he was among the top finishers. He thought a couple of the boys looked up to him. They showed him their secret fort.

In the afternoon everyone swam in the lake, except Billy couldn't swim. A camp counselor told him not to worry. They would teach him. But a girl teased him. She said he would melt in water because he was a warlock. He had never heard the word before, but the way she said it bothered him. He hated it. Day camp was supposed to be his new start, but nothing had changed. He felt like he was the bad kid, no matter where he went or what he did.

Later that afternoon a bunch of kids were hiking and Billy found himself next to the girl who started the teasing. He doesn't remember planning anything. He just grabbed her head and ran her into a tree. She screamed. Her nose bled, and a tooth was chipped. He was sent home. He doesn't remember if they didn't allow him back, or if he chose to stay away. But he didn't go back.

Billy realizes Hulk is slowing down and pulling off the road. "Hey H, what's going on? This can't be the turn. It ain't for another ten miles."

"Man, will you relax? I thought a little time in the country would jack you down a notch or two." Hulk skids onto a gravel parking lot. He's going a little fast and jerks the car to a sudden stop, spinning some gravel in the process. "I just wanted to get some beer while we're near Pinkerton's. Okay with you, chief?"

"Fuck you."

Hulk laughs and pulls a wadded-up ten dollar bill out of his pocket. "I've got this choke problem. I gotta' keep the beast running. Once this sucker gets hot on a hot day, if I shut it down I'll have a problem starting it back up." Hulk hands Billy the ten, "Get what you can with that. Okay?"

"Yeah." Billy swings the door open with enough force to dent the side of the big pick-up truck parked next to Hulk's Ford. "Whoops," he looks impishly back at Hulk, and they both laugh.

#

Hannah starts to open the screen door, but someone's in the way.

"Excuse me," she says. The man steps back and she moves through the doorway. When he turns, their eyes meet. Despite the unexpected context, the red eyes place him instantly.

The kid scowls, but his eyes are blank.

Hannah doesn't acknowledge him beyond the initial look of shock. She keeps moving, past the front of the pick-up, toward her car. She can sense him, behind her, still hesitating. She sees Fil, scrambling out of his car and rushing toward her. She races several yards across the gravel lot to the front of her Datsun. As she turns between her car and the pick-up, she steals a glance back.

"You fucking bitch." The kid starts toward her.

She grabs her door handle and hears the screen door open again. From the corner of her eye she sees the red-eyed kid turn back toward the door for an instant. The burly man in suspenders walks out with a case of beer under his arm and looks at the kid with a cold, hard stare. The boy glowers back. The two face off for a second, neither moving out of the other's way. Hannah opens her door, keeping her gaze on the boy. Fil heads back toward his car. The burly man ignores the red-eyed boy and walks around to his pick-up and gets in. Hannah slides in her front seat as Fil scrambles inside his car. They slam their doors. She turns her key, the engine responds, and she slides the gear shift into reverse. The boy leaps off the porch and is instantly at the front of her car. She hits the gas. Gravel flies as she shoots her car back ten feet. As the boy rushes toward her she swerves her car around, facing the road. Her maneuver leaves the boy on the passenger side of her car. He grabs for her door handle as she shifts into drive.

She guns it and gravel flies again. Fil has backed up farther down the lot. He swerves around the boy and heads out right behind her. Dust fills the air, but she can see the kid through her rearview mirror, standing in the gravel lot, glaring. He flips her the bird and shouts something, but she can't make it out.

19

Three overstuffed chairs and a long couch furnish the wide basement room. Several folding chairs are stacked in one corner. Two card tables, heaped with flyers and books and loose papers, are positioned along one wall; a poster featuring the four members of the band, Skrewdriver, hangs above the tables. On the opposite wall a big Confederate flag is accompanied by swastikas painted directly on the white concrete wall.

"This isn't bad," Billy says, nodding his head and looking around. "What you need is a picture of Adolf Hitler," he points at an open space near the Skrewdriver poster, "right there."

"That would be cool," the skinny kid responds. "I've never seen where you can get a poster of Hitler. Can you get them in Portland?"

"No problem. We get them directly from White Nation," Billy glances at Hulk, including him, "A guy in Omaha makes them. We'll get you one." Billy situates himself in one of the overstuffed chairs, pulling it around so he sits at the head of an oblong space. This is how Hanson must feel, he thinks.

Bob, the skinny kid who answered the phone, is just as Billy had imagined, but with a clear complexion. His friend, Dewy, is a little pudgy around the middle, with muscled arms. Both have shaved heads, and wear jeans and t-shirts. They seem to be about sixteen. Bob's girlfriend's name is Mary. Her head is shaved on top with a bright red tuft of hair in the front, hanging over her eyes. She has several earrings in each ear. Dewy and Mary sit down. Bob stands next to them with his hands in his jean pockets. Hulk takes a seat next to Billy.

"You guys are like the first link we've had to White Nation," Dewy says.

Billy winks at Hulk.

"So what's the deal with this place?" Hulk asks, looking at Bob. "Your parents live upstairs and leave you alone down here, or what?"

"My dad lives upstairs. He travels a lot, and I have the place to myself most of the time."

"Cool," Hulk responds.

"The TV is busted." Bob points to a set in the corner.

"Fuck TV," Billy says. "We never watch that shit. Too full of niggers. Nigger actors, nigger jocks. Every goddamn show, every goddamn commercial. It's another jungle monkey shitting in your face."

Bob and Dewy look at each other and shrug their shoulders. Bob lights a cigarette and offers one to Billy, who takes it. Bob offers Hulk, too. He declines. Dewy and Mary pull out their own cigarette packs and light up, filling the dank and musty smelling room with tobacco smoke. Hulk breaks a beer off one of the six-packs and passes the rest on.

"So is this it?" Billy asks gesturing toward the three of them. "Or do you have other members?"

Bob responds. "We're the core. We've got a few friends who hang with us, but nobody who is dedicated like we are."

"That's why we put out the flyers," Mary says, looking directly at Billy.

Her voice is friendly, but Billy doesn't like her unflinching eye contact. He thinks it's cocky. He looks at Bob. "So what kind of response have you got — to the flyers?"

"You guys," Bob says. He grins, then looks away from Billy, down at the floor. He takes his hands out of his pockets, puts them back in.

"That's it?"

Mary says, "We just put them around this week."

"I'll tell you what you need," Billy mimics Hanson, puffing himself up and taking in the small group, "You need to grab some attention. Let people know you're here."

"Like what do you mean?" Mary asks.

Billy looks right at her. "Like rat pack some queer. Torch some Jew store." He stares at her with his hard glare.

Mary doesn't respond. The three local skins look at each other. "I don't get it," Bob finally says. "Won't that just get us busted?"

Billy laughs, and Hulk starts laughing a half-second later. "You don't get caught," Billy says, sneering.

Bob and Dewy chuckle. Mary looks evenly at Billy, waiting. Billy studies the local trio. Bob sits back in his chair with his hands gripping the armrests. Dewy fingers the end of a pencil in one hand, the other hand shoved in his front jean pocket. Both boys look scared, tensed, on the verge of flinching. This must be what it feels like to be Hanson, Billy thinks. Or even Hitler. To be able to read people's fear. But he can't gauge Mary so easily.

"You make a statement to let people know you are here, but not who you are. They just know a group dedicated to white supremacy and separation of the races is present and serious. The law will come down on you, roust you; you have to expect that. That's part of the price we have to pay to make a white nation. Get people scared, first. Fear is the key. Once people know somebody with balls is operating in their backyard, somebody who is committed, they'll come to you."

"So, like what do we do — I mean exactly?" Dewy asks. His voice quavers ever so slightly

"Do you have a Jew store around here?" Billy asks.

"No, nothing like that," Bob says.

"Man, I'm not sure there are any Jews around here," Dewy whines. He looks at Bob and Mary for confirmation.

Billy notices Dewy slip the pencil into his shirt pocket. It's practically chewed clear through on the end. What an idiot, Billy thinks. "It's something you need to work on. I'm sure you got some fags or dykes around here."

He pauses for dramatic effect, but Hulk jumps in first.

"Hey, Billy what about that ni —"

Billy puts his hand up, silencing Hulk. Billy's jaw tenses. His fist tightens. His dramatic moment is messed up.

Goddamn Hulk, Billy thinks, and glares at him. Hulk had stopped as soon as Billy put up his hand. He looks away from

Billy's stare. Billy struggles to hide his anger. He looks at the floor. Everybody remains quiet. He looks back up. They're looking at him, waiting.

"I happen to know that you've got a race-mixing monkey right near here," he says, triumphantly.

Nobody says anything for a few seconds. Then Bob asks, "How do you know that? Where?"

"I just saw this jungle monkey and his white girlfriend when we stopped to get beer. Now, you guys need to do some scouting and report back to me. Ask around and find out where these people are. This is your neighborhood. You need to know this shit."

"How do we know it wasn't just somebody stopping to get beer who doesn't live around here — somebody passing through?" Mary asks.

Billy shakes his head, sighs. "We don't know for sure, but if you do your jobs instead of questioning everything I say," he pauses, looking right at Mary, "we will know for sure."

Hulk fidgets. "Hey, Billy, in the meantime, how about turning these guys on to some White Nation philosophy?"

"Yeah, cool," Bob says anxiously. He releases his grip on the armrests of this chair, runs his hands to his knees, then puts them back on the chair. He looks away from Billy. Hulk reaches over to the two remaining beers and pops the top off one and guzzles it.

Billy hesitates, thinking. "Okay — White Nation solutions," Billy announces the words like the title to a lecture. The tension eases; the three local skins and Hulk scoot their chairs in closer, listening attentively.

"An all-white homeland will be established in these five states:

Oregon, Washington, Idaho, Montana and Wyoming." Bob and Dewy look at each other and exchange enthusiastic looks. Mary glances at them, but her stare remains neutral. Billy continues his recitation from Hanson's White Nation pamphlets. "This area will provide us with the forest and farmland we need for production. We'll have seaports with access to fishing and shipping, too. In White Nation, health care will be provided to all citizens of the homeland by the government."

Mary clears her throat and half raises her hand. Billy looks at her.

"How will the government pay for this universal health care?" she asks.

Billy looks down at the floor, then back up. He doesn't remember most of the details from Hanson's material, but the tax was one of the easy parts. He looks at Bob and Dewy as he answers Mary's question. "Everything will be paid for by a ten percent tax. This will be a ten percent tithe which is based on the Bible." He looks at Mary as he changes his tone from explanatory to condescending, "That's a straight tax on personal income." He looks back at Bob and Dewy. "There will be no personal exemptions of any kind. No deductions, no loopholes. No Jew tricks." Billy laughs, and everyone except Mary joins him with forced laughs.

"Of course," Billy resumes, "only those of pure white ancestry will be allowed citizenship in the homeland. Anyone found out as not pure white will be immediately deported."

Bob reaches down and grabs the last beer and hands it to Hulk. "I got more upstairs," Bob says. "I'll be right back."

Nobody says anything for a moment. Dewy fidgets. Billy smirks. Bob comes back with two more six-packs, and hands one to Dewy to pass around.

"So tell us more," Bob says.

"Like what?" Billy asks. "There's tons of stuff. What do you want to know about? Education? Ownership?"

"Tell 'em about Hanson's program for kids and the family," Hulk volunteers.

"You tell em, H."

Billy begins to glare, angrily, at Hulk; but catches himself. He wants to be seen as the composed leader, in total control. He glances quickly at their faces, attempting to detect if anyone noticed his reaction to Hulk's kids and family comment. They're smiling, waiting for more.

Except Mary. When his eyes meet hers, she's staring back, with a slight glint.

20

Fil watches pork fat drip onto the glowing coals of old pear wood and sizzle. Smoke twists its way up, affixing its flavor to layers of baby back ribs.

"I marinated them in fresh ginger root, garlic, wine, and tomatoes and hot peppers from the garden," Max tells him.

The scent teases Fil's nostrils.

He watches as Max flips the ribs with tongs, takes a thick, round basting brush and dips it in a pint Mason jar half-filled with his sauce. Max dabs more than paints, sticking the thick sauce in the crevices of the meat. The racks of ribs are scattered on a three-foot by three-foot grate which tops a one-foot high semi-circle of odd-shaped rocks, each about the size of a football. Max flips and paints the ribs one last time, then drips honey over them before piling them on a big platter and hobbling over to the picnic table. Fil follows.

Max's barbecue rocks and grill are several feet from the creek banks; the picnic table is twenty yards closer to the house, around the side and under the shade of a towering maple. The huge leaves will begin turning in less than a month and fall, like giant, reddish-yellow, baseball-mitt-size snowflakes.

"If you think it's hot, try hanging out over that fire for a while," Max says as he sets the platter in the middle of the table. Fil slides in to a spot between Hannah and Gretchen. Everybody has a plate and a fork. A couple of shared towels are passed around. Gretchen made potato salad, a garden salad and a vegetable plate. Heather brought out the glasses while Hannah set three quart Mason jars of ice water on the table.

Fil notices Michelle doesn't help out. She appears to be moody. Gretchen has to call her to dinner three times.

"We've had hotter days," Gretchen says, pushing the bowl filled with potato salad toward Fil. "But not so many hot days in a row."

"I don't remember fire danger this bad for this long," Max says.

Gretchen starts the big wooden bowl filled with lettuce, cucumbers, tomatoes, and carrots moving around the table. Max limps around and slips into his seat between his daughters, across the table from Fil, Hannah and Gretchen.

"Those are all from the garden," he tells Fil. Max has been bragging to Fil about his barbecued spareribs and seems anxious for a reaction. Fil is being polite, though, looking around to make sure others are eating first.

"Eat already," Max says putting on his thick, mock-New York, Jewish accent and grabbing a hunk of rib in his paw. He bites off a mouthful.

Fil doesn't need much coaxing. He had been torturing himself for the past half-hour, smelling the smoke. He follows Max's lead and takes a rib in his hand and bites off a hunk.

He feels a dab of sauce dribble down his chin, and grabs the towel to catch it. He hasn't finished chewing, when he starts bobbing his head up and down. "These are the best ribs I've ever had. Flat out. "He wipes the sauce from this chin, takes another bite and proceeds to eat.

"I think you've outdone yourself, Max," Hannah tells her brother.

"Good ribs, Dad," Heather says.

Some blackbirds nearby start making a fuss. Heather looks up and twists her head around, but she can't spot where the complaining birds are coming from. Michelle pokes at her food.

Fil licks his lips and wipes his face again. "What is it about Jews and pork, anyway?"

"What do you mean?" Gretchen asks.

"I mean all my Jewish friends have always loved pork."

Hannah rolls her eyes at Fil. "Forbidden fruit, I guess."

"What's forbidden fruit?" Heather asks. The adults look at each other, hesitating.

"Chocolate chip cookies," Hannah finally responds, and everyone laughs. Fil figures Heather doesn't get it. But she seems content to work on her father's ribs and her mother's potato salad, anyway.

"You've only known left-coast-Jews, huh?" Max asks Fil.

"Left-coast-Jews? I've never heard that one before."

"Another Maxism." Hannah raises her eyebrows.

"There are plenty of Jews who would never dream of eating pork," Max says. "I think kosher is a little more fundamental back East."

"But it's obviously no big deal to you."

"We grew up kosher," Hannah says. "My parents died never having tasted pork. It was a big deal to them."

The group is silent for a moment except for the sound of chewing and silverware clinking.

Gretchen places a plate with carrots, celery and tomatoes in front of Heather. "How about some more of these, kiddo?"

"Okay," Heather says, grabbing a few carrot sticks.

"I'm done," Michelle says, getting up. "May I be excused?" Max looks at his daughter's plate, then at Gretchen, who just shrugs her shoulders. "You hardly ate anything." Max says.

"The ribs are too spicy."

"Heather is eating them."

Michelle mouths back, Heather is eating them, but doesn't actually say the words out loud. Max looks at her sternly. "Michelle."

"What?" she responds, her voice filled with protest.

"I want you to sit with us and have some dinner."

"I'm not hungry, and I don't feel like just sitting here if I'm not eating. Okay?" The last word is spit out, defiantly.

"Where are you going?"

"I don't know. Just off." Michelle maintains a nasty edge to her voice. Max looks at her with a stern expression.

"Okay, but no treats later. You know that?"

Michelle doesn't answer. Once she hears the okay, she turns and struts away, heading into the house. Max looks at Gretchen, who looks back with a resigned sigh. Max glances over at Hannah, who gives him a sympathetic smirk.

Fil represses a laugh.

"Teenagers," Max finally says, obviously feeling a little self-conscious about his daughter's tone in front of their guest.

"I thought you said she was eleven?" Fil says, looking at Hannah.

"Eleven going on sixteen," Max explains, and Fil laughs.

"Eleventeen," Gretchen adds.

"Eleventeen?" Heather asks.

"That's just an expression, honey. There is no eleventeen. It goes ten, eleven, twelve, thirteen."

Heather smiles at her mom. "Can I be excused, too?"

Gretchen looks at Heather's plate. She's made short work of her small portions. "I guess so. Where are you off to?"

"To see what Michelle is doing."

"Don't bug your sister!" Max shouts as Heather runs toward the house.

For a moment a silence engulfs the table. Fil thinks about Michelle and the skinhead kids he's encountered. Some aren't much older than Michelle. Thirteen, fourteen, fifteen years old. She seems so innocent.

The hum of crickets intensifies with the descent of evening.

"So Fil, tell Max and Gretchen your take on Robert Hanson," Hannah says.

"Thank God we don't have to worry about him anymore," Gretchen says softly.

Fil lets out a short, disgusted laugh. "I wish you were right. But we haven't seen the last of Robert Hanson."

Max says, "I thought the paper said the settlement will effectively end his organization."

Fil shakes his head. "He'll find a way — through somebody else's name or some scam. He's not done."

Everybody is quiet. Crickets carry on their own discussion.

"Here's the really scary thing," Fil resumes. "Decreasing Hanson's power could play into the hands of some other neo-Nazi leader. The main reason these thugs don't unite is because their egos get in the way. But the potential of one strong fascist uniting millions of disgruntled, lower-class white kids frightens the hell out of me."

"Like Germany in the thirties," Hannah says.

"I doubt that," Max says. "I don't think we're even close to Hitler and the thirties."

"And you're willing to take that chance?" Hannah asks.

"What am I supposed to do?" Max raises his voice. "Or anybody for that matter? Look at our fire suppression work. We praised ourselves every season for the great work we did. Think of the acreage of beautiful forests that would have been lost if we didn't work our butts off to stop the fires. But now, ten years later, it turns out all we did was save more fuels to make for hotter, bigger, and more disastrous fires later. If we had let nature take its course, we probably would have been better off."

"You aren't suggesting we let *human* nature take its course, are you?" Fil asks.

"Sure. Why not?" Max responds.

Hannah raises an eyebrow. "Here we go."

Gretchen smiles at her.

Fil catches their exchange, then turns to Max. "It sounds

like you're saying, let people hate each other, don't fight racism or injustice."

"How do you force people to not hate each other?"

Nobody responds. Max shrugs his shoulders and takes another bite of rib.

"Mad and Sarah told me about this study," Fil says. "It indicates kids who attend church schools and Sunday school are much more likely to hate gays than kids who don't attend these schools or church."

"That doesn't surprise me," Max says, wiping his mouth on a towel. "But it says you can teach kids *to* hate. You still haven't told me how you get people to *not* hate."

"I don't claim to have all the answers," Fil says. " But I know I have to keep doing what I'm doing."

"You must get scared, tracking these groups," Gretchen says. "I mean, at some point they must know about you, too."

"Yeah, I am scared. But trouble can find us, anyway. Look at the skinhead kid that went after Hannah."

"Or, the women I've been staying with," Fil continues, "They're not activists, they don't bother anybody, they live off in a very remote place, and somebody is giving them grief because they're lesbians."

"What about what happened to Gretchen?" Hannah nods toward her sister-in-law. "She's out here in the middle of nowhere, too, and she's not even from a — a — targeted group."

Gretchen's head is down, as if she were staring at the table.

"There's an important difference." Fil hesitates. He looks at Gretchen and lowers his voice. "It doesn't make what happened to you any less terrible." He turns to Max and Hannah. "But that was a random act of violence. What's happening to this group of lesbians is a hate crime."

Gretchen clears her throat. Her voice is hard, but she keeps her head down. "What happened to me was a hate crime."

Everyone is silent. The quiet lingers. Hannah moves toward Gretchen, but she puts up her hand. After a second, Gretchen steadies herself and raises her head. Her eyes are angry and watery. She snaps out her words.

"I felt their hate."

21

"Man, I can't believe this shit. I'm goddamn Clint Eastwood."

"It's cool, Billy, huh? And the pay is great, too." Bob laughs. His apprehension about being alone with Billy subsides a bit.

Billy and Bob perch high on a huge forested hill overlooking a series of hollows. With the naked eye they can see a trailer in one direction and a house, garden and vehicles in another. With the aid of Bob's binoculars they can make out tomatoes ripening on plants in the garden. Peering through an early morning mist, they follow the path of a bearded man as he lugs two five-gallon jugs filled with water. He disappears from their view for a while, the angle blocked by the thickness of the woods.

Eventually the man comes back into view, winding his way through the forest. He stops, barely in their line of sight, and moves from spot to spot, pouring water around the base of tall, thick flowery shrubs. Billy pulls the binoculars away from his eyes and hands them back to Bob.

"That's the shit, huh?" Billy asks.

"You got it, man. Merry Juana."

"So why don't we just go down there as soon as he's done and take that shit? Is it booby-trapped or what?"

"It's not ready yet, man. We can wait, and it'll be worth a lot more."

"Yeah, but what if this guy harvests his pot before we do? Then we get nothing."

"These hippies never harvest their shit this early. I'm telling you, man, we can wait a month, but we'll just wait two weeks. We'll be totally cool."

Billy reaches over and takes the binoculars back, brings them to his eyes and moves about, seeking the man's whereabouts. A turkey buzzard circles overhead, playing with the currents. The dark fowl has a wider view and a sharper eye than the kids on the hill. After several seconds Billy moves the binoculars back down and looks over at Bob. "So tell me about these Warriors for Christ fuckers."

"They're totally cool, really."

"I know. I know. I just want to hear every detail, okay?"

Billy appears calm. Bob has already witnessed Billy's hard glare and his sudden rage, and he's become wary of it; but there's no sign of trouble, now, sitting on a hill in the morning quiet. Dewy made up an excuse to avoid the scouting expedition. Bob knew he was too scared of Billy to come along. Earlier, Dewy told Bob he didn't like how quickly the stakes had grown. Bob agreed. But he figures hanging out with Billy and going along for the ride is still the best plan. They can always back out later. Take away the temper, and Billy is just what the Führer ordered, Bob said, and they both laughed.

Bob turns to Billy, "The Warriors for Christ called us, like you and H, after they got hold of one of our flyers. It turns out Dewy knew them. He used to hang out with the little brother of one of these guys. They were just leaving school when we were freshmen, you know. They're like twenty-one or twenty-two. They're all right, really."

"I don't get this Christ shit, man."

"It's no big deal, Billy. They got into the CFV stuff. You know, Citizens for Family Values?" Billy gives Bob an irritated glare. Bob winces and continues. "They just formed their own group and called it Warriors for Christ. I mean there wasn't any White Nation stuff happening around here, that's all. I'm sure they agree with us. That's why we should link up with them. They need to hear what you have to say, Billy."

"CFV? How can any heads-up skin be into that family shit?" Billy shakes his head. "Lets be Ozzie and Harriet, dude."

Bob laughs. "I agree with you, man. I'm just sayin' they got some good points."

"Like what?"

"They've already been fucking with this bunch of dykes, man. Just like you said we should do, and they could use our help, they said; really fuck these bitches, man."

"Like shit, man." Billy takes Bob by surprise. He thought he was reading Billy, but the hard edge suddenly explodes. "All we've been doing is scoping. The real shit hasn't begun yet."

"That's what I mean. They've already shot up the dykes' house. They've made their presence known, just like you said we should do." Bob hears his own pleading, whiny tone, but he can't help himself. He wishes Dewy had come along. Or that he hadn't.

"Then why hadn't you heard of them before they called you?"

Bob feels Billy's surge of anger and wants to disappear. If Mary or Dewy were here Billy would be easier to take. But he reminds himself that someone has to hang with Billy, and they can't just sit around forever talking theory. They have to take action eventually. He shrugs his shoulders, and Billy answers his own question.

"Because they're chickenshit motherfuckers, that's why. They're just playin' around the edges. They're scared to really fuck somebody."

Bob withdraws from Billy's abrupt rage, looks away, off to the horizon, waiting for the storm to blow over. But Billy won't be ignored. He gets in Bob's face and forces eye contact.

"You get me, man? I'm no pussy. I came down here to fuck somebody. I keep trying to tell you and your friends. Fear is the key. Either people fear you, or you fear them. Now are you a chickenshit motherfucker, or are you willing to go all the way to hell with me?"

22

Hannah and Fil return to their tent to discover Michelle and Heather have taken up residence. Hannah had pitched Max's old pole tent around the side of the house, figuring the ten-foot by ten-foot canvas shelter would provide a little privacy for a few nights. She covered the ground with padding and old sleeping bags, which made the cozy hideaway too attractive for cubbyhole-seeking Michelle and Heather. But Hannah still enjoys a respected aunt status with Michelle, and she manages to chase the girls out simply by requesting a little time alone before dinner.

Hannah and Fil lean back against some big cushions. Tomorrow afternoon Fil will swing by Mad and Peggy's to say good-bye to them, then head back for Eugene. Hannah has a couple more weeks at Max's and will have to return to Portland to get ready for the new school year. Then, a long distance relationship. It doesn't seem so insurmountable now. Of course, she reminds herself, race and age differences never rear their ugly heads in the comfort of isolated worlds of acceptance.

But the encounter at the store has kept her on edge. Running into the red-eyed boy at all was bad enough, but out in the middle of nowhere turned her stomach upside-down.

What would have happened if the kid had gotten to her before she got to the car? And Fil seems so matter-of-fact about these dangers. She wonders if he's really scared, underneath. Is it a macho image thing? He couldn't be that naive, but maybe he makes himself oblivious as some kind of denial.

"Why do you do your work?" she asks.

"You mean my skinhead and neo-Nazi documentation?"

Hannah nods.

"You know why. The more we know, the better chance we have of stopping them."

"Do you really think you can stop them?"

"Of course I do. It isn't easy. We lose a lot of battles. Like I told Max, I don't have all the answers, but I wouldn't do this work if I didn't believe in it. You face just as hard a road with teaching. You must lose your fair share of battles, too. But you keep trying. You believe in what you do."

Hannah looks into Fil's eyes. They're imploring, sincere.

"No. I don't." Hannah surprises herself. "I quit believing the day Anthony died."

"You've been pretending you care all this time?" His jaw slackens.

"I'm afraid so."

"I don't believe you."

Hannah doesn't know what to say. She feels like she just confessed her greatest sin. She would like to think Fil is right — that she hasn't quit believing.

Fil reaches over and takes her hand. "You were winning. You did the right things for this kid, and he responded. He turned his life around."

She sees Anthony, finally excited about reading. Tears suddenly well up in her eyes. "And then they killed him."

"You know his murder was a chance occurrence. Awful, but random. It doesn't discount what he did, what you did."

"It does too." She fights to hold back her tears. "What's the use? You help one kid, and another comes along and murders him."

"I know this is hard to take, but what you do, matters. Anthony is proof of success. Not failure."

Hannah is quiet. They pull apart, she dries her eyes. Things have felt too good with Fil. It's the damn feeling again. If things stay this good much longer, something bad will happen. She realizes how convoluted that sounds, and laughs.

"What?" Fil asks.

She wipes her eyes. "Nothing, really."

"Hey, no fair to laugh and not tell."

"What about us, Fil?" she asks, "Do you think we'll see much of each other after tomorrow?"

"You know we will. If you still want? That's what made you laugh?"

"I wasn't laughing at us," Hannah says. "I was laughing at my own convoluted superstitions. But there's something serious here for me. I mean there's stuff we haven't talked about. You must think about it. I know I do."

Fil gives her a puzzled look.

Hannah sees him, waiting for her explanation, but she wants

him to say something first.

"Doesn't our age difference bother you?" she finally asks.

Fil laughs. "Is that what's bothering you?"

Hannah doesn't laugh.

Fil looks away with a sheepish look that reminds her of Anthony. "I'm sorry," he says. "But the age thing is like — some invention. You know — ageism. It's not like racism. Racism is the plague. By comparison ageism is like a sneeze or something."

"So what are you saying? My being white bothers you?"

Fil starts to laugh again, but he stops. He seems to grasp the gravity of Hannah's mood. "No. Your being white doesn't bother me." He sounds condescending. She feels herself stiffen. He continues. "I think it's a problem the world throws at people and we have to deal with it. I thought you saw it that way, too."

"I do. What I'm saying is the same applies to our age difference."

Fil shakes his head. "No way. They just aren't the same."

"Maybe if you were in my shoes you would see it differently. I'm a woman."

"You are that." Fil rubs his hand across her breast and squeezes.

"Ow."

"Sorry, I didn't think it was that rough."

Hannah sits up and looks at Fil. She doesn't like feeling irritated. It wasn't that rough. And now she wishes she hadn't brought up age at all. "So, the age thing doesn't bother you?"

"No." He smiles. "It doesn't bother me. Apparently it bothers you?"

"That's what I'm trying to tell you. You know, Fil, the point is we have at least a couple strikes against us already."

"So what are you saying? Maybe we shouldn't try to keep seeing each other?" Fil looks shocked.

"No. Oh God, no." She reaches over and softly strokes his cheek, then reaches down and takes his hand. "I guess I just have to know how you feel."

"Well, I don't feel like we have two strikes against us. I think of it more as one negative canceling the other out and making a positive."

She smiles. "You sound like Max. Please tell me this isn't a Max theory."

"Worse," Fil laughs. "It's a Filbert theory. I'll save you the agony of hearing it, if you promise to not take our age difference too seriously."

"And race?"

"The problem there isn't us, as much as it's the way the rest of the world will treat us. Strangers, and friends."

"I think the same is true with age." Hannah thought they were pulling out of the argument, but now she thinks he still doesn't get it.

"I suppose. I guess you worry about the age-stares as much as I worry about the race-stares. I just don't think anybody will kill us for being different ages."

#

Max promised Heather that after dinner he would tell the story of Maurice the Mouse and Howard the Magnificent Teddy Bear. Heather looks like a ball in a pinball machine, as she bounces from Hannah to Fil to Gretchen, eliciting enthusiasm for the storytelling. But Michelle pulls her now-regular routine of sulking off before dinner is fully underway. As if that isn't upsetting enough to Heather, at twilight, Hannah and Fil slip off for one last walk alone. With everybody else gone, anyway, Gretchen decides to get the dishes started.

"Gee," Heather says, her face in a pout, "this is no fun at all." She looks like she's on the verge of a full-blown cry.

"Well, that really hurts my feelings," Max says.

"I'm sorry, Dad." Heather rushes over to comfort him. "I want you to tell me the story, but I wanted Aunt Hannah to hear it, too."

"We'll tell it to her another time. She needs to spend some time with Fil right now because he's leaving tomorrow. Okay?"

"But it's not fair. Ever since Fil came, Aunt Hannah doesn't play with me."

"You got a lot of time with your aunt, honey, and I'm sure she'll spend some time with just you in the next couple days. You have to share people like you have to share things."

Heather scrunches her forehead. "Will you still tell me the Howard and Maurice story — right now?"

Max lifts his daughter on to his lap. "You bet, sweetheart."

"The long version?"

"The long version." They settle themselves in, and Max is about to begin when she suddenly stops him.

"Wait, Dad. I have to get Charles." She jumps up and runs into the house. In a few seconds she comes running back out with her teddy bear in tow, hops back up and hugs Charles close to her.

Max smiles and begins. "Once upon a time there was a naughty little mouse named Maurice who lived with his mom and dad and brothers and sisters in a little mouse house inside the walls of a human house." Max sounds as if he were telling the story for the first time. "Sometimes, because he was mean, Maurice would trick his brothers and sisters and try to get them to take a piece of cheese from a mouse trap —"

"Dad?"

"Yes."

"I don't think I want to hear the story right now."

"Really?" Max sounds surprised when the protest arrives on schedule. "You know once we get past the bad part the story gets better."

Heather gets a sad and pensive look. "Maybe we could wait and tell it with Aunt Hannah."

"If you like, sweety." Max kisses Heather on the forehead. "But the beginning of the story will still be sad."

"I know, Dad, but at least we won't have to be sad alone."

23

Billy slouches in one of the overstuffed chairs, pretending to read a comic book, but he listens to Mary, wondering if she really knows what she's talking about. She's lecturing Bob and Hulk on the history of skinheads in England. Dewy hasn't arrived yet.

"So, in 1986, Ian Stuart gets out of jail and returns to Kings Cross, in London."

"When did you say he went in?" Hulk asks.

"He served six months of a twelve-month sentence. He attacked a nigger. A fuckin' year for that. Shit. Anyway, it didn't matter, he was recruiting more effectively inside than out."

Billy can't keep quiet, and jumps in. "I heard Nazis from all over Europe were visiting him in London."

"Yeah, they were. Before and after the prison term."

"You made it sound like he was doing better inside than out."

"Well, okay, so he was doing a good job either way."

"Shit, Billy, what's the difference?" Hulk says.

"The difference is she's no fuckin historian if she can't get it right."

"Just ease up, okay."

"I'll ease it up your ass, H. Why the fuck don't you back me up instead of always jackin' me up? Huh?"

"Why make such a big deal of little shit, man?"

"Fuck you."

Hulk stands up, takes a step toward Billy. Billy tenses. Hulk turns away.

Billy shoots him a triumphant smirk. Hulk hesitates. He looks like he's one leer away from going after Billy.

"So what year did Skrewdriver actually get started, Mary?" Bob asks. He yanks on his ear, then squeezes his hand into his pocket.

Mary glances at Billy, who isn't looking up. Hulk sits back down. "Stuart had another band called the Tumbling Dice. I think he started it in 1975. In 1977, there was a turnover in band members, and they renamed it Skrewdriver. They reformed again in 1981 and hooked up with White Noise records in 1982 —"

Mary stops. They all hear the familiar clomp of Dewy coming down the stairs, only his steps seem to have a skip to them. He comes through the door, beaming.

"Wait till you hear this shit," he says.

"What is it?" Mary asks.

Billy straightens up and leans forward.

"You guys remember Harry?" Dewy looks at Mary and Bob, but they stare back with blank expressions. "Well, anyway," he continues, "Harry lives on Rock Creek Road where this side road leads a short ways to a dead end. He says some family lives up there. Anyway, sometimes his little sister hangs out with one of the kids and she says they're Jews." Dewy pauses, waiting for excited responses. The other four are looking at each other, with half-smiles.

"Yeah, go on," Billy says.

"Well — one day a week ago — or maybe a week and a half, this nigger comes drivin' right up that road just as plain as day. Listen, Billy, Rock Creek Road is just a couple miles from Pinkerton's market, where you and Hulk saw that monkey in the first place."

"Yeah," Billy says, and gets up and paces back and forth, everybody watching him now. "We could get these kikes, we can scope this place out and leave 'em a little gift."

"A gift?" Bob asks.

"Fuckin' goddamn," Billy mumbles. This could be them, he thinks. That same fuckin' nigger, and the bitch is a Jew, to boot. Billy suddenly realizes he has a big, shit-eating grin on this face. Everyone is looking at him, wide-eyed, waiting. As long as there's action instead of history lessons, he's in charge.

"Listen, Billy," Dewy says. "Harry says he's been back a couple times. The nigger — he's been comin' around. He might even be stayin' up there. I mean Harry hasn't exactly been watching for him, you know, but he says he's seen him."

"What about?" Bob stops himself. He takes his hand back out of his pocket and yanks on his ear again.

"What about what?" Billy raises his voice a notch.

Bob looks at the floor. "The Warriors for Christ. And these dykes."

"What about them?" There's an edge to Billy's voice.

"Nothing," Bob says. "It's just that we're all set to jack with these guys. They're counting on it. I mean, this other deal sounds good, but we don't know the first thing about this place or these people."

"You don't know shit. We know they're a bunch of kikes with a race-mixing nigger. We know where they live. What more do we need to know?"

"Nothing. Its just the other deal, man. The dyke deal is all set to go down."

"So the fuck what?" Billy raises his voice to a shout.

Everyone is quiet. Billy takes a breath. He turns away, walks to the wall. He knows the local skins feel like they're getting in over their heads, but he figures he can get them excited about moving beyond talk and theory. He walks back to the chair and sits down. His voice is calm, but commanding. "We are going to do both. The kikes will be our little gift to the Warriors in exchange for the dykes. Kikes for dykes."

Billy laughs and everybody laughs with him. "We have to scope this place out. We have to get on this fucking nigger in particular. I want that monkey." Billy pauses and looks around, making eye contact with each person. "We're gonna' make ourselves known."

"Kikes for dykes," Dewy sounds like a six year-old. Bob snickers.

Billy stares at him, and Bob looks away. Billy gets back up and puts his arm around Dewy, giving him a hard, but affectionate embrace. "Way to go, dude. The kikes are for the Warriors, and the dykes are for us."

Dewy turns his head awkwardly toward Billy, gently trying

to pry himself away. "So, what about the nigger, Billy? Is the nigger for you?"

Billy hears the whine and fear in Dewy's voice. But he lets go. He turns away, and whispers, "The nigger is for Joe."

"Joe?" Dewy asks.

"Joe's our buddy," Hulk says.

"Joe is laid up in the hospital in Portland, beat half to death," Billy says turning back toward the group. "He's gonna' spend the rest of his life with only one nut and a steel plate in his head."

"No shit?" Bob asks. "Did a bunch of niggers get him?"

"Goddamn right," Billy says without hesitation. "And we're gonna' get even for Joe. We're gonna' get this nigger for Joe."

24

A spooky yew tree marks the spot where Michelle turns off the road. Hannah thinks it's odd her nieces aren't at least a little frightened. The arms of the reddish brown yew twist about in all directions, as if ready to grab a wayward soul.

Michelle told Hannah she wanted to take her to the secret place before she left. She even told Heather she could come along.

From the yew, Michelle takes her travelers up a steep bank and down the other side. For a few minutes they walk easily beneath the canopy of older firs. Then, a ground cover of ferns gives way to viny maple, and passage becomes impossible, but a tunnel leads through the thick plant growth. The burrowed walls consist of tangled blackberry and maple vines. Numerous cut-ends reveal Michelle's considerable effort with clippers and sheers in carving out the passage. Michelle and Hannah have to get down on their hands and knees. The trek would be easy for Heather, except she brings Charles and has to carry him. After several yards of crawling, the shaft opens into the secret place.

The little four-foot by five-foot cubbyhole is carved entirely out of plant life. The ceiling, made of vines, branches and leaves, is only a few feet high. An old blanket covers the ground, and a couple of turned-over cardboard boxes serve as tables. Heather has been allowed in only twice before. She's never brought Charles, until now, and snuggles up with him in one of the corners. It's early evening, still light outside, but the thick forest and the cubbyhole's plant-life walls and ceiling make it seem like night. Michelle pulls a big flashlight out from under one of the boxes and turns it on. She pulls the box into the middle of the space and places the light on it.

"Here." Michelle reaches over and takes Charles off Heather's lap and props him up facing one side of the cardboard table. "C'mon Heather," Michelle motions to her sister to sit on another side of the box, talking to her in a friendly voice. To Hannah, it sounds like she's calling a dog. Hannah keeps quiet, though. Heather doesn't seem to mind. She's in heaven, getting all this attention and being in the secret place.

"You sit here, Aunt Hannah." Michelle has arranged them on the four sides of the box. "You're the only adult who has ever been allowed in my secret place."

"I'm very honored, Michelle."

"Owly?" Heather calls Michelle with a quavering voice, "I don't want to tell ghost stories."

Owly. Hannah hadn't heard the nickname in a long time. When Michelle was younger, Max sometimes called her Owly. She seemed to have no fear of the dark — oblivious to the scary shapes that kids conjure out of the blackness. She would just get up and walk out of the house in the middle of the night. Max and Gretchen became worried, and Max quit using the name once he thought it encouraged her. Max had dropped Owly by the time Heather came along. Hannah figures Michelle must have told Heather about the nickname. It seems appropriate in her darkened secret place.

"It's okay, Heather," Michelle says, "We're not going to tell ghost stories now."

"Can we tell another story?"

"Okay, if Aunt Hannah wants to hear a story."

"Oh, I would love to."

"She hasn't heard how mentriloquism works and all about Howard the Magnificent Teddy Bear and Maurice the Mouse," Heather says, unable to contain herself.

"Do you know the whole story, Michelle?" Hannah asks.

"She does, Aunt Hannah, she tells it real good." Heather turns to Michelle. "Please, Michelle, tell it, please."

"I thought Dad just told you last night, Heather. She never gets tired of that story, Aunt Hannah."

Heather crosses her arms and pouts.

"I didn't say I wouldn't tell it. Geez, Heather, don't be a baby or you won't be allowed to come to my secret place again."

Heather brightens, but doesn't say anything.

"Okay, I'll tell it."

Heather bounces up and down, excitedly clapping her hands, looking at Hannah. Michelle gets very serious.

"Once upon a time there was a little mouse child. His name was Maurice." Heather and Hannah look at each other and exchange excited giggles. Michelle continues. "He had grown tired of always being told what to do. His father mouse and mother mouse wouldn't even let him play jokes on his brothers and sisters...."

#

Fil cruises along Sylvan Lane, his head bopping from side to side, singing loudly, "I feel good —" He takes his hands off the steering wheel and beats imaginary drum sticks on the dash. "Like I knew that I would now."

He puts his hands back on the wheel in time to control his car. He spots mile-marker twelve, slows way down and turns onto the gravel road that winds and twists its way to Mad, Peggy, Sarah and Dana's. He hits the final long straight-away and picks up speed again, bumping along on the rutted gravel incline.

The half-mile stretch is extremely narrow, bordered by a steep embankment on one side and a sharp drop off on the other. About a third of the way, the road widens, allowing a vehicle to pull over and let someone pass coming the other way. Fil takes a close look at the 1950s dark Ford pick-up that occupies the pull-off space. As he gets closer, still from behind, he sees the backs of two heads, either bald or shaved; he passes by and turns his head, peering into the cab and sees the occupants — young skinheads. Shit, he thinks, as he drives on by. These have got to be the guys who shot the place up. The Ford pulls out behind him. His heart kicks up. He'll soon be at Mad and Peggy's. It's gonna' be okay. After the next bend, there's two more curves in the road and he's there. Relax, he tells himself. Be cool.

He picks up as much speed as he can on the bumpy, gravel road. The pick-up is still behind him, closing. After a couple hundred yards, Fil has to slow down for a curve.

He slams on the brakes. A dirty, dust-covered white station wagon blocks the narrow drive. Fil looks back to see what the pick-up is doing, but he's too late. The driver smacks the truck right into Fil's car, snapping his head and torso forward and back.

The kids scramble out, wielding bats. Five more race toward him from the direction of the dusty white wagon. He looks to the woods, but realizes he'll never make it. Reflexively, he pushes down his button and rolls up the window. Fil gauges the space around the wagon, wondering if he can crash around it. He would never make it.

Three of the five hooligans in front of him are only a few yards away. One is a woman with bright red hair, one of the other two is a big, hulking kid. He seems familiar. Then Fil sees the third one. It's the red-eyed kid from the courthouse and the store.

Fil's jerks his head forward as his rear window shatters. Shards of glass fly. He twists around in time to see the next blow coming. The bat cracks the driver's side window and Fil lurches sideways. He scrambles toward the passenger door even though it offers no escape.

The skinheads set upon his car swinging their weapons, chanting, "Nigger. Nigger. Death to race-mixers."

#

Hannah sees a tear in Heather's eye. Before Hannah can say anything to her, Heather interrupts Michelle's telling of the story, "I don't want to hear this part, Michelle. Can't we skip over it?"

Michelle clenches her teeth. "God, Heather, you always do

this. You can't skip over part of the story. Why do you always ask to hear this story and then freak out?"

Heather starts to cry, and Hannah slides around and puts her arm around her. "It's all right, sweetie. Your dad can tell me later if you don't want to hear it right now."

"No." Heather wipes her eyes. "Go ahead, Owly, but do the short version of this part." Heather takes Charles and lays him down in the corner, looking away from them. "I don't want him to hear this part. It makes him too sad." She places one of the cardboard boxes over him.

Hannah stifles a laugh. Michelle sighs.

"Don't you want to hold Charles, sweetie?" Hannah asks.

"No. I want to sit on your lap, okay?"

"Sure." Hannah switches her legs, crossing them the other way to let the blood circulate. Heather slides onto her lap. Michelle lets them get settled and finally tells the story, but talking rapidly with an irritated tinge in her voice.

25

In Bob's basement, Bob, Mary and Dewy pace like rats in a cage. Billy sees the look in their eyes. They want to slow down, but they're too hyped up. They're exhilarated. And frightened. In way over their heads.

Dewy sits down in one of the chairs and gets back up. Mary and Bob sit down, but they can't relax. Bob keeps shoving his fingers in his jean pockets and taking them back out. Billy realizes Dewy chomped his pencil right in half. He smirks. He's in a zone, reading them. He knows they're all fighting an urge to bolt. They're afraid to speak.

Hulk isn't freaked out like the local skins, but Billy knows where Hulk's at, too. Enough is enough. Hulk wants to kick back.

Billy snorts more speed, offers some to Hulk. He shakes his head back and forth. "I've had enough for now."

Billy reaches the canister toward Bob. "Speed, Bob?"

"No thanks." He turns away.

Billy walks along side Dewy, who keeps pacing back and forth. He puts his arm around his shoulder. "Did you see the look on that nigger's face when he saw me?"

Dewy glances sideways toward Billy and shakes his head.

"The fucker knew it was me." Billy laughs. "And then that Christ Warrior — what's his name?"

"Dick," Bob says.

"Yeah, fuckin' Dick. He smacks the rear window and that coon started turnin' colors. What a stupid son-of-a bitch. He actually put his buttons down." Billy laughs.

Bob puts out a weak laugh. Dewy and Mary stare at the floor. Hulk looks at Billy with an even gaze.

"C'mon, Bob. I seen you hit that mother with a blow that must have busted his arm in half. I could hear it crack."

Bob looks at him. "Yeah?"

"How did it feel, man?"

"I don't know." Bob looks at Mary and Dewy. They look away.

Billy slides over to Hulk and puts his arm around him. "And the ol' H-man." He turns to the local skins. "Did you see him grab that coon and yank him through the window? He's kickin' and screamin' and gettin' the shit cut out of him on those jagged pieces of glass."

Hulk pulls away from Billy and takes a few steps. He doesn't say anything.

"What's with you?" Billy glances from one to another. He takes a couple steps toward the chair where Bob is sitting and looms over him. "We won, dude," he shouts, then turns back toward Dewy and Mary. "Get it? We bagged a nigger." He looks at Hulk, who shakes his head back and forth.

Billy feels like the star player in the locker room at halftime.

He's going from one teammate to the next, exhorting them on for the second half. But they stare back with empty expressions. He puts his arm around Dewy, again, who can't stop his pacing.

Billy turns back to the others. "When that coon saw us swingin' that noose, I thought he was going to shit his pants right then and there." Billy laughs.

"You wanna' know my favorite part?"

Nobody responds.

"When Dick busts his bat in two. Do niggers have hard heads, or what? I thought I was gonna' fall over when I seen ..."

Suddenly Mary screams. "Enough! Enough already."

Everybody else looks at Mary. Billy pivots, facing her. "Enough? I'm tryin' to have a little fun, and you're all sittin' here like we got the shit kickin'. Enough? We've barely begun. All we got was one lame nigger. Better strap on your boots, skins. That Jew family is up next."

Nobody says anything. Mary looks at Dewy and Bob, but they look away. She looks at Hulk.

He looks at Billy. "Chill."

"Don't tell me to chill, H. Fuck you. You're the one always wants action. Now you got it."

"We had it, Billy, and we can have more next week. I wanna' kick back. Lay low."

"Sounds good," Bob agrees. Mary and Dewy nod their heads. They're all looking away. They can't look Billy in the eye.

"Fuck you." Billy simmers. He's got to rein Hulk in. These kids are scared of him. They want a break, but they'll do what he wants — if Hulk doesn't blow it for him. "Word's out now. We have to strike before it's too late."

"That's exactly why we can't strike now," Hulk says. "Because word's out. Let's wait until things cool down, then hit the kikes."

"Fuck you." Billy gives Hulk an intense glare. Hulk stares back.

"I thought the point was to strike a blow," Mary looks right at Billy this time. "Let people know we're here but not get caught."

Billy jumps up and heads toward her. Mary tenses and puts her arms up, defensively. Billy fakes a blow to her stomach, and she falls for the fake. She's too easy, Billy thinks, and smiles. His strange grin distracts her for another second, and his right fist explodes into her cheek. Mary reels back, crashing to the floor. Hulk grabs Billy from behind. Everyone is up, muscles tensed.

"Enough, Billy. Enough." Hulk has him in a firm grip. Billy relaxes. Hulk lets go. Billy turns around and looks Hulk in the eye, glaring, but his muscles remain slack.

Nobody says anything. Bob and Dewy look at the floor, glancing sideways at each other. Mary is shaking as she slowly gets off the floor. Hulk looks at Billy, waiting. Billy glares back. Fucking traitor, he thinks.

After a moment, Billy looks over at Bob. "Give me the keys to your wagon."

Bob hesitates. Then he reaches in his pocket and tosses him the keys.

26

Hannah can't tell how late it is by the light, but it's dark in the cubbyhole and she sees Heather yawning. "It's getting late, girls. Don't you think we should head back to the house?"

Michelle shines the flashlight on her watch. "It's 7:45."

"Well, it's been getting dark earlier. Let's get going."

"I have my flashlight, darkness is no problem," Michelle says.

"I don't think your Mom and Dad feel that way. Besides, isn't eight o'clock Heather's bedtime?"

Heather doesn't protest. Hannah figures the woods are looking spooky to her.

"You and Heather go ahead, then, Aunt Hannah. I'm not ready to go back to the house."

Despite Max's stories about Michelle's lack of fear of the dark as a little tyke, Hannah finds the youngster's courage in the woods at night startling, and wonders if it's some kind of bluff to test her. "I don't think we can find our way back without you as our guide. Particularly with it getting dark out."

"Oh, I forgot. Okay, I'll take you out of the woods." Michelle sounds like Lois Lane taking care of Jimmy Olsen. Hannah smiles inwardly.

They crawl back through the plant-walled tunnel and emerge on the other side, Michelle leading the way and shining the flashlight back, lighting up the path for Heather and Hannah. The going is more difficult in the semi-darkness, but after a few thorny scratches they find themselves in the comparatively open, tall-forested area that's just ahead of the embankment to the road. The last bit of day lingers in the post-twilight hour. Their eyes, if given a chance, could spot things in the partial-blackness, but use of the flashlight prevents the eyes from adjusting.

Hannah feels a crispness in the air she hadn't felt before. Max said the weather was due for a change. Even in the forest, she feels the wind picking up. They begin to wind their way through the stand of firs, Michelle in the lead, Heather and Hannah close behind, when Hannah grabs her niece and points.

"Quick, over there, point the light."

"What is it?" Michelle sounds scared, and Hannah wishes she had been calmer, but she sees eyes in the dark, and they startle her. In the blackness it's hard to tell. She knows she saw something move, and it sounded big. Hannah pulls Heather close and keeps one hand on Michelle.

"I thought I saw something near that tree. Point the light lower, I think."

"What is it, Aunt Hannah?" Heather asks. "I'm scared."

Hannah hears rustling to their right and straight ahead, clearly something moving and more than one of them. The sounds send a shiver up her spine. Hannah quells her pounding heart. Her nieces move closer to her, touching and holding on.

"Give me the flashlight, Michelle, quickly."

"Owly, Aunt Hannah," Heather whines.

Hannah reaches for the flashlight, takes it, Michelle giving it up reluctantly. Hannah shines the light toward the closest noise, several feet to their right. The night marauder, mask and all, is caught in the light. Hannah, Michelle and Heather all jump back. Then, just as suddenly as they gasped for breath, they breathe collective sighs of relief.

"A raccoon," Michelle says.

Hannah shines her light straight ahead and farther off; moving the light side to side, she eventually focuses on two more. They stare back, as curious about the humans as the humans are about them.

"They're so cute," Heather says.

"But still dangerous," Hannah warns. She keeps the light on them, but they don't seem spooked. The animals keep staring back, running back and forth, keeping a watchful eye on the humans.

"Look at their masks," Michelle says. "They are really cute, aren't they?"

"They're adorable," Hannah agrees.

"Can we pet them?" Heather asks.

"No way, sweetie," Hannah gives her a little, loving shake. "They're wild animals. They're not like cats or dogs."

"I bet they know where Cinderella is," Heather says.

"Yeah, if we could only talk to them, they could tell you what happened to your cat." Michelle says it with disgust, but Heather doesn't seem to pick up on her sister's mocking tone. Then

Michelle whispers to Hannah so Heather won't hear her, "The raccoons probably ate Cinderella."

"Hey," Heather says. "Maybe Charles could — oh no —"

Heather starts to cry but keeps the words coming out. "I left Charles in the secret place." Hannah doesn't want to drag them all back through the tunnel and knows Heather is tired and could easily throw a fit. She sighs, feeling like she might suddenly lose it, too.

"Sweetheart," Hannah says, squatting down and pulling Heather close, "Charles is a bear. I think maybe he stayed behind because he wanted to spend a night in the woods. Maybe we should let him stay, and Michelle can get him first thing in the morning."

Heather keeps up a mild sputtering cry, threatening a full-blown wail.

"I can go back and get Charles," Michelle says.

"And leave us here in the dark without you and the flash-light? No way!"

"I can go without the light —" Michelle starts to argue, then apparently has a second thought. "Oh, maybe not tonight." She turns to her sister. "Heather, Charles will be all right. I promise. I'll get him first thing in the morning, okay?"

Heather hesitates, her lip quivering. "What if the raccoons hurt Charles?"

Hannah thinks maybe all three of them should just trek back in and get the bear. It will only take a few more minutes. If they don't, Heather might remain unsettled for hours.

Her thoughts are interrupted by a sudden crackling followed

by the low boom of thunder. The forest lights up. The raccoons and the girls are silhouetted against the thickets. Dry lightening could engulf the woods in flames in an instant. Hannah decides against going back.

"They won't hurt Charles," she says, imagining the raccoons tearing the teddy bear's stuffing out. Meanwhile, the little beasts keep running back and forth, still curious about their forest visitors, and agitated, now, by the impending storm. "Remember, Charles and the raccoons are friends. He might even find out where Cinderella is without a bunch of people around to mess things up."

"Okay," Heather sniffles as she relents.

27

Hannah, once again sleeping indoors in the alcove, is awakened by the sound of breaking glass. She smells smoke, senses the urgency and is up quickly, sliding into her tennis shoes, forgoing the two or three seconds necessary to pull the backs of her shoes over her heels, and flops in them like she might wearing oversized slippers. She's wearing the t-shirt and underpants she sleeps in.

Max is already racing from his bedroom doorway as she exits the alcove. Dragging his foot, he looks like Grendel emerging from the swamp. He gathers speed, rocketing toward his daughters' room. Hannah is a step behind him. The crackle of fire taunts them from the other side of the door.

"Stay low," Max shouts. They both know the smoke will subdue them first. "Get Heather, I'll get Michelle." Opening the door will fan the fire, but Hannah figures Max sees no other option.

He takes a huge breath, swings the door open, and dives to the floor, scrambling madly on all fours toward his daughters. Hannah drops low, too. She's quickly at Heather's bed.

"She's not here, Max!" Hannah grabs and pats all over the bed in the smoke-filled darkness. She ducks down to look and feel under the bed when she hears her brother.

"She's here." He coughs. "She's in Michelle's bed. Help me." He coughs again. The fire crackles and pops, and yellow flames devour the far corner, but thick, black smoke obscures the rest of the room.

In the smoky haze, Hannah moves more with her ears than with her eyes. She feels Heather in her arms, placed there by Max, and drops down, carrying her like a mother gorilla would carry her young. Max is right behind with Michelle.

Gretchen stands ready with the extinguisher waiting for the doorway to clear.

"Here," Max coughs it out as he places Michelle down and slides her toward her mother. "Get them outside and away from the house." He takes the extinguisher from Gretchen and turns back toward the room.

Outside, Gretchen turns to Hannah. "There's another fire extinguisher in the barn just inside the door. I'll stay with the girls if you'll get it."

Hannah has already pulled the ends of her shoes over her heels and doesn't waste another second answering. She turns and runs the seventy yards down to the barn, quickly locates and grabs the extinguisher, then races back toward Max and the fire.

#

Gretchen, wearing a robe, sits down in the yard, crosses her legs, lifts Heather onto her lap and pulls her close. Michelle, like her sister, is in pajamas. She sits down, locking her arm inside her mother's arm, and leans her head against Gretchen's shoulder.

"Owly, I need Charles." Heather mumbles in a spooky monotone.

"Oh Honey," Gretchen pulls her daughter tight and kisses the top of her head. She's not sure what to say about the teddy bear being consumed by the fire. "Let's not think about Charles right now. We're so lucky both of you are all right."

"Mom?"

Gretchen turns her head toward Michelle.

"Charles wasn't in the house. He spent the night in my secret place." She twists her head around to get in front of Heather and talks gently. "Heather, you want me to go get Charles for you?" Heather shakes her head affirmatively.

Gretchen is shaken. She doesn't have any extra energy for a kid's drama in the middle of the night while Hannah and Max are still battling to save the house. From Gretchen's view, the flames don't appear to be spreading, but she can't see what's going on inside. "Michelle, now isn't the time. Heather will be all right without Charles for a little while. Especially if she already spent the night without him. How did that happen, anyway?"

"She spent the night with me in my bed. She accidentally left him up there. It was too late when she realized it."

"Too dark," Heather says, still in a spacey monotone.

"Well, it's still too dark. How could you possibly find your secret place now?"

"I could get the flashlight out of Dad's truck, Mom. I can find my secret place blindfolded," she says proudly.

"No, Michelle." Gretchen barks. "Please, honey, I have enough to worry about right now." The tone of her mother's voice silences Michelle.

#

The black, smoldering wood, covered with foam, is a depressing sight. Still, Hannah and Max look at each other with elation. They can finally ease up. Max had been holding his own, keeping the fire from spreading, when she joined him. With Hannah wielding a second fire extinguisher, the blaze quickly succumbed.

"Is it out — for sure, I mean?" Hannah asks.

"I think so, I think so," Max responds. The exhaustion suddenly catches them. "I'll call 911."

"I'll meet you outside."

Hannah heads out the front door and down the porch steps. An eeriness overwhelms her, as if a dark shadow had passed over them. She approaches Gretchen, still sitting cross-legged on the ground with Heather in her lap. Hannah doesn't see Michelle.

"What happened?" Gretchen asks.

"I think we were firebombed."

"God, why? I mean who would firebomb us — oh God!"

"What?" Hannah sees that something has clicked for Gretchen. "What is it?"

"The rapist. The other one —"

Max walks up. "What are you saying?"

"The other rapist came to get even because we had his buddy arrested. God, Max, he could still be around here." Gretchen looks around and hugs her sleeping child tighter. Her voice becomes frantic. "Michelle. Where's Michelle?"

"I thought she was with you," Max says.

"She was — she was here a minute ago — oh — damn. She wouldn't do that — she wanted to go to her secret place —"

"That's only a couple hundred yards," Hannah nods up the direction of the road.

"God!"

From a long way back in the woods, smoke billows up into the night sky, and a reddish glow emanates from the distance. Max starts to hobble toward the road.

Hannah stops him. "Max. I'll go. I can go faster than you, and I know where the place is — I was just there."

Max hesitates.

"The guy could still be around here, Max," Gretchen pleads, frantically. "Stay with me and Heather. Let Hannah go."

They can see that the smoke and fire glow are a long ways back in the woods.

"If Michelle is at her secret place she shouldn't be in any danger," Hannah says. "And she has no reason to go deeper into the woods." Hannah doesn't want to think about where else she might be.

"Okay." Max relents. "But you better hurry. I don't like the way the wind is kicking up." He reaches down to help Gretchen up. She's still holding Heather. "Stay close to me. Let's go in and call for more help."

"Didn't you call, yet?" Gretchen asks.

"Yeah, but I didn't tell them there was a forest fire. I said I thought an arsonist torched our house and we had the fire under control. I thought we just needed mop-up help and to report it to the sheriff."

Hannah races over to her car, grabs her flashlight and starts up the road, running as fast as she can on the uneven surface in the dark.

#

Hannah wonders if she'll have trouble recognizing the yew tree, Michelle's entry-marker, in the dark. When she reaches the curve she easily spots it, turns, and scrambles up the embankment that leads down into the woods. She can see the fire, beyond Michelle's secret place. There's no need for panic, she tells herself; as long as Michelle is there, they'll be fine. But she can feel the wind and wonders how out of control this fire could get and how quickly. "Michelle! " She shouts, then stops and listens.

Nothing.

"Michelle!"

"Aunt Hannah?" The voice is faint.

Hannah moves forward, slowly now, through the wood's entanglements. She must be nearing the spot. "Michelle!"

"Aunt Hannah, I'm right here." The voice is loud and clear. Hannah points her flashlight and is caught by a beam of light coming toward her. She squints, and turns momentarily away from the light.

"Michelle?"

"Yes." Michelle points the light down at the ground between them. "There's a fire in the woods back there, Aunt Hannah," Michelle gestures with the flashlight, past her secret place to the woods beyond. "We better get out of here."

Hannah laughs at the earnest, adult expression. The laugh almost turns into a cry. She realizes she's emotionally wrung out. Michelle has the flashlight in one hand and Heather's teddy bear tucked under her other arm. "Yes, we better, sweetheart."

The scent of burning wood admonishes Hannah to hasten her pace. Their flashlights cut through smoke, already drifting through the thickets like fog rolling off the ocean. An unearthly quiet ahead of them plays against the crackle and hiss of the wildfire chasing them, growing louder. Hannah gauges the fire. It's no longer at a safe distance. She feels a stiff breeze gust through the forest. The wind is gaining strength, pushing the blaze toward them. There's no time to waste. She takes Michelle by the wrist, Michelle's hands occupied with the flashlight and the bear, and they maneuver at a quickened pace through the woods toward the road.

Suddenly, Michelle's voice vibrates and whines and carries an urgency. "Aunt Hannah!"

The red-eyed kid's menacing glare is disrupted by the concentrated beam from Michelle's flashlight, but he refuses to squint or turn away. He must be blinded by the light, Hannah thinks, but he continues to glare, his body tensed, ready to strike. He can't be more than ten yards away, standing between them and the road. Hannah bends down to Michelle's level, and speaks into her niece's ear in a hushed tone.

"When I tell you to run, you run," she says, firmly. "No matter what is happening to me, don't turn around or stop. Go as fast you can and get your Dad. Understand?"

Michelle shakes her head affirmatively, but doesn't speak. Hannah worries Michelle could freeze up. She places one hand on Michelle's shoulder and begins to gently nudge her sideways and forward. At the same time, Hannah steps forward, putting herself between the skinhead and her niece. The woods are too thick for them to move to the side, especially in the dark. The garish boy blocks their exit. Hannah feels the fire looming behind her, and she moves closer to the boy, gripping her flashlight like a weapon.

He moves slightly, attempting to escape the focused beam of Michelle's light. He reaches in his pocket and Hannah watches as he pulls out a knife and opens it. Quickly, she shines her flashlight on the ground looking for a bigger weapon. She kicks around, too, feeling for anything.

Branches of various sizes lie all around. She squats down quickly, keeping her gaze riveted on the red-eyed kid, shifts the flashlight to her left hand and grabs at the forest floor with her right. She grasps a branch and begins to lift it up, but it crumbles in her hand. Rotted, decomposed wood.

The kid sees what she's doing and moves toward them. Hannah grabs frantically, and feels another branch. She wraps her fingers around it and squeezes. This branch doesn't give way.

"Now!" she commands Michelle and, using her left forearm, gives her a gentle push in the direction of the road. They separate.

Michelle follows her aunt's orders and doesn't look back or sideways, and doesn't see the skinhead lunging for her, his knife poised. The fire is moving, too; gaining momentum, racing to cut off their flanks, picking up speed as it devours the dense, dry fuel.

Smoke is the vanguard for the advancing conflagration, and the irritating gray matter engulfs them. The woods are lit with orange and yellow flames, but vision is obscured by the smoke. In the eerie haze, Hannah hones in on the boy's hand, and strikes with the branch. The knife flies out of his grasp and is lost to the forest floor. He turns from the fleeing child and smacks Hannah across the face, sending her sprawling to the ground. She feels the sting on her jaw and cheek, the jab of branches in her buttocks.

"Run, Michelle, run!" she shouts. "Don't stop! Run!" Hannah starts to get up. The boy hesitates. He looks at Hannah and glances back in the smoky darkness at Michelle. He goes after Michelle. Hannah springs up and leaps on his back and shoulders, bringing them both to the ground. She can't see Michelle, but she imagines her scrambling easily on her familiar path, putting distance between herself and the fire.

A powerful gust of wind funnels through the trees, chasing smoke and debris. The fire's intensity kicks up, crackling and popping as it races through the bone-dry woods. In an instant the blaze is at the road. Red-orange flames bound off young, parched trees, attempting to leap to the tall trees on the other side of the narrow, dirt divide.

Hannah and the snarling skinhead come to their feet, face each other again. A nearby stump explodes, showering fiery coals into the air. The conflagration erupts through the thick low growth, completely cutting off access to the road. The woods crackle. Smoldering branches crash down, as the flames surround them, and close in; more dangerous to both, now, than either is to the other.

The fire is mesmerizing. They watch, like children, in complete wonder at the awesome power. Swirling, suffocating, smoke envelops them.

Hannah shakes herself from the fire-induced trance. She focuses on the blaze, her training, her instincts, fighting off the disorientation brought on by the sudden fury.

She considers a gamble. At Silver Woods, fire-tents allowed them to get low and let the raging force pass. Perhaps survival can be found in the muck and mire of the low spot near the spring, allowing the swampy mud and water to act as a fire shelter. That strategy leads away from the road and the house, along the edge of the fire's frenzy, but Hannah can formulate no other way out of the raging holocaust. The wall of flames between her and the road looks impenetrable. She sees the red-eyed kid standing in front of her with the look of a little, lost boy, frozen by the flames. She recognizes the look. It's the same gaze that peered back at her at Silver Woods, when that swirling inferno stunned firefighting veterans.

Hannah knows the boy must be responsible for the fire, but she doesn't have time to weigh her feelings. She looks at him and pulls his gaze to hers. "Follow me!"

The kid looks at her. The heat of the fire presses him. A snag a hundred feet away erupts, sending dead, dry pulp flying in all directions. He coughs from the smoke. He says nothing.

The fire is roaring. Hannah can barely hear herself. "Follow me, now!" she screams as loudly as she can, urging him again.

Her gaze holds his. She puts out her hand. Still he hesitates. Does he hate her so much? More than he values his own life?

He glares at her — a hateful glare. But he also holds the look of a frightened animal caught in the flames. Paralyzed.

"Now!" Hannah screams.

Perhaps he senses the urgency of the moment more than he feels the loathing that grips him. Perhaps some primitive survival drive takes over. Whatever the cause, the desire for life, for the moment at least, triumphs over hate.

The red-eyed boy takes her hand, and they run into the heart of the inferno.

28

Michelle's mouth is moving, but she's too far away for Max to make out the words. Behind his daughter the flames have crossed the road, forming a solid wall of fire. He sighs at the sight of her, running safely in front of the blaze. But his tension remains. Hannah is nowhere to be seen. He fights to catch his breath and center himself.

"A scary boy," Michelle gasps for breath, "is back there with Aunt Hannah."

Max stares at the woods. He sees no opening in the wall of flames. Gretchen asks Michelle, "A scary boy?"

"He looked mean, and he had a knife. Aunt Hannah told me to keep running." Michelle starts to cry, holds it back, "I wanted to help her. She said I had to keep running and get you, Dad. No matter what." Michelle breaks down completely, sobbing. Heather, still in her mother's arms, starts crying too.

"Aunt Hannah. We have to get Aunt Hannah," Heather screams.

Max stares at the woods and thinks of attempting what he knows would be suicide. He can't see an opening anywhere. He looks at Gretchen, hoping for some sign of support, a signal to go for it despite the odds. Gretchen returns a hard stare.

"Gretch ..."

"No." She gestures toward the wall of fire. "There's no way in the world you're going into that, Max."

Michelle is sobbing, and Heather is screaming. Max can't think. The faint wail of a siren breaks his paralysis. A county sheriff's car appears first around the embankment, followed by a state police car. Neither have sirens on, though. The fire engine is behind them and cuts its siren as it comes into view.

The county sheriff gets out of his car. He wears a gray uniform and no hat. One of the two state police officers is on the car phone, calling for a full response to the forest fire; the other state police officer, a tall, stiff-shouldered man dressed in dark blue with a broad brimmed hat, joins the sheriff as he approaches Max, Gretchen and the children.

The county sheriff is older and a bit pudgy, but his frame is solid. He gestures toward the fiery woods and asks, "What's going on here? The report we got said you suspected an arsonist firebombed your home, but everything was under control."

"We thought it was. My sister is up there." Max gestures toward the blaze. "Maybe the arsonist, too. We have to get her out."

"I'm sorry," the sheriff says, "but we have to get you out."

"Excuse me, Jim," the second state police officer, also dressed in a blue uniform and wearing a broad-brimmed hat, joins the small group. He looks at the county sheriff. "State's got several firefighting crews on the way, and three local outfits are already battling the perimeter just this side of 122. Someone spotted it thirty minutes ago from the air. We've got our people evacuating a half dozen families on the other side of the ridge, but it's just a precaution. They think they can stop this thing at the top. We better get these folks out of here now, let the crews get a line dug."

"The fire's moving that way." Max points toward the left of the road, where the land slopes upward. "Once it came out of the tree line and the land fell away, it turned. Our house isn't in danger. Besides, it's not going to jump the creek. Look. There's nothing within twenty yards of here for it to do anything with."

"You're probably right, sir," the second officer says stiffly, "but we have to evacuate you as a precaution."

"We'll get a local crew coming in here any minute," the sheriff says. "They'll get a fire break dug, and your place'll be a lot more secure. You best leave it to them. We'll get your family out of here."

Max looks at Gretchen. "Take the girls and go with the officers." He turns back to the sheriff, "I'm going to stay and help."

"I don't think anybody has a problem with that, but if you're thinking of trying to go in there, you're crazy. Nobody -"

The sheriff stops, looks at Gretchen and lowers his voice. "Why don't you go ahead with these officers, ma'am?" The sheriff gently places his hand on Gretchen's back and gestures with his other hand toward the state police officers.

Gretchen begins moving, still holding Heather and taking Michelle by the hand. She turns back. "Don't do anything stupid, Max. You can barely walk—."

"I won't. I won't. I just can't leave. I can't walk away right now."

"I know how you feel," the sheriff says kindly. His eyes shift away, gauging the distance of Gretchen and the kids. He lowers his voice. "I gotta' tell ya, buddy. Nobody's alive in there. Unless your friend got out the other side..."

"My sister," Max corrects the sheriff.

"Your sister. Maybe she got over the ridge before it got going."

"She just went up there several minutes ago. The fire was already moving this way from over there." Max points to his right.

The sheriff raises his voice. "She went up there after the fire was already going? What on God's earth for?"

"To get my daughter."

The sheriff softens again. "And your daughter?"

"That was her." Max cocks his head toward his family, getting in the state patrol car. "My sister got her out, but — somehow — she must have got tangled up with the arsonist."

"Do you have any idea who this guy is?"

"Not really. He may be the friend of a guy my sister just helped to bust, a rapist."

"John Cooper? That's your sister who helped us collar that guy?" The sheriff's eyes light up and get watery at once. Max forgot Hannah had met the sheriff. He feels his throat harden.

One of the two state officers returns to the sheriff's side. He appears to have something to say, but Max talks first.

"My daughter called the guy up there a boy. Why would he set the woods on fire?"

"I don't think he did," the state officer says. "Apparently this blaze got started on the other side of this rise. I expect one of those lightening strikes sparked it off."

The three men stare at the fire for several seconds.

"The wind picked up about midnight," the state cop finally

continues. "The fire must have really picked up a head of steam when it hit your place."

Two crummies rumble around the bend, past the sheriff's car, and a dozen fire fighters scramble out of each of the long green vehicles. They look like giant station wagons from the front but are two and one-half times as long, enabling them to hold full crews of firefighters.

The crew members look young to Max, but the sight of the yellow-clad, hard-hatted youngsters comforts him. He glances at the pile of tools they've tossed on the ground: axes, shovels, and pulaskis. He thinks about grabbing one and heading up the road.

"According to the latest word, we're in real good shape," he hears the apparent crew leader say to the rest of them. "Ray Holland's crew got an early jump on this baby, and she's already contained on three sides. We got to work our way around to the left here, head off this flank. We'll let her have the crest of that hill." He points toward the top of the rise to his left.

"If we can stop her in that little saddle up there, we'll be in great shape. We can hope to hook up with a couple state crews around the other side there." He points to the left again." I need three people to head to the right and make sure there isn't anything flaring up behind this house." He gestures with his thumb over his shoulder toward Max's place.

"I don't need to tell you," another guy speaks up. Perhaps the other crew leader, Max figures. "We got some new people on this crew. I don't want you new people paired up with each other. You all know the drill. Our job is to contain. Contain the sucker and let it burn itself out. What's lost is lost."

29

Mary sits in Bob's overstuffed chair. Bob and Dewy pace.

The skin's basement hangout seems smaller to Hulk. As if it shrunk. He leans his back against the wall. "We're in deep shit," he says. Dewy and Mary nod in agreement.

"We're still in the clear," Bob grumbles. He says it without conviction.

"You wanna' wait 'til it's too late?" Hulk shouts. Bob, Dewy and Mary wince. Hulk calms himself, lowers his voice. "Fuckin' Billy is outa' whack. We gotta' figure our next move."

"What should we do?" Bob asks. "Anybody got any ideas?"

Mary and Dewy shake their heads.

"It's not like any of us killed the guy," Bob says.

"Are you nuts?" Mary glares at Bob, shakes her head back and forth. "We were there. We helped."

"Legally, we're on the same hook as Billy," Dewy says.

"Legally?" Mary says. "You're suddenly a lawyer, Dewy? None of us have a clue how much trouble we're in. But you can bet we're in deep."

"Geez, take it easy, Mary. That's what I just said. We'll take the same rap as Billy."

"And I still say we won't" Bob looks at Dewy, then Mary. "We meant to rough the nigger up. And that's exactly what I did. Then I quit."

Mary opens her mouth, about to go at him again, but Bob hurriedly resumes. "You guys, too. We all quit. It was Billy that went nuts. None of us ever intended to kill the guy."

"So what are you saying?" Mary has her hands on her hips. She moves her right hand to her face as if she were holding a phone. "Excuse me officer, I want to report a killing. Yes, I was there. I helped beat the guy up, but I didn't have anything to do with killing him."

Bob looks at the floor. All three of these punks are idiots, Hulk thinks. He's got to get out. Nobody says anything for a while. Hulk wonders what they're thinking. Maybe turning on Billy. Maybe turning on him, too. Bob starts in again.

"Look, Billy wanted to go after the Dykes, too. Right then and there, but we talked him out of it. All four of us. That's gotta' count for something."

"You just don't get it, do you?" Mary shakes her head. "We're accessories to murder."

Her words hang in the air. After a few seconds Mary sits back down. Bob slumps against the wall and slides to the floor, resting on his butt. Dewy keeps on pacing.

Hulk suddenly brightens. "I'll call my Uncle Kirk. He's been in some heavy shit before. He'll have a plan."

"What kind of shit?" Mary asks. "I mean, how can he help us?"

"Just trust me, okay?" Hulk walks over to the old rotary phone and dials his uncle's number.

"Just hold up a second, okay?" Mary is forceful. "I trusted this whacked-out friend of yours, and look where it's got us. I don't want anybody else to know about this. You know?"

Whacked-out friend? As pissed off as Hulk is at Billy, he still doesn't like Mary putting his guy down. He decides to let it go. "Okay, you got a good point, but my uncle is an ex-con. He would never rat anybody out."

Mary seems to accept this, but Dewy is concerned now. "How do you know that for sure?"

"Shit." Hulk can't think. How is he supposed to know everything? He just wants to call his uncle and have him figure it out. "That's the way these guys are. Okay?" Hulk raises his voice and nobody responds.

He picks up the phone again. Everyone is drained. They watch Hulk.

As he dials the number, he realizes his uncle wouldn't appreciate him saying what he said. Hulk doesn't dial the last digit, pretends to be listening, tries to think. He needs to talk to his uncle alone. He hangs up the phone.

"This is really weird," he says. "My Uncle Kirk is not a phone guy. I mean his line is never busy."

"At this hour, too? In the middle of the night?" Mary asks.

"Yeah, I don't get it. I think I better just go over there."

"Why not try again after a while?" Mary asks.

Hulk paces for a while. Bob sits down. Dewy is smoking, puffing nervously.

"Goddamn. I never should have given Billy the keys to my wagon," Bob moans.

"Maybe we oughta' all just clear out of here," Dewy says.

"Do you have any places in Portland where we could hang out for a while?" Mary asks.

Hulk doesn't answer. The mention of Portland reminds him of Joe. Maybe Joe is lucky he was too busted up to join them. At least he's out of the hospital, recuperating at home. Hulk's gotta' get out of state. Disappear. Uncle Kirk will help him. "I'm goin' over there," Hulk finally says.

"I'll go with you," Bob jumps up.

"Maybe we all should go, you know, stick together," Dewy says. They're all on their feet.

Hulk shakes his head. "Nah. I don't think so. Uncle Kirk wouldn't dig it. I'll talk to my uncle alone. He'll know what to do. Then I'll swing back over here or call you guys."

30

The conflagration sweeps through the low-lying brush, consuming grasses and vines, blackening the earth. In places, the ground is too hot to touch. Above, the fire rages in the tree tops. Hannah, with the red-eyed kid in tow, picks her way toward the spring and swamp. Her eyes dart back and forth, seeking openings in the flaming debris, looking warily for falling branches or an exploding snag. The mesmerized boy, his pupils wide and glassy, seems like a tourist, relishing a macabre satisfaction from the blackened and burning woods.

Hannah, her mind engaged in survival, has no time to analyze her actions with the boy. She believes she's heading toward the marsh, but the blaze alters the terrain. Familiar trees and paths are gone, replaced with rivers of fire and clouds of smoke. Hesitancy and doubt are luxuries she can't afford. She pushes on.

The danger is less to the right than the left, where crackling, orange flames form a nearly solid wall. She steps quickly, dragging the kid with her. The path closes up. The right is worse now. Thickets turn instantly into giant bonfires, funneling smoke skyward. She doubles back a step and races forward and to the left. The area twenty yards ahead is completely engulfed, but it looks clear beyond. She has to angle around it somehow. The forest floor, tantalizingly, offers openings between dozens of individual spot fires, but with the wind shifting and the earth so dry, the fires can merge quickly and trap anything that ventures inside.

A flaming tree sways. It's coming down, but she can't tell if it's falling toward them or off to the side. She backs up, yanking the boy and dragging him with her. It crashes to the ground twenty yards in front of them, revealing a clearing beyond. Streams of fire race from the fallen tree, snaking along the forest floor, threatening to instantly close any access to the clearing. Hannah dashes for the opening, hurdling over the fire, but she loses her grip on the boy. Without her pull, he comes to a sudden stop.

She reverses her momentum and turns back toward him. He stares at the blazing woods. She motions for him to follow her, screaming, "This way. Come on." But he doesn't respond. She shakes her head, then jumps back over the spreading, low-lying flames.

"This way," she screams, nodding toward the clearing. He doesn't respond. She looks in his eyes, but he doesn't acknowledge her. He's gripped by the high flames in the tops of the trees, as if he were watching a movie, in no danger at all. She grabs his wrist again. Jerking hard, she pries him from his spot and drags him across the burning ground. She feels the heat scorch her feet through the thin rubber soles of her shoes. Once past the river of fire, the clearing provides a brief, partial respite, extending for thirty yards before the terrain thickens again with fiery undergrowth and trees.

A rocky protrusion to her left seems familiar. The swamp should be nearby, around the other side of the boulder and down. She heads toward it, but several tall fir look like they could come down in an instant. She works her way around them, dragging the boy far to their right, before circling back to the left toward the rocky knob. One of the giant trees sways, then teeters, smashing into the protrusion, resting against it, continuing to burn. She grips the boy tighter and ducks under the tree. Burning embers sting her. She lets go of him and frantically smacks at her hair and shoulders, knocking the fiery cinders away. The boy stands motionless, oblivious to the ash and embers on his shoulders. She slaps them off, then grabs his wrist again.

Tugging him along, she races around the edge of the boulder and spots the low-lying marshy area down to her left.

The middle of the swamp is free from fire. Hannah sighs. She was right. The bottom land is filled with muck and standing water, and can't burn. If they can only get there, they might survive. A combination of tall, flaming trees and blazing thickets surround the wet, grassy plain.

She turns to face the boy, to prepare him for a charge through the flames, but the face looking back at her is blank, except for a glaze that seeps from his dark, red eyes. Hannah blinks. Is he crying? The hard, yellow-orange droplets look like sap oozing from a burning tree. The heat scorches her. They have no time. She turns back toward the fire-encircled marsh.

She grasps the boy's hand tighter, and with a hard jerk on his arm, bolts into a wall of flames. Her skin feels like it's melting. Her hair singes and curls, her eyes burn, but an updraft keeps the smoke from overwhelming her. She looks down, reassuring herself her shirt isn't on fire. She reaches the open, sloping land that falls away to the swampy bottom. The fire's intensity lessens. She expects to hear a sizzle as she feels the sloppy muck below her heated feet. She points herself toward what she estimates as the center and low point of the swamp and dares a glance upward. The towering maples and oaks that surround the clearing wave long flaming branches. A massive branch dislodges. She ducks, jerking the boy with her. The branch crashes down into the muck less than fifteen feet away. It continues to burn as giant hunks of charcoal.

Hannah's pace is slowed by the muck and standing water. She lifts her left leg up high and places it back down, sinking in up to her calf. She lifts her right leg up, looking skyward for the falling branch that will end her life, then sets her foot down, sinking deeper still. Her balance falters, and she lets go of the boy's hand, steps high again with her left leg and squeezes it into the muck nearly up to her knee. She has trouble wiggling the right foot free. It's time to get down.

She looks back at the boy, standing still, staring. "You have to get down," she shouts.

He looks at her, but his stone face shows no recognition of who she is or where he is.

"You have to submerge yourself in this muck." She points down, but he doesn't respond. A huge flaming branch crashes down no more than twenty yards away; the glowing embers reach them and sting them. Hannah looks up, attempting to locate the most open space. She tells herself to find the safest spot available and hunker down.

She grabs the boy and pulls him down, submerges him in the watery muck, and arranges him so only the top of his head is exposed, his face forward in the tall wet grasses. Hannah lifts her leg up out of the muck and places it back down again.

Laboriously, she moves several feet beyond the boy. She pulls her t-shirt off, soaks it in the muck and wraps the top of her head with it. Her hair could act like kindling, she reasons; the fine fibers a quick, easy fuel for the flames. She wiggles down into the swampy water, scooping the muck up and around herself for protection from the heat, flames and falling embers.

31

The sun emerges from deep in the woods, its red-orange glow mimicking the previous night's fire. The dim light reveals hesitant smoke, sifting amongst the charred woody giants. Fire crews, positioned on the far side of the blaze, still battle for containment. Where the fire has been, inside the fire's perimeter, embers glow and flare up in search of new fuel. The earth is hot and black; otherwise, the fire is through with Max and Gretchen's land.

"Look," Max pleads with the sheriff, "I'm a veteran of wildfires, I know what I'm doing."

"I know you are — you've told me enough times — but your safety is my concern. I can't let you go in there. Nobody is alive in there. All you can do is get hurt or killed by some falling piece of burning wood."

Fucking bureaucrats, Max thinks.

"You're wrong," he says. "I know the chances are slim, but I know my sister. And I know this piece of land. If she got to the swamp, she might have survived. I can get most of the way there on the old road. It won't be too dangerous that far; then I'm willing to take my chances. That's my right. It's my life."

"Look, I feel for you, buddy, but it's not your right. I've got jurisdiction in a civil emergency. And a wildfire is an emergency. You are not going up there. That's final."

The sheriff hears a call on his car radio and heads over to answer it. Max looks at the woods straight ahead and at the sheriff from the corner of his eye. He could take off. But with his bum foot, he wouldn't get far. He can see the sheriff talking and looking at him, then motioning for him to come back to the car. Max thinks again about bolting up the fire-blackened road but bides his time instead.

"We found a station wagon back here," the sheriff says. "Off a side road with access to your woods up there." He pauses.

"Yeah?" Max asks.

"Well, there was a bunch of bloody baseball bats in there, and the thing stunk of gasoline. Sure looks like it had something to do with the arson of your place. The car is registered to a Robert Moore. He's a local kid. We've had an eye on him, but he's never done anything except petty stuff."

Max stares at him. "Bloody bats?"

"I don't suppose you know a guy named Filbert Childs?" the sheriff asks.

"Yeah, he's a friend of ours. He just left here, late yesterday afternoon."

"I don't know how to tell you this any other way but to just say it." He pauses and takes a breath. "He's been found, dead."

Max's throat hardens. "Dead? How?"

"Some women on Sylvan Lane found him. He was hanged.

My deputy says he was worked over pretty bad, first. Probably with those bats. His car was all smashed up, too; then pushed into a ravine."

The sheriff pauses and looks at Max. "I won't know till we look into this a lot more thoroughly, but it sure looks like whoever killed this Childs guy firebombed your house, too."

#

The woods can be hushed, but rarely mute: water trickles and bubbles, a breeze rustles leaves, crickets rub their legs, birds chirp and sing. In the aftermath of the fire, even the muted sounds of the forest are gone. Hannah has never heard such stillness. She takes it in, along with the blackened world around her. Then, slowly, she begins to hear things. A crackle in the distance and two faint sounds, nearby. A bubbling noise created by the slightest movement of water, and breathing. It's her own breath she hears, moving in and out.

She explores the terrain, remaining focused on a point directly ahead. She's behind the boy. She figures he has no way of knowing she's there unless she gives it away. She stays immobile, submerged in the watery muck, the top of her head covered with her shirt, which is caked with mud and ash. The boy isn't moving. Perhaps he's dead, but Hannah isn't taking chances. She watches and waits, content to savor her survival.

Hannah figures the safest thing is to assume the worst — that the boy will return to his aggressive mode and attack her again given the chance. And more danger looms above. Charred branches poised to crush anything below. Wait, she tells herself.

The journey out of the fire-scorched woods will only get easier with the passage of time.

#

It takes Billy a while to focus. He only vaguely remembers how he got here. He jerks his arm up and twists his head around. That bitch, he thinks. He's in a fucking rice paddy or some shit. He takes in a broader survey of his surroundings; he sees the burned landscape, the increasing light. Goddamn, he tells himself, he better get his ass in gear. He's not sure where to go, but he pulls himself out of the mud and stands.

"Gotta' get the fuck outa' here," he mumbles. He looks up each slope, weighing the possibilities. Everything looks the same. Just pick a route and go, he prods himself. He lifts one water-soaked, mud-covered leg out of the mire and sets it back down. He sinks in deeper. He turns to go the other way and spots something odd to his left. He freezes. He thinks he saw something move in the mud. He tenses. It could be a goddamn snake. He tries to jump back, but the mud holds him in place. He peers at the spot in the muck where he spotted the movement, but it's still now. He waits, staring.

He looks around for something to poke at it with, sees nothing, and slowly backs away, lifting one heavy, mud-laden leg out, following it with the other. "I gotta' get the fuck outa' here."

#

Max doesn't know how much time has passed. He's not even sure if he dozed off or just spaced out. He looks at the light and guesses at least half an hour has passed, maybe more. He's sitting cross-legged with his back against the tire of the sheriff's car, still staring toward the woods. The crackle of the sheriff's radio brings him back. The sheriff comes around the side of the car and looks down at him.

"I just talked to my dispatcher. They've cleared your family to come back in here. Apparently they're on their way now. Anyway, I'm pulling out of here, buddy. It's been a long night."

"Yeah," Max gets up, using the hood of the car to pull himself straight. His knee bites at him first, then his back stabs him for good measure. "Listen, I appreciate everything you've done. As far as our disagreement, I know you're just doing your job." As the words come out Max realizes once the sheriff leaves, he'll be able to check out the woods.

"Those woods are still dangerous," the sheriff says. "You know there's lots of snags and whatnot that can crash down and kill you as quick as anything. If anybody lived through that, we woulda' known it by now." The sheriff pauses. "Shit, buddy, if you like, I'll walk up the road a piece with you, just for the hell of it."

"No need to, really. I'm pretty beat, I think I'll lie down until my family gets back."

"Like I said, they'll be here any minute. Sure you don't want to walk a hundred yards up the road, just to look at the damage?"

"Well, okay, if you're up for it now." Max decides he can go back later and look for Hannah.

They walk side by side, slowly, gawking at the blackened forest. Max points at the standing, charred remains of a giant tree. "Twenty-four hours ago, that was one gorgeous cedar.

Look at it now."

The sheriff shakes his head. They walk on in silence. After a while, he says, "I don't know what to tell you. I think you wander off this road you're asking for trouble. Give it time to settle, for things to shake out on their own, for the wind to kick up again and knock the loose shit down."

They stop and stare out at the woods. The sheriff shakes his head at the devastation.

Max looks at the burned woods, but he plays a stronger image in his mind's eye. He sees himself picking his way to the marsh and finding Hannah buried in the muck, but alive and smiling. A sudden, crashing sound unnerves him. He and the sheriff look up first, the reflex for survival warning of danger from above, but everything is motionless. They hear it again, like a startled deer coming toward them. They remain quiet, looking toward the noise. They see him at the same time, long before the scruffy, mud-coated boy sees them.

"What the fu —" Max cuts himself off and grabs the Sheriff.

"I see him, too," the sheriff whispers. Max keeps his gaze on the figure moving toward them. Slowly and steadily, the sheriff pulls out his gun.

"Goddamn it," Max whispers, "that's got to be him."

The mud-covered figure hasn't even located the road yet. A straight line would take him to the road in twenty steps. Instead, he keeps angling through what he apparently believes is the path of least resistance. On this route, he will intersect with the road in seventy or eighty more steps. Max smirks as he watches the boy struggling to find a way out.

The sheriff motions Max to stay behind him. Together, they begin to move back down the road, keeping an eye on the mud-covered suspect.

The boy is within ten feet of the road before he spots the wide, rutted lane. He looks down the road first, toward Max and Gretchen's, then back up. He sees the two men coming at him. He starts to turn and run back through the woods.

"Hold it right there, son." The sheriff is commanding, his gun, compelling.

The kid stops, his exhaustion evident.

The sheriff carefully steps over the uneven ground and low-lying plant growth. He keeps his gaze on the suspect while talking softly but authoritatively to Max. "Don't do anything stupid, friend. I'm going to handle this."

"I got you," Max responds evenly. "Do your thing. Just let me ask him about my sister."

The sheriff gets to within a couple feet of the boy. "Turn around and put your hands on your head," he says.

The teen complies. The sheriff brings one of the culprit's hands down and cuffs it, then the other. He frisks the kid and tells him his rights.

Max remains on the road, watching intently. He imagines a generic movie scene, where the angry loved one jumps over the officer and begins strangling the villain. He tells himself to calm down.

The Sheriff and the kid reach the road. The handcuffed juvenile maintains his defiance, greeting Max with a hard glare. Breathe, Max reminds himself. Be cool. The sheriff eyes them both, uneasily.

"I want to ask you something," Max says as they begin to walk down the road. "Do you know where my sister is? The woman you — encountered — last night?"

The boy looks at Max but doesn't say anything. Max hardens his stare to match the boy's. "Look, all I'm asking is where she is — if you have a clue, tell me."

"I don't know what the fuck you're talking about," the kid says coldly.

"Yes you do. My daughter saw you. You attacked her and my sister." Max raises his voice. "What happened after that?"

"Fuck you." The boy spits the words at Max. The sheriff pulls the boy toward him and away from Max.

Max is suddenly overwhelmed. He's losing the movie image. He tries to keep the mental picture, to keep from going crazy on this kid, but the young thug's venomous words dissolve the image and another replaces it — Hannah's bruised and charred body, dead on the forest floor.

Max attacks the boy. The sheriff intervenes.

"Max!"

The three men freeze at the sound of a woman's shout, turn, and look up the road. Hannah's bare legs are covered with mud. Her t-shirt, back on, is wet and muck covered. Her hair is scorched, her face cut and bruised.

Max begins to hobble, then bolts back up the road. His limp makes his run more of a gallop. He wraps her in his arms. After a long hug, they turn and start down the road, his arm around her shoulder, her arm around his waist. Max looks back at the boy, staring up the road at them. The sheriff moves the kid toward his patrol car.

Max's elation suddenly evaporates. He looks at Hannah, knowing what she doesn't know, knowing he has to tell her about Fil.

#

Hannah and Max reach the sheriff's car. The four face each other. She tries to make eye contact with the boy. Safe now, she wants questions answered, but she doesn't know what they are. He's looking down, avoiding her. The sheriff opens the door and begins to maneuver the kid inside. The red-eyed boy glances back one last time.

Hannah's eyes meet his eyes. Hers are open, searching. His are cold, unrevealing.

She can't believe this is it. There must be more, some break in his armor; even the slightest crack that could become a crevice, a place to hold onto. She refuses to let go. She rivets her eyes to his, imploring him to acknowledge her, to respond.

For one split second, she sees a glimmer of recognition. Then it's gone.

"I killed your nigger," the boy hisses.

Hannah is stunned. His words come out of some dark abyss. She doesn't understand them. She looks at Max. His tender, watery eyes confirm the horrible truth. With a surge, her body is taken over by a pounding from within. It's in her heart, in her throat. Something thunderous that makes no noise yet is so deafening it silences every other sound in the world.

32

Everybody must see her red eyes, Hannah thinks, as she sits down to dinner. Nobody says anything. She expects Heather to ask, but she keeps quiet, too.

Hannah can't taste the food or register words. She nibbles, nods and smiles, as dinner becomes a blur. She wonders if this speedy, aching feeling will ever leave. It's been nearly a week since the calamitous night.

She realizes her plate already is gone. Michelle is clearing the table. Gretchen is at the counter, cutting into a blackberry pie. She places a slice in a bowl, scoops a big dollop of vanilla ice cream out of a silver cylinder and plops it on top of the slice of pie. Michelle takes the first bowl and puts it in front of Hannah.

"Eat it right away," Gretchen says over her shoulder. "The hot pie will melt the ice-cream."

Gretchen hands Michelle two more bowls of pie and ice cream, and the youngster takes them to Max and Heather. She comes back and gets one for herself and sits down. Gretchen follows with her own bowl.

Everybody's quiet, slurping up melting ice cream and blackberry juices. Hannah sticks her fork in the pie, but she doesn't lift it.

"This is the best pie I've ever had, Mom," Michelle says.

"Great pie, Gretch," Max says. "Man oh man, do I love pie ala mode."

"Daddy," Heather says impatiently. "It's not alamo pie, it's blackberry pie." He laughs.

"Sweetheart," Max starts to talk with his mouth full of pie and has to wait a second. "Ala mode means with ice cream. This is blackberry pie ala mode."

"Ala mode," Heather says, delighted by the sound of the words. "Blackberry pie ala mode." Max, Gretchen and Michelle laugh even though Heather is obviously hamming it up.

For Hannah the laughter feels too close to tears. And reminds her of Fil. She considers excusing herself and leaving the table, but she knows she feels better when she's engaged with people. She looks up and sees Michelle looking at her with a sympathetic gaze. Hannah gives her a half-smile, and Michelle smiles back. Hannah looks back down. She cuts a small wedge of pie with her fork and lifts it to her mouth. After she gets it down, she looks at Michelle again.

"Are you excited about starting middle school?" Hannah's voice feels flat.

"I wish you could be my teacher."

"Do you know who your teacher will be?"

"Polly told me her name is Ms. Collins. But she doesn't know anything about her."

"I don't know how she'll approach things, but you should be

studying culture and heritage and geography."

"What's heritage?"

"Your family history. Your roots. In my class all the kids talk about their own heritage and we study cultures from around the world, too."

"She'll love geography," Max says, looking at Hannah. Then he turns to Michelle. "You've always loved looking at the Atlas."

"Why don't you get it, Michelle," Hannah says. "I'll show you some things."

Michelle has already finished her pie and ice-cream. She looks at Max, then at Gretchen. "Can I?"

They both nod. "Sure." Max says.

"Me too?" Heather asks.

"Don't you want to finish your pie ala mode?" Max smiles and his eyes twinkle.

Heather sticks a forkful of ice-cream-coated pie in her mouth as Michelle and Hannah get up and head into the living room.

#

Gretchen scrapes at a suds-filled pan with a plastic scrubber. "I'll finish up, Max, if you want to join Hannah and the girls."

"Thanks." He wipes his hands on a towel he's holding and hangs it on a hook next to the sink, then wraps his arms around Gretchen and presses up against her from behind.

"I sure do love your pie ala mode."

She responds with a light laugh.

He gives her a kiss on her neck, turns and walks into the living room.

Hannah and the girls are on their knees, huddled over the big Atlas.

"See this one?" Hannah asks, enthusiastically. "The colors show precipitation." She turns to Heather. "How much rain and snow there is." Then back to Michelle. "The dark blue is the wettest, and the yellow has the least precipitation."

"Look at how much rain South America gets." Michelle says.

"That's mostly Brazil. Look at how much we get." Hannah points to a little sliver of dark blue along the Pacific Northwest coast.

"Which one is South America?" Heather asks.

Hannah points, then points to Africa. "And this is Africa. See how dry it is in the north, and how wet it is in the south?"

"Can I turn the page?" Michelle asks. "There's a map I don't understand." She flips through until she comes to a full-page photograph of North America. The background is black and the entire continent is red. Closer scrutiny reveals reddish browns and numerous spots of gray and white. Hannah studies it for a moment.

"This was taken from a weather satellite. The vegetation comes out as red. See these brown areas?" Hannah points to the southwestern United States. Michelle shakes her head. "That's desert. And some of these little gray spots are cities that show up."

"What's vege — " Heather pauses.

"Vegetation?"

Heather nods.

"Trees, grass, all the plant life. Everything green. "

"Then why is it red?" Heather puts her arms out with her palms up.

Hannah laughs. "That's a very good question. It's the way it shows up on this kind of photograph."

"They show population, too," Michelle says. She turns the pages until she finds the one she's looking for. Four maps cover the two-page spread, one large one and three smaller ones across the bottom. Michelle points to the middle, bottom map.

"This one says religion. But I don't get it." She points to the eastern half of the country. "It's yellow, and the little box says yellow means Protestant. We have lots of different religions in America."

Hannah studies the map for a second. "That means there are more Protestants in that part of the country than any other religion, but you're right. Lots of people there are Jewish or Catholic or Muslim. I'm sure there are Buddhists and Hindus, and other religions, too."

"What's Oregon?"

"You tell me."

Michelle leans over to get a closer look. "Light blue. Mixed Christian. What's that mean?"

"Probably no one Christian group has that many more people than the others. It's mixed. Catholics, Protestants, Mormons."

"I'm mixed," Michelle says, proudly. "Heather, too. We're half-Christian and half-Jewish."

"That's what we mean by heritage. Do you know what makes you half of each?"

"I do." Heather pipes up.

"What?"

"Because we believe in both God and Santa Claus."

Hannah and Michelle burst out laughing. Heather had a serious look, but laughs, too.

Max leans against the living room door-frame, grinning.

#

Hannah looks straight ahead at the garden, avoiding the charred forest to her right. It's her last twilight at Max's. She still can't face the devastation. The lingering scent of burnt wood won't let her completely ignore the gutted land, but she refuses to turn and view the desolate woods.

"What are those, Aunt Hannah?"

She didn't hear Heather approach. "Oh, these?" Hannah looks down at the pile of manila folders.

"Did they come in your package?"

"Yes, sweetheart. These are folders. They tell me things about my new students."

"What kind of things?"

"Hopefully, things that make me a better teacher."

"Aunt Hannah?"

"Yes."

"I wish you didn't have to go back to Portland."

Hannah reaches out, envelops Heather in her arms and squeezes her. "I love you so much, honey." She pulls back and looks at Heather. "School starts next week, and my students will need me."

"Do you love your students?"

Hannah smiles. "I haven't met them yet, but they become very important to me as I get to know them."

Heather gives her a blank look, then runs back into the house.

Night is descending earlier, which is fine with Hannah. Darkness suits her. Streaks of pink and gray cut across the dusky, blue sky. The orange sun rests on the horizon.

Max limps up and slides into his rocker next to her. He has a couple blankets and hands one to her.

"You're going to need this."

She takes it, but sets it aside.

"I guess you've made up your mind," he says. "But I'll tell you one more time. You can stay here as long as you like. I don't mean days or weeks. Years." He smiles. His eyes are twinkling and watery at the same time.

"A room full of kids with raging hormones awaits me. You can't expect me to give that up for the peace and quiet of the country."

He laughs.

They sit quietly for a while, watching the sun set. The last slice of orange slowly disappears. A wide stretch of light blue spreads out along the horizon. Above it the pink streaks have deepened into purples, fanning out, giving the illusion of an ocean filled with dozens of mountainous islands. After a while they disappear, and the sky takes on a dark, rosy hue.

Hannah shifts her weight. "I had a strange dream last night." She says it looking straight ahead, without inflection, in a somber monotone.

"Yeah? Tell me about it."

"I'm back in the courthouse hallway waiting for the Hanson trial, and the hall is filled with Nazi skinheads. Nobody else.

Dozens of them — looking hateful. Only I'm not afraid. I'm encased in this glass-like bubble. I know it doesn't sound protective, but you know how dreams are."

She gives Max a wry smile. "I feel totally safe and confident. It's a wonderful feeling. I can see them all, observe them. The feeling is like — well, it's like I can be totally safe and figure them out. I'm excited rather than scared because I'm onto something and I'll be able to tell everybody — to tell you and Fil."

As Hannah gets excited, life comes back to her voice, but when she mentions Fil, her throat catches, and she stops. Max puts his hand on her wrist but doesn't say anything. The crickets have started their nightly racket. The colors are nearly gone from the sky, except for a deep, dark purple.

Hannah hangs her head, collecting herself. After a moment, she takes a deep breath and continues. "In the dream I remember that —" she can't get Fil's name out — "that he's gone, but I don't know how. Then I look at the glass bubble and see a small crack forming. At first I just look at it, but when it cracks a little more, I place my palms and fingers against it to try to stop the crack from spreading. But once it starts I can't stop it." Her voice becomes tense.

"Fissures run in every direction and I know the whole bubble will shatter any second. My heart is pounding. All my calm and confidence disappears. I'm in a total panic."

"Then I woke up. I wasn't sure which was worse — the nightmare or reality."

Max rubs her arm. "I know it doesn't seem like it now, but things will get better."

"You know, Max," she can feel the tears, ready to flood again. "I believed that Mom and Dad's deaths somehow made me stronger for dealing with death. I thought that's how I was able to be strong when Anthony was killed." She shakes her head. "What a fool I was. There is never anything —"

Max reaches over and puts his arm around her. He doesn't say anything. After a moment, Hannah continues.

"Sometimes, over the years, I've wanted the hurt I felt right after they died, because they keep getting farther and farther away. I don't want it now. I forgot how awful this is."

She stares blankly into the distance. He stays close, but doesn't say anything. After a while, she shifts in her rocker, fumbling with the folders on her lap.

"How did you pull that off?" Max nods at the folders.

"Lynn, the school secretary."

"I figured as much. It looks like you're doing more than going through the motions."

"I'm just trying to put one foot after the other."

"Like in the fire?"

"As I recall, you're the one who's against fighting fires?" She manages a half-smile.

"I admit I can't help myself, but I'm still not sure it does any good in the long run."

"Saving one tree is reason enough for me." Gretchen's voice startles Hannah. They look up at her, standing in the doorway, her arms wrapped around her chest. When they look at her, she looks away.

"The girls are in bed," Gretchen says after a moment. "I'm

turning in, too. Stay out as long as you like, Max. I just wanted to let you know."

"I'll be right there," he says.

"Good night, Hannah."

"Good night, Gretchen. She turns and heads back into the house.

"She's doing better, isn't she?"

"Her good stretches are getting longer. Gretchen said rape is like losing someone to death. Something is gone forever."

Hannah doesn't respond. Night has fallen, but the sky begins to lighten again. A slice of the moon has emerged at the edge of the blackened woods. Hannah resists looking.

She closes her eyes and sees Fil's head making his strange back and forth shaking motion as he bursts from a halting series of laughs into full-blown laughter. The vision makes her chest heave, and she starts to cry. She tries to convince herself that her loss is nothing compared to the world's. That Fil touched so many people, so deeply and for so long. That, by contrast, she barely knew him at all. But her mind games are easily defeated. She openly sobs.

Max holds her, then pulls her tighter with one arm and softly strokes the back of her head.

After a while, he straightens up. "I'll stay with you if you like."

"No. Go to bed. I want to be by myself."

He looks into her eyes, hesitating.

"Really, Max. I'll be fine."

"Okay." He kisses her on the cheek. "Good night."

"Good night."

Hannah feels a sudden chill and wraps herself in the blanket. The darkness encourages her to turn and steal a peek at the devastated hillside. The earth is scorched, the forest incinerated. She can barely make out shapes or details in the blackness, but the ascending moon reveals skeletons of charred trees still standing here and there, exposed and naked. They look like the bodies of dead soldiers, propped up to discourage the enemy from another attack. The formerly impenetrable terrain is open. The thickets of blackberry and viny maple that buffered and crowded the woods are gone, consumed by the pillaging flames.

The barren landscape overwhelms her. She turns away and thinks about the new school year. A few kids stuck out from the information in the folders. She reaches down and rummages through her stack. The moon has separated from the horizon, revealing its round, fullness, lighting up the night, allowing her to read the reports and comments. She confirms her thoughts about a couple kids and makes a note to call their parents and set up meetings.

Hannah looks straight ahead at Max's garden. Beneath the radiance of the full moon she can distinguish the ripe, red tomatoes from the green ones. She turns back toward the woods.

Now that she finally sees the fire-plundered earth, she can't quit looking. Many of the tall fir are completely gone. Others are blackened, but standing. She can't distinguish a madrone from an oak, or a fir from a cedar by their charred ruins. Nothing green clings to the slope. Dozens of dead, standing trees remain. The moon's beacon exposes the ravaged, desolate hillside, allowing Hannah to survey the gutted, sooty land in detail. She moves her gaze from one dead, standing tree to another, until, suddenly, the sight of a live tree startles her. Perhaps it's an illusion. She peers harder.

In the dark, and from the distance, she can't determine if it's oak or maple. Or perhaps madrone. But the branches protrude with leaves shimmering in the night sky. Encouraged, she searches for more, zig-zagging her gaze back and forth amongst the dead standing trees. Again, she spots a live tree. Then three or four more in a cluster. She can't tell if they're fir or cedar or pine, but they're clearly evergreen, perhaps scorched, but alive.

She moves her gaze closer, working her way back down the slope until she spots another live tree, alone and isolated. The unique yew is unmistakable. Thin, wiry branches loaded with flat, dark green needles are clearly silhouetted in the light of the moon.